Horse
sense

Horse sense

Kevin Bryan

Tate Publishing & *Enterprises*

Horse Sense
Copyright © 2009 by Kevin Bryan. All rights reserved.

No part of this publication may be reproduced, stored in a retrieval system or transmitted in any way by any means, electronic, mechanical, photocopy, recording or otherwise without the prior permission of the author except as provided by USA copyright law.

This novel is a work of fiction. Names, descriptions, entities, and incidents included in the story are products of the author's imagination. Any resemblance to actual persons, events, and entities is entirely coincidental.

The opinions expressed by the author are not necessarily those of Tate Publishing, LLC.

Published by Tate Publishing & Enterprises, LLC
127 E. Trade Center Terrace | Mustang, Oklahoma 73064 USA
1.888.361.9473 | www.tatepublishing.com

Tate Publishing is committed to excellence in the publishing industry. The company reflects the philosophy established by the founders, based on Psalm 68:11,
"The Lord gave the word and great was the company of those who published it."

Book design copyright © 2008 by Tate Publishing, LLC. All rights reserved.
Cover design by Stefanie Rooney
Interior design by Stephanie Woloszyn

Published in the United States of America
ISBN: 978-1-60696-022-6
1. Fiction / Christian / Suspense
08.12.30

Dedication

This book is dedicated to my parents, Jack and Jean Bryan, who provided the inspiration for the characters Jake and Jan, and who taught me to pray.

Acknowledgment

I would like to thank my three daughters, Faith, Angela, and Sarah, for encouraging me to keep writing. And I would like to especially thank my wife, Marsha, who tolerated all my hours of concentration on this story.

1

Gail's trademark ice-blue eyes didn't exactly spring open at the sound of the soft knock on her hospital room door. They did come open, though, and their glare was not too polluted by the pain meds that were playing tag through her system.

It wasn't quite as bad now that she was in an actual room. At least the staff on the floor didn't know her as well as those in ER. If she heard one more person wearing scrubs tell her that it was about time someone sent her in for treatment instead of the other way around, she was gonna taze them on the spot. It was a good thing they had taken her firearm when they had admitted her, or the emergency room at Saint Charles Hospital might be a really exciting place.

She couldn't think of one more 97702 Blue that might pay her a visit and fertilize the potted plants in her room. Every individual on her team had taken their turn, from her lieu to her latest trainee. They all knew how to lay it on pretty thick, too. She was glad that the perp that put her here was 1,000 pounds and sported four feet, but Gail wished the name could've been something other than "Babe." Stupid stinkin' hay burner was lucky she hadn't turned her into coyote bait right there in the middle of the trail.

Her dad hadn't helped her mood with his, "I always told you those lousy nags weren't good for anything but barbeque!"

So, figuring that whoever was knocking wasn't going to bring anything worse than what she'd already suffered, Gail gruffly hollered, "Yeah, what do you want?" When Mollie's big brown eyes peeked around the privacy curtain, it was a welcome surprise.

Pals at Rosland High School better than ten years ago, they hadn't spent a lot of time together since. They got together just often enough to commiserate about their lack of luck with men and to compare notes about which of their classmates had managed to escape from Central Oregon. And they were there for one another when disaster struck in whatever form. This horse-induced broken back of Gail's was the most recent of the problems.

"Hey, girl," Mollie began, "what some people do for some time off! But couldn't you have just broken an arm or sprained a wrist? It ain't gonna be easy to hang at the lake with a broken back! Dang, can't you plan ahead?"

"Hey Mollie, how are you? How'd ya hear?"

"You might think you can drive fast, but you know nothin' compares with the speed of a cell phone in the hands of one of our mothers." Mollie entered the small room and placed a black and yellow backpack on the floor as she sank into one of the hospital's notoriously uncomfortable visitor's chairs.

"Did you have a hard day at work?" Gail asked, noticing how Mollie wilted.

"Yeah, you know how it is. Bust your chops all day, but there's never a client who is glad to see ya," Mollie replied.

"Boy, do I know. That's one thing that a police officer has in common with a dental hygienist. No one is ever glad to see us, but our clients keep comin' back," Gail laughed.

"Too true," Mollie answered. "Anyway, I brought ya this backpack full of my favorite DVDs. Thought they might break the monotony for you during your recovery. I don't think you're goin' be doing much dancin,' and I want to keep you distracted while I'm out there buildin' loops to rope the cowboys while you are out of commission."

"Huh! Good luck," Gail grunted. "Like there are any decent Cayuses left out there that aren't wearin' a brand. I hope the DVDs aren't a bunch of goofy romances."

"Mom mighta snuck a sappy love story or two into the stack, but I think most of them are adventures. There is nothing as exciting as your day-to-day stuff…but better than staring at the ceiling and less frustrating than stacking marbles. I better run and let you get some beauty sleep. It looks like you've been missin' out lately! Hope ya get well soon. If there's anything ya need, just holler," Mollie said as she prepared to make her exit.

"Thanks for stopping by," Gail responded. "Why don't cha hand me that backpack of treasure before you leave, so I can check out my future viewing pleasure. Man, there must be fifty of those suckers in there! I'll get 'em back to ya. Soon, I hope."

"Yeah, there are fifty at least. What else can a girl do on a cold winter night in wonderful Rosland, Oregon, while recovering from the side effects of faulty horsemanship?" Mollie quipped as she headed out into the hall. "And don't worry about gettin' 'em back in a hurry. Summer's comin,' and I won't be sittin' around watchin' movies again till fall."

2

Three Months Later

Gail's recovery from the horseback-riding fiasco was nearly complete. A couple more weeks of therapy, and she should be good as new. And a good thing, too, since she was moving from a rental house in Redmond to her very own brand-new home in Prineville. She wasn't able to provide much muscle to the move, but between a little logistical support from her parents, and even her mother's parents, and an enormous amount of muscle and brains, not to mention trucks and trailers, from her friends and coworkers at the Bend P.D., the move went relatively smoothly.

As the dust was settling and most of the friends were leaving, Gail found her mother, Amy, putting some finishing touches on the towels and soaps in her new master bathroom. "Mom, thanks for all your hard work. Everything looks so good. I can't believe we got all my junk moved, and a lot of it put away in one day," Gail said with a tired but grateful tone.

With a motherly look of concern, Amy replied, "I'm so glad I got to help. How's your back holding up? I bet you're gonna be sore tomorrow."

"I think I'm okay. I let everyone else do the heavy stuff. Pretty good planning, wasn't it? But Mom, could you do me one more favor when you leave?" Gail asked.

"Sure, what is it?"

"Please take Mollie's DVDs back to her. I don't know when I'll get out to Rosland, and now that I'm in my new place and feelin' pretty good, I don't think I'll be watchin' any more of 'em," Gail answered.

"No problem. I'll be seeing her mom next week. I'll just give them to her."

"That'd be great. Thanks so much for all the help. Here, I'll get the backpack," Gail said as they headed for the front door.

Out front at the curb, Gail found her dad, Nate, haranguing the last of her cop buddies at the scene about who was going to eat the last of the donuts that had been purchased to bribe the moving crew. "Dad, you'd better be careful. The next time you see Russ he's going to be on duty, and he'll probably give you a ticket for loitering—while you're driving at your old man speed through town."

Nate scowled and replied, "You know I don't go to Bend but about once a year, and I doubt this 'ere owl hoot 'ill recollect me by then. Besides, you guys are too busy chasing excitement to take time to harass an old man for driving too cautiously."

"Whatever. Hey, Dad, will you do me one more favor? I have a big box of junk for Grandma. It's for her garage sale tomorrow. Can you take it to her for me?"

"Sure, but I hope it is good valuable stuff. Both Grandma and Grandpa are worn plumb out, and the stupid sale doesn't even start until tomorrow."

Russ raised his eyebrows and asked, "Your grandparents are havin' a garage sale tomorrow?"

"Yeah," Gail replied. "They are hosting a great big garage sale monstrosity to benefit a teenager in their church. He has a reoccurring brain tumor, and they're trying to help the family out."

Nate added, "Monsterosity is right! People have been dropping off all kinda trash for weeks. Gramps and Granny have been sorting, culling, pricing, and pitching junk for days. One thing is certain, we'll all be pleased as punch when the whole thing is done! It has been entertaining, though."

3

The next morning dawned bright and clear; perfect garage-sale weather. Nate got up early, gathered Gail's donation to the sale, and headed to his parents' home, which was all of about one hundred yards away. They lived on side-by-side one-acre lots. His parents weren't all that thrilled to get more stuff, but most of it looked like it would sell, and they had everything ready well before the advertised 8:00 start to the sale.

Things started slow for everything but DVDs. "They're sellin' like hotcakes. Looks like we should have priced them a mite higher," Gramps said, referring to the movies.

"Yeah, maybe, but just be glad they're gone. At least we won't have to worry about how to get rid of 'em." Nate replied.

The first thing that caught Amy's eye when she stopped on her way to work at just after 9:00 was a black and yellow backpack with a $3.00 price tag on it. From the look on her face, the thing must have been wearing serious HAZMAT tags. "Is…is…that…Mollie's backpack over there?" she asked, pointing at the deflated pack.

"Yeah," Nate responded. "Do you think it's priced too low?"

"No, I don't think it's priced too low. It's not supposed to be in the sale at all. It's Mollie's. Where are the DVDs?" an edge of panic was creeping into Amy's voice.

The stately ponderosa pines that stood as silent witnesses to this stomach-turning mega-mess got a lesson in looking green. You couldn't find a sicker-looking bunch than the crew at that garage sale. Fifty or more prime DVDs that weren't theirs to sell had been sold for less than what one of them would cost to replace.

"Wait," someone said with a faint tone of hope. "I think one woman purchased most of those, and she wrote a check for them."

"That's right," Nate, who was acting as the money man, offered. "The check's right here. There's a cell phone number on it. Don't you think that if we call and offer a little incentive money, we might be able to get 'em back?"

"Sure. Once we explain what happened, I'm sure she'll be glad to give 'em back," Amy confidently stated. "I just don't want to be the one who has to explain this to Gail."

"Forget about Gail. I'll tell her. You start worryin' about how to tell Mollie," Nate replied.

Aside from that one not-so-tiny problem, the garage sale was a success. The stuff that was left over could be taken to the dump in one trip, and a fair amount of cash was raised to help the family in need. Throughout the day, one or another of the workers would try the phone number listed on the check that had been written to purchase the movies, but no one received a response. Then finally, that evening, on Amy's first attempt after she got home from work, she got an answer. Nate could tell that it wasn't going well by the expression of Amy's face, and then by the exasperated sigh that escaped when she put the phone down.

"What'd she say?" Nate asked anxiously.

"Well, first she didn't know what I was talking about," Amy replied, voice dripping with frustration, "then she said that it was too late. She bought the movies for her son in Iraq, and she shipped them to him this afternoon. She sounded high, drunk, stupid…or a combination of all three."

"Oh, now, that's just great," Nate returned. "But she looked way too old to have a kid in Iraq. And, hey, wait a minute. How'd she ship 'em? This is Saturday. The post office is closed!"

"I dunno," Amy said. "Maybe she shipped them through one of those 'Mailboxes Are Us' places in Bend."

"You didn't deal with this lady," Nate replied. "If you had haggled with the penny pinchin' bat, you'd know that there is no way that the tight wad would spend the extra dough that those places charge. No, she just flat lied to ya. I'd bet my BVDs she ain't shipped those DVDs nowheres, no wise. But I guess it don't matter none, 'cause we ain't gonna get 'em back."

"What do we tell Gail?" Amy moaned.

"I told you I'd take care of that. She'll understand. But how are we gonna make this up to Mollie? That's the big question," Nate answered.

4

Two in the morning is a dark time in the pine forests of Central Oregon, when the moon is new, a hundred-foot trip from a carport to a house can turn into an adventure. It's so dark you can get lost in your own backyard. Get into a clearing or above the trees, though, and the night sky on one of those moonless nights will amaze even the most stoic. The sky is awash with stars.

> *It didn't seem dark to Eliab or Yanoa. They didn't see things the way people see them. And the stars didn't draw their attention either. It was the two pillars of light that shone through the roof at the back of the little house nestled in the giant ponderosa trees on West Pine Cone Way that drew their interest. At times it appeared that the light was shining down through the roof, and then at other times it looked like the light was shining up.*
>
> *The warriors had witnessed these light shows on a multitude of occasions; but, the mighty pair could not help but be nearly overcome with wonder. The King was communicating with mortals, and the mortals were not consumed! And that usually meant that things were going to get interesting. There was the smell of battle in the air!*

For Jake and Jan, nearly sixty years of sharing a bedroom had changed almost everything. Almost. Each not wanting to awaken the other when they were lying awake was one of the few constants. And so on this dark July night, they each maintained silence in order to not disturb the other. Both were engaged in the same activity: prayer.

Their approach was totally different from one another, as was their approach to almost everything. Jan was organized. She prayed down a list—literally. Had it been light right now she would have had her list in front of her, but she mostly had it memorized, so lying in the dark, she went through it in her mind. Funny, she couldn't remember so many things anymore, but the prayer list wasn't among them. Her list was by category: Kids, Grandkids, Great-grandkids, Siblings, Neighbors, Old friends, Kids in her Sunday school class, People in the Church, People she wanted to introduce to Jesus. She didn't pray through the categories in any particular order, but within the categories, she was methodical. No one got left out. Unless she got stuck on someone, then things could go on for a while. Or, unless she fell asleep before she made it through the list. If she did, matter of fact, even if she didn't, she'd start again in the morning, right after her Bible reading.

Jake's prayers were different. There was no structure with him. He prayed for people or circumstances as they came into his mind. Sometimes he'd spend an hour on one thing, praying about it from every different angle. It was in those times that he "knew." Knew things he had no way of knowing, knew the things that were on people's hearts or things about the future. He almost never told anyone about this "knowing." It scared folks. Shoot, it scared him! So he'd just pray; lying in bed, mowing the grass, walking through the woods. He'd just talk to God about what he knew or about what he didn't. Lately he'd caught himself even talking to God out loud. He knew he needed to watch that. Someone was going to see him and think he'd completely lost it. But then, maybe he had.

Tonight, both Jan and Jake were stuck on their eldest

granddaughter, Gail. Neither of them knew why, but both of them could not quite pray past her. So they just prayed all over her. This certainly was not the first time that Gail had been the subject of a prayer-a-thon for her grandparents. The police department that she worked for had their officers on a schedule of two twelve-hour day shifts, followed by two twelve-hour night shifts, followed by four days off. It seemed that, more often than not, Gail would become the recipient of an extra dose of prayer on one of the night shifts nearly every shift cycle. Her recent back injury had placed her in the prayer spotlight as well. But her back appeared healed, and she was not on duty tonight, so it seemed odd. Jake didn't "know" anything either, he just felt an overwhelming sense of darkness.

5

Gail took three quick strides across the deck, spun on her heel, and returned to stand in front of her mother. "What do ya mean she won't give 'em back? That's the biggest batch of crock I've ever heard. She hasn't shipped those DVDs to Iraq. I can't believe you let her feed you that crap."

"What was I supposed to do Gail, call her a liar?" Amy responded, with her eyes studying the boards of the deck.

"It'd be great to reach right down the phoneline and throttle the witch," Nate added. "But I've never been real successful at that. My hands must be too big."

"I dunno," Gail snapped as her eyes scanned the green grass and thick pines that surrounded her parents' yard, as if she were looking for a target on which to unleash her fury. "But give me that stinking check. I'm gonna go out to her house and give that woman a good old-fashioned talking to."

Nate got out of his lawn chair and walked over to the edge of the deck. Their two labs saw him move and came running, hoping that the movement meant he was going to throw one of their toys for them to chase. Luke, the two-year-old yellow lab, let out a short high-pitched growl and spun and wiggled so much that Nate said,

"Settle down, you knot head, before you turn around inside your skin. Maybe that's what already happened, and that's why you never know where you're goin.'"

Nate turned back to Gail and matched the intensity of her glare with a stubborn look of his own. "I'm sure you're right, Gail. If she bought those DVDs to send to Iraq, she hasn't done it yet. And bein' it's the weekend; we haven't put the check in the bank either. But I don't want cha goin' out there alone. That's right on the Chiloquin County line. You know how rough it is out there! Most people who live out there moved there just so no one official would be around to bother 'em. And I can't go with ya because your ma and I have some people coming over this afternoon."

"Dad," Gail barked, "I go to those kinds of places for a living. Do ya think that everyone in our jurisdiction is nice and polite? Besides, I won't be in uniform, so no one will know I'm a cop!"

Nate knew from experience that he wouldn't win this argument. The fact that Gail had come out on a Sunday when none of her nieces or nephews was there and it wasn't a holiday was evidence enough that she was serious about getting those DVDs back. "Gail, it was my fault, not yours that those DVDs got away. I'll make it right with Mollie. None of those things could have been that valuable."

"It's the idea, Dad. Mollie lent those movies to me. I'm gonna do whatever I can to get 'em back."

"Okay. I'll go get the check. The address is on it. But couldn't Russ or someone go with you?" Nate asked.

"Russ is on duty today. But if it will make you feel better, I'll check in with Mike Divetti before I go down. He'll know if there are any really bad hombres at the address."

Mike was the sergeant for the southern portion of East Lake County Sheriff's Department. Gail had graduated from Rosland High School with him, and he and Nate worked out at the same gym. Both Gail and Nate liked and trusted him.

Gail called the county dispatch office and asked to speak to Mike and was told that he would be off duty until Thursday. She offered to patch Gail through to Mike's voicemail.

6

Jake would have been raking pine needles from the flowerbeds in his front yard on any other day. That was the downside to the beautiful big Ponderosas that stood along the driveway, all those needles. During burning season, raking was almost enjoyable. The bright flames consuming the piles of needles made quite a sight; but during the dry summer months the danger of forest fire made burning not only dangerous, but illegal. All you could do with the needles during this time of year was pile them up and wait for the fall rains. Oh, you could haul them to the dump, but Jake sure wasn't interested in paying to get rid of something he could burn for free.

Some people only raked during burning season. But more needles came down every time there was a little wind. A brief thunderstorm last evening had brought enough wind to provide a pretty good crop, and Jake hated the way they looked among his carefully tended flowers and carefully manicured grass. But they'd have to wait until tomorrow. Jake took Sundays off.

He finished his inspection tour and headed for the house. Just as he was going through the door he was struck by an almost overwhelming concern for Gail. Jake didn't know why, but often God would burden him with the need to pray for one of his kids or grandkids. When he got that burden, all he could do was pray. So he went into the house where Jan was busy putting the finishing touches on their Sunday dinner. He headed for his recliner but stopped in the kitchen long enough to speak to Jan, "We'd better be bringing Gail before the throne. I don't know what the child is up to but I gotta strong hunch that she needs our prayers."

"What do you suppose is wrong? She's not working today," Jan replied. "Besides, I think I saw her rig pull in next door."

"Don't know, don't much care. Just know I gotta pray," Jake said, settling into his chair. "Maybe she'll stop by before she heads out."

Eliab and Yanoa had gotten orders to head to an area a little to the south of Rosland. They never thought to question the directions or object. When the King spoke, they obeyed with eagerness. Nothing could have suited them better than to praise and worship the sovereign through obedience to His bidding.

When they arrived at their destination, the smell of battle was strong, and the air was full of the sounds of the conflict. They had no more than arrived then they realized they were being surrounded by a host of the army of darkness. The warriors of light were greatly outnumbered. Still, success would have been so simple, had only the mortals been asking the King for victory. But so few asked, and fewer still put on their armor. Didn't they know they were in a war? The King had told them in the Book. Couldn't they understand that victory was theirs for the asking? But they had to ask.

7

"I just don' like ya goin' out there alone, is the thing. You can't never tell what a nest full of hornets you're gonna stir up when ya go off into the pucker brush in the south part of this county," Nate argued as he pitched a knotted rope across the yard, his two big labs grabbing it before it had a chance to bounce. "Why don' cha let me go out there with you tomorrow after I get off work and see what we can do together?" he grunted as he wrestled the rope from Luke.

"Dad," Gail answered with a practiced smirk, "tomorrow after work may be too late. She'll probably have mailed 'em by then. And I don't want to drive all the way back out here tomorrow anyway. Besides, do you really think that a card-carryin' member of the 50/50 club would be that much help?"

Nate knew he shouldn't ask, but he just couldn't keep from rising to the bait, "The 50/50 club?"

"Guys that are over fifty years old and fifty pounds overweight!"

"Oh, now, that's cold. That was designed to hurt my feelers. But I tell ya what, I think this fat old man may have every bit as good a chance with folks as your pals in the 44/4 club."

Gail didn't give her dad the satisfaction of asking what the 44/4 club was. She already knew: size forty-four coats and size four hats. In other words, all muscle, no brains.

"I'm not gonna argue with you about it, Pops. I'm not goin' out there to arrest someone or get in a brawl. I'm just going to stop by and try to talk her into givin' those DVDs back," Gail said with frustration as she headed for her Toyota pickup.

"Get back here, you bozos," Nate shouted at his dogs as they ran down the driveway in the dust behind Gail's pickup. Both quickly turned and ran back to him. "At least you boys got enough sense to listen to me," Nate grumbled.

Next door, Jake and Jan watched the Toyota drive by with a mixture of disappointment and trepidation. Jake would wander over next door later and find out what was going on.

8

"Let's see," Gail muttered to herself, "the numbers get smaller, with the evens on the right, as I head west. That means the next place on the left should be 16173." There was what looked to be a driveway of sorts through the bitterbrush, but there was nothing to indicate the address, or even if it really was a driveway. She would never admit it to the old man, but finding homes out in the pucker brush, as he called it, wasn't quite like locating an address in town. The next turn to the left was marked with a white rock with 16069 painted on it. That goat path back there about a quarter mile had to be the place she was looking for.

The driveway, if that's what it was, was pure dust. There had obviously never been any gravel on it. Someone had just cleared off the bitterbrush and started driving between the trees. That worked all right, if you didn't mind dust, in this land where the volcanic eruptions that formed the Cascade Mountains had left six feet of pumice powder on top of everything. The ground was so porous that any precipitation ran right through; you never had to worry about mud bogs or puddles, except during spring thaw when the ground was frozen and the accumulated snow was breaking up, then it didn't matter what you'd done, the road was going to be a mess.

That meant that almost everyone who lived in this country drove four-wheel drive vehicles. But then, they were needed to negotiate the heavy snows in winter anyway.

About 200 yards after leaving the road, Gail got a glimpse of a pole barn up ahead on her right. Then she noticed a small manufactured home. Both buildings were old and in a sorry state of disrepair. Off the pole barn to the west was a rough, sorry-looking corral, fashioned from pine poles. Two blaze-faced sorrel horses were trotting around the small enclosure. As Gail rolled closer to the buildings, a black and white Border collie bounded off the porch, barking and growling like he was prepared to eat the pickup, starting with the tires.

She came to a slow stop and sat in her rig as the dust slowly drifted in the still air. The dog's tail raced its nose around the truck three times before it stopped beside the driver's side door. Now it stood staring in the window, right at her. Every couple of seconds it would lunge at the truck and snap and bark.

Gail's two years of experience as a community service officer, prior to her being promoted to police officer, told her that her best move at this point was to stay in her vehicle until the dog settled down. She used the time to carefully observe the door and windows of the house that were visible from her position. She saw no movement inside.

Expanding her observation to the outside, she noticed that at some point someone had made a feeble attempt at some landscaping. Red lava rocks outlined what had once been rectangular flowerbeds on either side of the porch. An oval of the same rock marked an aborted effort at a flowerbed in the center of the driveway's turnaround. The dry ground inside these borders sported nothing more than a few straggly yarrow stalks and a scattering of dwarfed lupine. A liberal spattering of beer cans provided the primary colors.

At least one of the horses in the corral had a taste for pine. The top poles forming the enclosure had been cribbed nearly in two in places. But then the brutes needed something to chew, for not a blade of anything green was visible in the pen. If Gail hadn't been mad at horses she may have felt sorry for them, especially considering the way that the animals were taking turns nosing the hay rack in their corral, flipping their tails at flies and shaking their heads.

As the Toyota's engine cooled and clicked, the dog began to lose interest. Finally he decided that he wasn't going to get to a chance to put his fangs into the occupant of the pickup, and he trotted back to the porch where he began entertaining himself by licking the inside of his food dish. He was so intent on finding the last taste or hidden crumb that he pushed the dish off the steps, and then started barking at the racket it made clattering down the steps.

That move reminded Gail of the doggie treats that she had in the pickup's glove box. She always carried a few milk bones to try to buy the affection of her dad's dogs. Locating the bribes, she rolled down the truck window and clicked her tongue at the dog. He responded instantly by running back to the truck, sitting on his haunches, cocking his ears, and holding his head at a quizzical angle while looking in the open window. Gail tossed a treat, and the dog deftly caught it and swallowed it in one move. The sharp bark that came next was all begging and no aggression, so Gail felt safe in opening the door and swinging her feet out of the truck. She tossed the little mercenary another treat and climbed out of the rig and started toward the porch. The dog trotted beside her like a lifelong friend, a move that bought him another piece of doggie cookie.

The house had an empty feel as Gail knocked on the door. She didn't really expect a response; if anyone had been home they would have heard her drive up, not to mention the dog's greeting. She called out anyway, "Anybody home?" The words echoed back at her. Peeking in the window beside the door, she could see that the residents were not long on neatness inside any more than out. There was considerable debris strewn around, and on the table was a white plastic bag from the local grocery store. From what she could see it looked very much like it could contain a pile of DVDs. Knowing better, she reached out and grabbed the doorknob. It was unlocked, and the knob turned easily in her hand. Coming to her senses, she let the spring in the knob turn it back to the latched position.

Before the temptation to enter the house became too great to ignore, she moved away from the door and made her way over to the pole barn. It was not a large barn, about twenty by thirty feet. Gail looked in the barn's only window, a small opening framed in beside the man door. The interior of the building was illuminated by daylight that entered the building through transparent panels in the roof. The barn appeared to be about ninety percent full of high-dollar alfalfa hay. Odd, Gail thought, these people live in a dump and drive old beater cars but feed their horses the best hay money could buy.

The horses snorted and bucked when she got close to the corral. The old bathtub that was being used as a watering trough for the horses was dry. Without thinking she opened the hydrant and began to fill the tub. At the sound of the running water the dog came trotting, put his front feet on the side of the tub, and tried to drink all the water as it came out the short piece of frayed green hose attached to the hydrant. The horses forgot they were broncs when they heard the water. They had their noses in the cold water that escaped the dog and were making loud slurping noises before there was an inch of water in the tub.

Once the tub was filled, Gail closed the hydrant and turned and headed slowly back toward her rig. She could feel the small hairs on the back of her neck stand on end. She was sure that someone was watching her. Slowly turning a complete circle, she scanned the trees and brush for any sign of movement, but she couldn't see anything.

Puffs of dust mushroomed around her feet when she started walking again. This place was too quiet, creepy, she thought.

When the horses and dog had finished drinking there was no noise, not even a slight breeze to whisper through the lodge pole pine trees. She stood in the dust halfway between the barn and her Toyota, debating with herself about entering the house and taking the DVDs, and listening. Her years as a police officer had given her a kind of sixth sense about danger, and the sense was screaming at her. And it was driving her berserk because she couldn't see any reason for her fear.

The black and white dog made her decision for her when for no apparent reason it began running around her in a tight circle, barking and nipping at her feet, like it was trying to herd her away from the house. That was too weird, she thought as she compliantly headed toward her truck. The apparent success made the dog more aggressive. In an attempt to distract the dog, Gail reached down, grabbed an empty beer can off the ground and tossed it toward the porch, hoping the pooch would follow. Instead, the motion agitated the mutt even more, and out of frustration Gail tried to kick the mongrel as he nipped at her heels. She got bitten on the calf for her trouble.

Managing to get inside the pickup without further injury, she checked the bite. That little turd had broken the skin. There were two nice puncture wounds on either side of her calf muscle. "I oughta ventilate your flee-bitten hide, you worthless cur," she hollered, more to herself than to the dog who had made his way back to the porch where he stood panting and looking pleased with himself.

She sat in her rig, again looking the place over. Paint was peeling from all the trim on the house. The black three-tab shingles were curled on the corners from baking in the sun. The window screens were torn and hanging down from two of the windows. A stack of worn-out truck tires leaned against the southeast corner of the house. "Why in the world would somebody living in a dump like this spend money on DVDs?" Gail asked herself aloud.

The burning in her calf from the dog's teeth dimmed her apprehension about this place, but she still felt like she was missing something, and attempting to determine what it was that was freaking her out. For fifteen minutes she sat studying the house and surrounding landscape, trying to figure out what she was sensing.

Finally she decided that it was just her imagination running away with her, and she started the Toyota. She glanced at the horses as she swung the pickup around. She was surprised that they weren't watching her. Instead, they were both looking south intently, standing stiff legged, ears up sharp and pointing forward. She stopped the pickup and scanned the scrub pine and bitterbrush in the direction they were facing but could not see anything. Must just be a coyote or deer, Gail decided. Looking back at the porch, she saw the dog had plopped down and was already taking a nap. That was odd. If there were a critter out there, the dog should be as interested as the horses. She thought about getting back out of her rig and doing some more investigation, but she couldn't shake the feeling of fear. Not wanting to admit even to herself, that she was spooked, she convinced herself that she was leaving because she didn't want to give the mutt another chance at biting her.

Gail drove back out the dirt drive feeling more like a frightened child than she had since junior high. About halfway back to the road, she noticed what she should have seen on her way in: No one had driven on the driveway since the thunderstorm yesterday afternoon. Her incoming tire tracks were the only tracks marring the raindrop-dimpled dust. Interesting, she thought, if anyone had been here last night, how could they not leave tracks in the driveway when they left today? And there were no vehicles in the driveway. She pondered the thirst and hunger of the animals. "I don't think anyone's been around for a couple of days," she said to herself.

Eliab and Yanoa were back in the ponderosas at Jake and Jan's before Gail had pointed her Toyota north on Highway 31.

Though they had been able to provide some assistance, it was far less than they knew was possible.

As much to break the creepy feeling as to keep her promise, Gail speed-dialed her mom's cell phone as soon as she hit the pavement and was headed north. "Hi, Gail," her mother answered.

"Hi. I just wanted to let ya know that I'm headed back toward Prineville."

"Any luck getting the movies back?" Amy asked.

"Nope," Gail answered, irritation spilling over in her voice, "there wasn't anyone at the address except a couple of old hay burners and a flee-bitten mutt. The place looked about as prosperous as a line shack on a hard-scrabble ranch."

"Did ya leave a note or anything?"

"No. But the mutt left a good mouth impression on my calf muscle. That dog is lucky I didn't pop 'im on the spot."

"Gail! He bit you?" Amy gasped, the mom coming out in her voice.

"Yeah, and he made a pretty good job of it too. Good thing I'm current on my tetanus shots."

"Do you think you need stitches? Did it bleed out good?" Amy's nurse training was starting to kick in.

"No, Ma, I don't need stitches. And it did bleed a little. I'll just rub some antibiotic cream into the holes when I get home, and I'm sure it'll be fine. Please tell Dad I'm okay, but he needs to start workin' on an explanation for Mollie," Gail said, her tone making it clear that she was getting ready to end this conversation.

Amy, mother and nurse, wasn't ready to leave it at that. "Why don't you stop here on your way through? We can fix you up with some supper, and I can make sure those bites are cleaned up good," she suggested.

"Thanks, Ma, but I think I'll pass. You guys have company, and I'd like to get home before too late. Tomorrow's my last day off before going back to work, and I have a bunch of yard work and laundry to catch up on," Gail answered.

"Okay, but Tim and Mary already left. Keep an eye on that bite. If it looks like it is starting to get infected, you need to have someone look at it," Amy insisted.

"It's not that big a deal, but I promise to keep an eye on it. Love ya. Bye," Gail disconnected quickly without giving her mom a chance for more concerned instructions.

"Well, Nate," Amy said when she had hung up the phone, "Gail didn't find anyone home when she went to retrieve the DVDs. But she did manage to get bit by a dog at the house!"

Nate turned from the Mariner's baseball game that he was watching on the TV with a look of astonishment. "That gal knows more 'bout handling dogs than a mail carrier. How in the world did she manage to let some mongrel bite her?"

"I don't know any of the details," Amy stated, throwing her hands up. "She obviously didn't want to discuss the event in detail. I just hope the wound doesn't get infected."

"Ah, Ma," Nate smiled, "ya know that girl is tougher than nails. Ya might start worryin' about the mutt, though. He might come down with a fatal case of foot and fang disease, or croak of instant lead poisoning."

"Laugh if ya want, but animal bites can be serious," was Amy's retort. "But what are we gonna do about Mollie's movies?

"We'll take her backpack to her with enough money to cover the replacement cost of 'em," Nate replied. "I just haven't figured out how to make her take the cash, or how to explain my stupidity. I guess I'll just have to blame it all on you."

9

At a little after seven on Friday morning, Gail was at the station trying to finish up the paperwork from her last shift. Nothing too exciting, a couple of domestic calls that went nowhere and a drunk driver arrest that demanded a lot of report writing. She was looking forward to her days off. The last couple of hours of the second shift that started at seven in the evening and ended at seven in the morning could get long. And they certainly had today.

"Hey, Gail," her sergeant, Bill Brown, said as he stuck his head into the cubical she was working in, "any idea why Divetti wants to talk to you? You guys workin' on somethin' together?"

"No," Gail answered, shrugging, "I left him a message a few days ago asking about an address. No big deal. I'll give him a call."

"Ya won't have to. He's on his way over right now. He asked me to have you stick around until he gets here. You sure this isn't anything I need to know about? Mike sounded a little growlish on the phone," the sergeant added.

"Ah, you know Mike. Probably had to buy his own breakfast this morning," Gail laughed. Mike Divetti was notorious for filching donuts out of the briefing room when he stopped by the station.

"Hey, Mike," Gail teased when he showed up a few minutes later, "did you come by to see how much better our blue uniforms look than your disgusting brown ones? Or are you here to steal pastries again? Ya know, ya might wanna go a little easy on the calories, they're startin' to show." Mike was an even six feet tall and weighed about two hundred and forty pounds, but didn't have an ounce of fat anywhere. His arms and chest were massive. She was sure she could harass him without hurting his pride, but looking at his response to her kidding, she began to think she had miscalculated. The last time she had seen Mike look this serious; he was failing a high school calculus exam.

"I just have a couple of questions for you. You remember calling me about that address down on the East Lake/Chiloquin county line?" Mike asked. When Gail nodded, he continued. "Why were you interested?"

"Oh, it wasn't anything urgent, just a little garage sale mix-up. I was hoping you might be able to give a little insight into the residents of the address. And since you're here asking, I'm guessin' that you do know something about 'em."

"I think I might need you to provide a few more details about this mix-up," Mike stated, his tone all business.

Mike's serious demeanor was starting to worry Gail. "What's this all about, Mike? Why are you so interested, and what's up with this Judge Roy Bean routine all of a sudden?"

"Well, the dude—guy by the name of Ron Shear—what owns the place you were asking about came home last night, after spending two weeks down in Lake Isabella California caring for his mother. She has terminal lung cancer and is normally cared for by her daughter, but Ron goes down for a couple of weeks two or three times per year to give his sister a break. Anyway, he came home to a bit of a surprise. The woman that he has been living with for the past eight years, a gal named Jodie Caddell, was lying dead on the living room floor. He called 911, even though she was obviously real dead. The hot weather hadn't been kind to the corpse. When the deputy, he's new with us by the name of Derek, arrived, he looked around and talked to Ron and they agreed that she probably had suffered a stroke or heart attack or something. There was no sign of a struggle, and nothing appeared to be missing, hard to tell in that mess though. Just about that time Pistol Pete showed up on the scene. You know he's the acting coroner for South County? He noticed right away that something was up. There were multiple abrasions and contusions around her neck. Derek hadn't noticed because the vic was wearing a turtle neck. So all of a sudden we have ourselves a probable murder, and I got called into it. Along with the Oregon State Police, of course. We don't get enough major crimes to warrant the equipment, or gain the investigative experience, to handle something like this on our own.

"It took me a while to remember why the address was so familiar," Mike continued. "In fact, I was trying to find the driveway when it hit me. The address I was trying to find was the address that you left me a message about. So, tell me. Why were you so interested in this particular address?"

Gail gave Mike the DVD story, start to finish. Then she admitted that she'd been on the premises last Sunday afternoon. "You're gonna find my prints on the front door knob and on the hydrant handle," she told Mike. "My footprints will be in yard and my tire tracks in the driveway. You've undoubtedly collected evidence from those spots, haven't you?"

"I know we lifted fingerprints from the door knobs, both front and back, as well as from a bazillion other places inside the house. An isolated thunderstorm went through there on Wednesday evening and dropped quite a bit of rain, so we didn't get any tracks from outside. I don't think anyone tried to get any evidence from out around the horse corral." Mike was talking to her like she was any other cop, then caught himself and put his professional face back on.

"We're not gonna find any of your prints or anything inside the house, are we?" he asked.

"No," Gail answered, "I didn't go in the buildings." She didn't volunteer the information about how close she came to being inside. "Ya got any suspects?"

"Besides you, ya mean?" he answered.

"Yeah, I mean real suspects."

"Not yet. We're running all the prints through AFIS. Hopefully that will turn up some evidence that suggests that someone was in that house that didn't belong there. And it would be nice if that someone had some motive for her murder."

"Please keep me posted," Gail requested when she saw that Mike was ready to close this informal interview.

"I'll let you know what I can. But you gotta remember that if we get a hit on your prints through AFIS, OSP is gonna want to talk to you. So far, I haven't told anyone about your phone call to me. But notes about this discussion are going to be in the file, and curiosities are going to be aroused. Let me know if you think of anything that might help the investigation. And stay outta trouble." Gail had the reputation for being a straight arrow among the law enforcement agencies in Central Oregon, but Mike remembered a slightly different person from their days in high school. The same could be said for him, he supposed.

"Do you have an estimated time of death?" Gail asked.

"We are not going to know anything conclusive until they get us an autopsy report. Pete's guess was sometime between Saturday noon and Sunday evening. He usually comes pretty close."

They walked out to the parking lot together in silence. As Mike climbed into his brown-on-white East Lake County Ford Explorer, Gail said, "Our uniforms are nicer, but you guys 'ave got the sweet rides. Oh, and Mike…thanks." He gave the two-finger salute as he drove away.

Gail settled in her Toyota and started it up, but she just sat behind the wheel in the parking lot thinking. Jodie Caddell had gone to a garage sale on Saturday morning, answered her phone Saturday evening, and then sometime between then and Sunday evening, had been murdered. Gail's mom could have very easily been the last person, other than the murderer, to speak to her. "This is way too weird. I wonder what would have happened if I had gone on in the house," Gail said to herself. "She was probably lying dead on the floor when I was there. The murderer may have been there too." Gail shook herself and headed her rig toward home.

10

During the forty-five minutes that it took Gail to travel from the Bend Police Department parking lot to her new home in Prineville, her mind worried the details of the events that had been put into motion by the simple action of her sending a back pack full of DVDs home with her mom and dad like a dog with a marrow bone. You could go back further than that, in fact, to her going for a horseback ride on a mare that had more spirit than she had riding experience.

When she was a preteen she loved to spend a warm afternoon playing in Paulina Creek, the whitewater stream that carried the snowmelt from the Newberry Crater to the Deschutes River. She lost whole afternoons in the cool shade of the majestic ponderosa pine trees occupied with nothing more than sending cones and sticks down the rapids of that small stream and watching as they spun and caught and then took off again in the violent swirling of that small mountain stream. She felt that she was in no more control of the events surrounding Mollie's DVDs than one of those cones spinning in an eddy on its way down that creek.

Normally she loved the morning drive from Bend to Prineville. Her commute began in the thriving activity of Oregon's fastest-growing city, with the torn-up streets, rapidly growing industrial parks, and exploding housing developments. Fifteen minutes later, the landscape was dominated by gentleman's ranches of five- to ten-acre parcels with a couple of horses, a cow or two, or maybe even a llama or alpaca sharing grass with a small flock of wild Canada geese. Fifteen minutes after that, and you were driving through alfalfa and cattle ranches with roots that went down five and six generations and that were part of a serious industry instead of a polite political statement of the gentleman acreages. Fifteen more minutes at sixty miles per hour, and you drove into Prineville, a small cattle town/mill town at the foot of the Ochocco Mountains, that had changed but little in the past seventy-five years. Rolling down Main Street, past the farm implement dealers, the feed store, the tavern with genuine batwing doors made everything slow down. By the time you reached the heart of the old town, with its magnificent stone courthouse and well-kept park and cemetery, life felt completely different.

People were different here too, she thought. Cowboys actually touched the flat brims of their Stetsons when you met them on the sidewalk. Old men sat in wooden chairs on the porch of the mercantile, spitting and whittling, while they solved the world's woes. Mothers tried to corral their broods of preschoolers. Life seemed slower and easier, like the idyllic days her grandparents talked about when they reminisced about their childhoods.

None of those things that she normally enjoyed so much on the drive home even registered in her thinking this morning. Her mind was completely absorbed in the mystery surrounding Jodie Caddell's death. What could the motive have been? Who was to benefit? Was there, as the detectives always said, money to follow? Was Gail going to be implicated? If she was, what did it mean for her future in law enforcement or for her future in general, for that matter?

Right now, though, she needed some dinner—or was it breakfast?

What did you call a meal eaten at eight thirty in the morning, before you went to bed? She'd go to work on trying to sort this whole mess out once she had eaten and gotten some sleep. It was too hard to concentrate when you were running on fumes.

As soon as she was in her house, she went to work in the kitchen. She started four slices of bacon frying then diced a slice of onion, chopped a quarter of a red pepper, minced half a tomato, and grated some Tillamook cheese. When the bacon was crisp she laid the slices on paper towel to cool and to absorb the excess grease. Meanwhile, she broke four eggs in a bowl, added a couple of tablespoons of cream, a healthy measure of ground black pepper, and whipped the mixture together. After pouring the bacon grease out of the frying pan and putting the pan back on the gas flame burner, she poured in the egg-and-cream mixture. While the mixture heated, changed color, and began to solidify she cut the bacon into chunks and sprinkled them over the cooking eggs. Then she added the onion, pepper, and cheese to one half. When the cheese had melted, she laid the tomatoes and folded the side without the vegetables over and let it cook for another minute and a half.

Fifteen minutes to a complete meal, the only real satisfaction or sense of accomplishment for the past three or four days.

While she ate, her mind kept going back to what she'd seen, or more likely what she may have overlooked last Sunday afternoon in southern East Lake County. Quickly finishing her meal, she cleaned up the kitchen, went in her bathroom, stripped, and took a quick shower. Then it was off to bed.

Just over four hours later, she jolted awake. The horses, something about the horses in that dirty little corral held a clue. She could picture them in her mind's eye, twitching their ears, pawing at the ground and switching their long tails. She clearly remembered the look of their lips as the brutes guzzled the water at the bottom of the tub. Then it came to her; the way their attention was intent as they stared south while she was leaving. They were immensely interested in someone, or something, in those trees. And Gail would have been willing to bet half her next paycheck that it wasn't a deer or a four-legged coyote.

She lay, staring at the ceiling of her bedroom, trying to decide the best approach to take in sharing her suspicions with Mike and the rest of the East Lake County investigative team. Would they believe anything she told them, or would it cast more suspicion her direction? The chirping of her cell phone interrupted her plotting. She wasn't expecting any calls; in fact, she meant to turn the phone off when she went to bed. She coveted sleep on her first day off duty.

Checking the phone's screen did no good, it simply said "private." Not knowing who was calling, she thought about not answering, but instead barked a gruff, "'Ello," into the phone.

"Gail, this is Mike Divette. How are you doing?"

"Oh, you know, just another day in paradise. Ya find something about your murder case already?" she asked.

"Well, actually, I'd like to talk to you about that," Mike replied. "I'm sittin' out front of your house right now. Ya mind lettin' me in?"

"Give me a couple minutes to get up and presentable."

"Okay, no hurry."

As Gail scrambled out of bed and into some sweats, her mind was racing at about 7,000 rpm. Why in the world would Mike come by her house? She'd talked to him less than eight hours ago. And this was Crook County, outside his jurisdiction, so why would he even be out here? She was sure it couldn't be good news.

She quickly ran a brush through her tangled hair, washed her face, and trotted her toothbrush through her mouth. Throughout the routine, Gail could not come up with a reasonable explanation for this strange, unexpected visit.

Mike was sitting at the curb in front of her house in his late-model quad-cab power-stroke Ford pickup when Gail opened her front door. The bright sunlight and heat of the day seemed out of place. On Gail's internal clock it was morning; everything else, including reality, said it was early afternoon.

She waved Mike in from her porch. As she watched, he closed his cell phone and climbed out of the big pickup.

"Come on in, Mike. Last night was my second night shift, so excuse me if I'm a little groggy. Let me get a pot of coffee goin'," she said, after pointing him to a stool at her breakfast bar. He was silent while she went through the motions of putting the coffee pot into action. As the brew started, she got a couple of mugs from the cupboard and asked, "Do you take cream or sugar?"

"No," Mike grunted, "I take it black."

More silence, an uneasy void.

"So," Gail asked as she turned toward Mike, "what's up? I don't think you drove all the way out here so we could rehash our glory days of high school. Did you find something interesting out about that murder case?"

"Yeah, we've come up with a couple of fascinating details. First, the coroner is sure that the vic did not die where her boyfriend found her. The body had been moved, post mortem. Second, she wasn't strangled like we had assumed. Her neck was snapped, a real professional-type job. There were rope fibers on her neck and wrists—apparently she had been tied up before she was killed. And third, the AFIS report contains a very interesting set of prints from inside the house."

"Really? Some frequent flyer or something?" Gail asked, with obvious interest.

"No," Mike returned, "yours."

"I told you that you'd find my prints on the door knob."

"Yeah, ya did. But remember, I specifically ask you if we'd find anything from you inside. You were quite sure we wouldn't."

"And I still am," Gail said. "Except, wait a minute, if the DVDs were in there, my prints would obviously be on those."

"Yeah, well, we didn't find any DVDs. But we did pick up a nice set of your prints from a beer can that was sittin' on a coffee table right beside where the body was found."

Gail sat, stunned, her mind revved up almost to the red line. Then it hit her: the can she threw to distract the dog! "I can explain that," she said. "I tossed a beer can in the yard to get that stupid mutt to leave me alone when I was tryin' to get back to my rig. Someone must have picked it up and put it inside the house."

"Well," Mike replied, "is that coffee ready?" As Gail poured, he continued. "There are a couple problems with that. First, the yard is pretty much littered with cans. Why would someone pick that one particular can up and take it inside? And two, nobody on the investigative team has seen a dog. We found a dog dish, and a lot of doggie landmines, but no pooch."

"Well, you better ask the boyfriend, what's his name—Ron?—about the dog. It's an ornery black and white Border collie. Here, if ya want proof, look at this," Gail continued as she pulled up the leg of her sweat pants to show off the nicely colored bruise and the four mostly healed puncture wounds. "This is where the mutt put the bite to me."

"I don't know anything about this biting dog, or any of that," Mike said, "but I do know that it is mighty odd that out of all the cans scattered around that yard, the one that you happened to handle is the one that ended up by the body."

"Look, Mike, you can't really think that I had something to do with that woman's murder. What possible motive could I have?" Gail asked.

"If I knew the motive, you'd be on your way to the tank right now, Gail," Mike responded. "As it is, you're pretty close to taking that ride. We don't have any other suspects at this point."

"What about the boyfriend? Have you checked his story? Or how about the neighbors? Or relatives, friends, acquaintances? Have you checked all of them?"

"Take it easy, Gail. I'm not haulin' you in or charging you just yet. And yes, we are trying to check everyone. But so far, we haven't got much. The boyfriend has gas receipts that match his story. We haven't been able to find many friends or relatives, and you've been out there. What neighbors? Can you think of anything else that might help us out?" Mike asked.

"I was just layin' awake thinkin' 'bout that when you called. I did notice something with those horses. When I was leaving on Sunday the horses were really intent on something to the south of their corral. At the time I thought there was some kinda wild animal out there. Now I'm wondering if that something might have been the murderer."

Mike knitted his thick brows together in thought and said, "You might be on ta something. Our guys didn't really search anything beyond the yard. Ted and Tony are big-time bow hunters, so they know how to read signs. I'll get them to go out there and check the surrounding woods for anything that might look out of place. Meanwhile, you need to be thinkin' about how you're gonna sweet talk the OSP crew when they come askin' questions about how your prints got inside that house."

As Mike was walking out the front door, Gail remembered to ask, "Hey, when you were collectin' your evidence, did you guys find the DVDs that got me involved in all this in the first place?"

"There were a bunch of movies in the place, but how we supposed to know if they were the ones that came from the infamous yard sale?"

"When I was peeking through the window, I thought I might have spotted them in a grocery bag on the table."

"There was a grocery bag full of paperback books on the table, but no DVDs that I know of. You're not still tryin' to get 'em back after all this mess, are ya?"

"I dunno. It'd still be good to get 'em back to Mollie. But more, I'd just like to know where they went."

"I'll check the evidence list and ask the officers that collected the evidence, but if I were you, I'd be more concerned about how to keep my backside away from the flames than about those movies."

II

Jake was raking needles, thinking and praying early Saturday morning. I'd rather be fishin,' he thought. In fact he was hoping that Nate would be along with a grin on his face and a cooler in the back of his pickup truck, headed for some hidden stream in the desert. Nate worked long hours during the week, leaving before five in the morning and not arriving home until after six in the evening. So on Saturdays he didn't usually get moving early enough to suit Jake. But about once a month, spring through early fall, Nate would stop by, pick up Jake, and they would head out to stalk eastern brook trout with their fly rods. Both Nate and Jake thoroughly enjoyed these outings. The enjoyment was pronounced by the knowledge that four and a half decades earlier, it was Nate waiting for Jake to take him on some fishing adventure.

 Jake was emptying the mornin's third wheelbarrow full of needles into the burning pit when he heard gravel crunching under the tires of Nate's pickup. He quickly took his yard-working tools into the tool/woodshed and headed for the garage to grab his fishing gear. Meanwhile, Nate had gone into the house to talk to his mother. This was a tradition; as soon as Jan knew that the men were setting out on an outdoor adventure she would go to work on packing them a lunch. She would put together enough food to take them through the day, and they would feign surprise and express appreciation.

"You guys better be careful," Jan told them as they arranged the lunch and other gear in the rig.

"We'll leave a few fish for seed, but the rest are destined for the smoker," Jake quipped as he climbed into the passenger seat of the Dodge. "See you sometime before dark. Women want me, but fish fear me."

They stopped in Rosland for fuel and then headed south and east, out into Oregon's high desert. The landscape changed from pine forest to sage and juniper. Driving through the pine forest, they stayed alert for deer. Even though it was seven thirty in the morning by the time they cleared town, having a deer jump out in the road was still a real possibility, and running over one was a sure way to ruin a good day. They spotted several doe-and-fawn pairs and one nice four-point buck, still in the velvet, but the deer were smart enough to stay on their side of the bar ditch.

"Did Gail make any progress on them DVDs the other day?" Jake asked as they sped south on Highway 31.

"Nah, but she did manage to get herself dog bit when she went out to try," Nate answered.

"Dog bit? How in the world did that girl let herself get dog bit?"

"I dunno. But ya know those crazy cattle dogs. Ya just can't trust 'em."

"'At's true enough, but she's the last person I'd expect to git bit. But you didn't have any luck fetching the movies, eh?"

"No, there wasn't anybody home, I guess."

About forty miles south east of Rosland, just before the little Town of Silver Lake, Nate turned the pickup off the state highway onto a logging road that headed west. This road took them into open rangeland, where having a herd of beef cows vie for right of way was a sure bet. The landscape changed quickly as they gained elevation. The desert vegetation of sage and juniper gave way to pine, and as the elevation continued to climb there were white fir and aspens mixed. This was the scenery that Jake and Nate loved. The plentiful greasewood bushes, currents, and Manzanita provided beautiful green undergrowth for the stately trees.

Jake filled Nate in on what was happening with Nate's brother and sister as they drove along, and Nate shared the latest news about his grandkids. Even living next door to each other, their schedules didn't allow much time for visiting, but these drives to the fishing or hunting grounds provided time to catch up on the latest news.

"Which crick are we gonna terrorize today?" Jake asked as they bounced along the dusty gravel road.

"We haven't hit Dixie Crick in awhile. The brookies in there should have forgotten us by now. I think we about wore the Sycan out last month. You got the lips ripped off near all the fish in that river," Nate answered while scanning the surrounding woods for wildlife. "Hey, look at that!" he said, hitting the brakes. "There's a badger!"

He locked the brakes on the Dodge and skidded to a stop on the side of the road. The emergency brake was set, the engine off, and Nate was out the door before the gravel quit flying. If he could catch up with the grizzled critter before it got to a hole in the ground, they could have some fun. Waving dust out of his face, Nate could see the thirty-pound animal heading up hill about twenty-five yards away. Sprinting as fast as a fifty-two-year-old fat man could, he closed to within ten yards before the badger could find a hole to go down. And that was as far as the animal intended to run; it backed up to a ponderosa pine tree that was about five feet in diameter and prepared to make a stand. With its teeth bared and hair standing on end, the badger made it obvious that it was not afraid of these interlopers in its domain. Nate got within about fifteen feet of the badger, and the badger charged him with its teeth snapping together and a ferocious growl coming from its throat. Nate gave ground, and the badger backed up against his tree.

Jake arrived with a stick about twenty feet long that he had broken from the top of a blown-down tree. The stick still had the remains of what had been the tree's branches attached, but it had been dead long enough that the needles were gone. Jake jabbed at the critter with the stick, and the badger exploded. The air was instantly filled with dust, chunks of dry tree limbs, and murderous growling. Within a second the twenty-foot long stick was reduced to about fifteen feet, and the badger retreated against his tree. Jake advanced and jabbed again; this time the badger fastened onto the stick with its teeth and jerked it out of Jake's hands, dragging it back to the tree, snarling and snapping.

Nate and Jake laughed and hooted likes kids on a playground while they watched the angry little animal reduce the treetop to bark mulch.

"Well, I guess he taught us a lesson," Nate laughed, heading back to the pickup.

"I'll say," Jake responded. "I don't think he wants to go fishin' with us."

"Must not a liked the fishin' pole you'd picked out for 'im," Nate laughed.

"Yeah, he wanted one a those new-fangled graphite rods. That stick insulted his delicate sensibilities."

"That boy has some serious anger management issues."

When the men were about halfway back to the road they turned and watched the badger waddle on up the hill and out of sight. They were still laughing when they got back in the rig and rolled up the road.

Well into the forest, they turned off the main logging road onto a spur road and then onto a branch of that spur road that was little more than a deer trail. They rolled slowly but churned up amazing volumes of the lightweight dust. Finally at a landing at the end of the spur, they parked and got out of the rig. There wasn't a sign of water in the area, so an observer, had there been one, might have concluded that the pair had lost their minds when they pulled on hip waders and grabbed fly rods before starting up a steep trail.

When they reached the top of the ridge above where they had parked, they stopped in the shade of a huge ponderosa, and each of them slathered on a liberal dose of insect repellant.

"How long we gonna fish?" Jake asked.

"I dunno. Couple hours, I guess. It's quarter to eleven now. What do you say we meet back at the truck at one?"

"That sounds good to me. Try not to catch more than ya can carry out without help," Jake said over his shoulder as he headed off on a trail that angled off the ridge to the north.

"Okay. Just up and pull the trigger on that big old hog laig a couple a times if you need any help," Nate teased, referring to the .357 his father had strapped to his hip like a gun slinger in the old west, which made a kind of strange picture being tied down above his black hip boots. "I'll come a runnin' to pick up the pieces of any cougar that might have tried sneakin' up on you."

"You're not gonna think you're so tough when one of those big cats grabs you from behind and drags you to her den for her cubs to play with. Don't ya remember those tracks we saw last time we were down in this draw? If that kitty get's aholt of you you're gonna be wishin' you was packin' a shootin' iron of your own."

"Ah, you'll have to come to my rescue when you come to get the keys to drive out of here, so I ain't afeared," Nate laughed as he took off the ridge on a branch of the trail that bore south.

"Okay, see ya at one."

Jake hit the creek about fifteen minutes later and immediately started fishing downstream. He had rigged up with a long leader terminating at a green scud. About ten inches above the scud a mosquito was offered. Except during the couple of weeks in June when the stoneflies were hatching, the scuds and mosquitoes were the ticket. On the second cast a nice fat brookie took the mosquito like he meant business. A short but fierce battle ended with a smile on Jake's face and a beautifully speckled trout in his cotton tote. During Jake's childhood, about the only meat that he had opportunity to eat was game that he caught or shot. Growing up poor in a family of thirteen kids during the depression made an impression. Those roots never left him; he wasn't much for "catch and release." Any legal game that presented itself was harvested.

The eastern brook trout in these mountain streams were an opportunity that was almost too good to be true. The Oregon State Fish and Wildlife Commission had decided that these fish were predatory, and their numbers needed to be severely reduced to enhance the environment for the bull trout and red band rainbows that shared the waters. Hence, there was no limit on the number of brook trout that you were allowed to harvest. While Jake did not agree with the agency's reasoning, he was more than happy to assist. Twenty-five or thirty of the brightly colored fish, smoked to a golden brown, would supplement his diet nicely.

Nate hiked for about half an hour before he turned and intercepted the stream. As he walked, he marveled at the beauty of God's creation demonstrated in this remote watershed. The multitude of shades of green displayed by the numerous types of trees seemed impossible. And the colors of the wildflowers that grew in the dense underbrush were spectacular. The orange of the Indian paintbrush blended with the purple of wild iris and pink of columbine and arrayed among a multitude of small white flowers that Nate could not name demonstrated God's ingenuity. Who else could create such variety?

The stream itself was a miracle. Like all of the creeks in the Sycan watershed, Dixie Creek had its source in the high elevations of the Cascade Mountains. As the snow, which accumulated during the severe winters, melted, it fed streams that flowed down into the Sycan Marsh. Instead of then flowing into bigger streams that eventually made their way to the ocean, these streams watered the marsh's lush grass and then disappeared. Nate suspected that the streams somehow went underground and then welled up again to form the Anna River, whose headwaters flowed up miles away to the east, but that was just his uneducated guess.

Because the streams were small and virtually landlocked, the fish in them never had a chance to gain much size. A fifteen- or sixteen-inch fish was a monster. Most were under a foot in length. Since there was no chance of scoring a trophy fish, and because the streams were so remote, they did not receive much angling pressure. That was the main attraction for Nate. He could fish all day without much chance of encountering another angler.

Once Nate estimated that he had left enough untouched water to keep his father busy, he cut to the creek. When he stepped up to the water, the first thing he noticed was that some critter had been here recently, harvesting the freshwater clams that were abundant in the cold clear water. Judging from the sign, it had been a raccoon, but Nate knew that the black bears that inhabited this region had a taste for these shellfish as well. He reminded himself to keep an eye out for bear signs. It would not be a good idea to startle a sow with her cubs. The next thing he noticed as he started to fish was that mosquitoes were out in full force. As soon as he quit moving he was surrounded by the little bloodsuckers. Within five minutes of the time he started fishing, when he looked down at his denim jeans and green brush shirt, they looked like a pair of gray coveralls, mosquitoes covering every square inch of material. It was a good thing he had lots of insect repellant. The high-pitched hum of the insects was easy to ignore, though, since almost every cast of Nate's scud and mosquito fly combination was producing a strike. Man, oh man, what fishing. The only thing that could make it better was if the fish were bigger!

When Nate broke out of the hypnotic stupor created by the woods, the stream, and the fish, he looked at his watch and realized that he was going to have to hustle to get back to the rig by one o'clock. He reeled in his line, broke down the pole, and headed back as quickly as the dense underbrush and blow downs allowed. With the amount of noise he was making getting through the brush, he sure was not going to have to worry about surprising any bears!

As he moved away from the creek, the undergrowth was less and less dense due to the lack of water, which made walking much easier and faster. When he broke out on the ridge above his pickup he could see that Jake was already there, sitting on the tailgate. Nate thought it looked like his dad was in animated conversation with someone, but he did not see anyone, or another rig. He must be singing, or talking to himself, Nate thought, but it is odd that he is making all those hand gestures. As soon as Nate left the vantage point of the ridge, the view of the odd scene was blocked by the surrounding vegetation, and he was left to wonder about what was going on. When he reached the rig, Jake was quietly sitting on the tailgate.

"Who were you talking to a few minutes ago?" Nate asked.

"Talkin' to?" Jake responded. "I wasn't talkin.'"

"Well what was all the hand wavin,' then?"

"I dunno. Just battin' skitters I guess. You catch any fish?"

"Yeah, I got a couple little ones; how about you?"

"I did about the same. Are you ready to head back?"

The blatant lying was part of their father-son ritual.

"Yeah," Nate said. "Let's chew on our lunch on the way out."

"Sounds good," Jake replied, closing the tailgate and walking around to get in the rig.

12

Both men were quiet on the bumpy ride out the logging roads to the highway. They busied their eyes, scanning the surrounding terrain for game, their minds with what they had seen while Nate was on the ridge and Jake was on the tailgate. Nate was extremely curious about what his dad had been doing, and he hoped the old guy wasn't losing his grip, but it was obvious that Jake did not want to discuss it.

> *Eliab and Yanoa were once again commanded to go to the area of the Chiloquin/East Lake County Line. When they arrived, the battle was still fierce. Their orders were to restrict their involvement to defense, and though their obedience to those orders was never in question, it frustrated them to know that the battle would easily be won if they and the other of the holy warriors on the scene were given the authorization to attack. But too few of the King's mortals were being obedient to the commands in the Word. The King's command to enter the spiritual battle on their knees, commands to bind, commands in regard to holiness, were being ignored by so many. The holy*

warriors were perplexed as to how these mortals could so easily dismiss the orders of the King! But hadn't it been so from the beginning? The Book promised that someday this disobedience would end, and they would be able to demonstrate the power that the King had placed at their disposal. Oh, for the day to come!

Jake had been so quiet on the forty-five minute drive up Highway 31 that Nate was having trouble staying awake at the wheel. From time to time he would sneak a glance at his dad. And each time what he saw was a look of concentration. What was going on in the old man's mind? He thought about asking but knew from experience that all he would receive were evasive one-syllable replies.

The men were sitting at the stop sign at the intersection of Highways 31 and 197 when Jake suddenly came out of his meditations. "Hey," he hollered. "That green Ford Taurus headed south, that's the movie lady."

"Are you sure?" Nate asked. "There are about a bazillion Ford Tauruses on the road, and the half of 'em that aren't brown are green. What makes you think that that is the one?"

"Look at the muffler, see how it's almost draggin,' wired up with balin' wire? I noticed that when she was at the sale. And that bumper sticker, how many bumper stickers in central Oregon read 'Spotted Owls are People Too'?"

"I dunno," Nate grunted, "but if you're sure it's her, we'll try to follow her."

"Oh, it's her, all right. I got a good look at her when she drove past. Ya can't miss that long straight white hair."

They sat trying to make a left turn onto the busiest highway in central Oregon, growing more frustrated by the second. A string of about a dozen tractor-trailer rigs were backed up behind a motor home whose driver apparently had no particular place to go. An occasional passenger car was thrown into the mix just for aggravation. By the time they turned onto the highway, the Ford was no longer in sight. They joined the parade anyway, hoping that they would catch a glimpse of the green Taurus in one of the passing lanes, but every time they got to a passing area, the guy in the motor home would speed up, making it impossible to get past the string of rigs that was between them and the lady in the Taurus. They gave up when they reached the small town of Gilchrist, fifteen miles south of Rosland. Disappointed, they turned around and headed for home.

On the ride north on Highway 197, Nate turned to Jake and said, "Ya knew, didn't you?"

"Knew what?" Jake answered, looking out the passenger-side window.

"You knew that you were gonna see that car on our way home from fishin.' That's why you were so quiet. You were waitin' to see that car."

"I thought I might."

"You thought you might, my hind leg! You knew. That's what was goin' on with you when I was up on the ridge watchin' you talk and wave your hands around. What do you see or hear?"

Jake was quiet for a long time, then he answered quietly, "I don't know how to explain it. I just get these kinda messages. Don't really want to talk 'bout it, okay?"

"All right, but someday we're gonna have to talk about it. It's just gettin' too stinkin' weird to ignore."

13

Nate headed right for his cell phone after dropping a gallon Ziploc plastic bag full of cleaned trout into the sink. The cell phone that Amy had gotten for him to take out in the boonies with him, the phone he always forgot to take with him. He and Jake had cleaned the fish at Jake's outdoor fish-cleaning station that stood behind his shop. He tossed a quick, "Hi," at Amy and picked up the phone.

"Who ya in such an all-fired hurry to call?" Amy asked.

"I gotta call Gail and tell her that her gramps and I saw the DVD lady today."

"What'da ya mean you saw her? Was she fishin'?" Amy asked, puzzled.

"Nah, we saw her driving down Highway 197. I want to get her address from Gail. I should have written it down before I gave Gail the check. I think she was probably headed home. If I go out there right now, I might catch her." Nate spoke quickly as he punched Gail's cell number into his keypad.

"Hey, Dad, what's up?" Gail answered.

Nate would never get used to people knowing who was calling before he even said hello. "Howdy, how're you?"

"Not too bad, I guess. I'm just gettin' set to go out to the Crook County Rodeo. Should be some good bull rides tonight. I heard they had some riders show some pretty good stuff in the qualifiers last night. What ya up to?"

"I need the name and address offen that lousy DVD check. Gramps and I saw the lady who bought them when we were comin' in from the desert this afternoon."

"What? You couldn't have, it's impossible."

"Well, I don't know why it can't be, I just know that we saw her," Jake replied, an edge in his voice.

"It can't be, because the lady is dead. She got herself croaked the same day, or the day after, she bought the DVDs—a week ago today."

"That's crazy," Jake nearly shouted into the phone. "We just saw her."

"You musta saw someone who looked a lot like her, 'cause she's dead," Gail shot back.

"Quit talkin' crazy and get that check and read me the name and address," Jake continued.

"I'm tellin' ya that you gotta stay outta this. They already think I might be involved since I was out there nosin' around while the lady was lying dead in the house. If you go out there now, things are going to get even uglier."

"Whoa, whoa, whoa, ya gotta slow down, here. They think that you might be involved? Who thinks that?" Nate asked.

"Well, Mike Divetti is heading the investigation, and that's probably the only reason I haven't already been drug in for questioning. But the State Po Po is involved too, so things are a bit dicey. They've got my finger prints from inside the house—don't ask, it's a long story—and then there's my phone call in Mike's answering machine asking about the address. Now please don't go makin' it worse by claimin' that you saw a ghost drivin' down the highway, or by chargin' out there like the lone ranger or something."

"All right, but I still want ya to read me that name and address. I gotta think about this mess," Nate said.

Gail hesitated, then answered, "Okay, but please don't do anything crazy. Here it is. Joanie Craddock…hey, wait a minute, that's not right! I gotta go."

Nate was left standing in his living room, staring at his phone as it went blank, listening to a dial tone, wondering what that was all about.

Gail paced as she listened to her phone ring in an attempt to reach Mike Divetti. After what seemed like an hour, on the fifth ring, Mike answered, "Yello."

"Mike, this is Gail." She was talking so fast she had to force herself to slow down. "What did you say that the name of the vic was?"

"Slow down Gail. Her name was Jodie Caddell. What's this about?"

"I just looked at the check from the garage sale. It was written by a Joanie Craddock! The victim of your homicide wasn't even the same woman that I was looking for. Has the boyfriend of the deceased mentioned another woman? Have you talked to this Joanie Craddock?"

Mike sighed and said, "Gail, ya gotta settle down and let me process some of this. The boyfriend hasn't said anything about anyone else living out there. And there hasn't been anything to indicate that there were any more than just the two of them using the address. Ted and Tony are on their way out there right now to nose around behind the house, looking for any clues as to what those horses were watching. I'll try and catch up with them. We'll see if he knows anything about this…what'd ya say the name was, Joanie Craddock?"

"Yeah, the name was Joanie Craddock. This is gettin' weirder and weirder, Mike. Could ya let me know as soon as you hear anything from your guys?"

"Depends on what they find. You are remembering that you are a 'person of interest,' aren't you? And hey, since we have this confusion going on with the name on the check, just to be sure, what's the address on your garage sale check?"

Gail looked at the upper left-hand corner of the check and read it to Mike. "16173 North Bonanza Road. That is the address I was at, isn't it?"

"That's the address all right. Look, I gotta give the boys a call and give 'em a heads up about this Joanie Craddock. I'll talk to you later."

"Hey Mike, thanks," Gail replied.

14

Ted and Tony were big ole' boys: Big like oxen. And they were about a matched team. Both were over six-foot-four. Neither tipped the scales at less than 290. With chests bigger around than an oak whiskey barrel and arms that were indicators of a lot of time in the gym, they could go to the Seattle Seahawks training camp and fit right in with the offensive line, especially at dinnertime. Aside from their size, they didn't look too similar. Ted was dark and sported a perfect military flattop haircut. Tony had a ruddy complexion and probably was a redhead once, before male-pattern baldness made him glad that a shaved head could be a fashion statement.

When either of them got in close quarters with a suspect, they were intimidating. Together they were terrifying. Only those who were very, very drunk, impossibly stupid, or incredibly high ever wanted to mix it up with them. Quite a few suspects had attempted to outrun them, but surprisingly enough, for big men, they were quick. And thanks to a lot of time on the treadmill, they had pretty decent endurance. Their unofficial motto was, "You can run, and you can fight, but that just means that you are goin' to jail tired and bruised."

They liked working as a team when the rare opportunity

presented itself—East Lake County sheriff's deputies normally ran one to a car—so they were looking forward to spending some time together scouring the bitterbrush and pine thickets searching for clues in the county's latest murder case. And the search would be a pleasant change of pace from their steady diet of drug investigations and domestic disputes. They were not too sure what they were supposed to be looking for; Divetti had instructed them to look for anything "suspicious." Good enough, they could do that. Especially on a sunny day that promised to be pleasant, thanks to a weak, cool weather system that was making the two-hundred-mile trip across the Cascade Mountains from the Pacific Ocean.

The timing was perfect; the weather was supposed to be back to normal tomorrow with high temperatures in the nineties.

Ted had Tony in tears, sharing the details of one of the traffic stops from his last night shift. "I kid you not," Ted said. "I pulled this putz over right down the street from Vic's Tavern at about two thirty. He was swerving a little and had a busted taillight, so I figured I got a sure-thing DUI. When I look inside the car the guy is wearing one of those World War II aviator's helmets, complete with goggles. That's when I notice that there's no windshield in the car. The glass is completely broken out, and the guy is drivin' around when it's like forty degrees outside."

"So what'd he say?" Tony asked.

"Well, I ask if it wasn't a mite cool for all that air conditioning. This old buzzard burps and says, 'Naw, but it shore was last winter.' Can you believe that he has been driving around with no windshield since last January?"

Tony was preparing to make some appropriately rude remark when the radio interrupted their story time. The sergeant wanted to know their location. When they informed him that they were about a mile north of the county line and preparing to turn off the highway, he instructed them to pull onto the shoulder at the intersection and wait for him to join them.

"I wonder what's up," Tony said.

Ted replied, "I dunno. It's not like Sarge to send us out to do a job and then not trust us to get it done."

"Yeah, something has gone sideways on this deal, or there sure won't be three of us goin' out there."

The two deputies did not have to wait long for their sergeant to join them. The dust they had stirred up when they pulled off the road had not finished settling before Mike's rig pulled in behind them. Both the big men climbed out of their patrol car and were met by Mike, who was coming up their patrol car.

"What's up, boss?" Tony asked.

"This morning I found out that there's a player in this drama that we haven't interviewed. It seems that there's another woman who, at the least, is using Shear's address on her checking account. I want to find out why he didn't volunteer this information," Mike told his deputies. "So, I want you to go to the door with me, to provide a little extra intimidation, in an attempt to get him interested in being a bit more honest. If he held back information about another roommate, who knows what else he hasn't bothered to tell us?

"I'll introduce you and then ask permission for you to do the search. Then while you're out playin' Davie Crockett and Daniel Boone, I'll broach the subject of the other woman.

"You guys roll in first, I'll be right behind you. Oh, and watch out for dogs. There might be a biter around. And don't either of you big oafs smash him if he shows up."

Ron Shear came out on his porch when he heard the two sheriff's department rigs pull into his yard. He was barefoot in jeans and a T-shirt, and his hair looked like he had just rolled out of bed. He held a mug in his right hand and had a quizzical look on his face. "Hey, boys, what's goin' on?" he called out when they got out of their cars. "You find something out about who killed Jodie?"

"No," Mike said as he, Ted, and Tony walked toward the house three abreast, like a band of really big lawmen out of a low-budget western. "We're out here hoping to pick up a couple more clues." Pointing to the men to his right he said, "This is Officer Williams and Officer Petz. If it's okay with you, they're gonna take a look around behind the house."

"Yeah, sure," Shear answered. "Go ahead on 'er. My property goes back about a hundred yards. From there on it's National Forest land for about a mile. Good luck findin' anything, though. It's nothin' but a brushy mess back 'ere. And the ticks can be a mite troublesome."

"By the way, Ron," Mike asked as the big guys started around the house, "I noticed a dog bowl and a chain there on the porch. Where's the dog?"

"That is a really good question," Ron said. "I ain't seen Zip since I got back. Kind of forgot all about him, what with all the excitement about Jodie, but realized the next day that he was gone. That dog likes to wander around, but he's never gone for more than a day. He never has liked to get too far from his food dish. I just hope some coyote or cougar didn't decide that the mutt looked like a good source of protein.

"Maybe he's at one of the neighbors,'" Mike suggested. "Could be that someone adopted him."

"Could be, I s'pose, but I doubt it. Neighbors are kinda scarce around here."

"Yeah, well, he'll probably turn up. Mind if I come in while the two officers take a look around?"

"That's fine. I got nothin' goin' on today. That's the great part about bein' retired—no schedule. Would you like a cup a coffee? I just brewed a pot."

"Sure. That'd be great. Black, please," Mike said as he looked around the living room/dining room area. The place was a mess; even worse than what you'd expect from a retired guy on his own for a week or two. A pile of newspapers, a bunch of outdoorsy-type magazines, a few dirty dishes, dust on the countertop, and a lot of junk everywhere. It looked like Mike's place, since his wife decided she didn't like being married to a cop.

"Say, Ron, you ever heard of someone named Joanie Craddock?" Mike asked after Ron handed him coffee in a Seahawks mug.

Ron got a puzzled expression on his face and said, "Why does that name sound familiar? Joanie Craddock. I've heard that name. Why're you asking that?"

Mike set the mug of coffee on the counter and carefully watched Ron's expression as he explained, "We have some reason to believe that she may be living here, or at least using this as her mailing address."

"That's nuts," Ron replied. "I've lived here for 'bout four years now, and there's never been a Joanie Craddock here durin' that time. Whoever told you that she was livin' here was *loco*."

Mike was still studying Ron's face when he replied, "We have a check that Ms. Craddock wrote last week. The address printed on the check by the bank is this address. We checked with the bank, and it's an active account with a fairly healthy balance. No one answers the cell phone number when we call it. Just thought that maybe you were lettin' someone use your address." Mike's 'con' meter was flashing red but he couldn't figure out why. Everything that Ron was saying sounded like the truth, even the inflection in his voice seemed genuine, but something intangible just didn't feel right.

"No. I don't know anything about that. No one is living here 'cept me, and Jodie up to a week ago. And I don't let anyone use my address! There's enough of that identity theft stuff goin' on without invitin' it."

"Well, then, have you got any idea why this lady's checks have your address printed on them?"

"No. But wait a minute, now that I think about it, that's why that name sounded so familiar. I've been gettin' mail for that person lately. In fact, I have some around here somewhere," Ron said as he started shuffling through the magazines and newspapers on the counter. "I've given it back to the mail carrier a couple of times tellin' 'em she don't live here, but I guess her name's too close to Jodie's, 'cause I keep getting it. Here's a piece right here; it's from some credit card company. I just figured that it was someone who lived here before me. You know how that junk mail just keeps comin' forever."

Mike took the envelope from Ron and tucked it into his black leather notebook. "Ya mind if I take this to the post office and see if they can tell me anything about it?"

"Be my guest. Tell 'em not to send any more of it out here, while you're at it."

Mike picked the Seahawks mug back up and took a sip, "I know you've been thinkin' about what could have happened to Jodie. Have you come up with anything? Did you think of any problems she was havin' with anyone? Are there any ex-husbands or boyfriends or family that she may have had a beef with or anything?"

"Nothin,'" Ron said, shaking his head. "Everybody liked Jodie. She has an ex-husband someplace in Idaho, but as far as I know, she hasn't been in contact with him for years. She has a sister in Portland. They'd talk on the phone at Christmas or birthdays, stuff like that, but they aren't close. Her folks have been dead for several years, and she never had any kids. We've both become almost like hermits. That's why we live out here in the sticks. Jodie preferred the company of her horses to spending time with people. I always told her that I thought if she had to choose between those horses and me, I'd be down the road."

"So the horses belonged to Jodie?" Mike asked.

"Yeah, and Zip too—maybe that's where the mutt is, maybe he's off lookin' for her. She was an animal lover. Some folks like to mess with the yard or a garden or play bingo or belong to a club or make quilts or something. Jodie, she just wanted to be with her pets. It was her idea to move out here so she could have horses. We lived in town before, but she had grown up in the country."

"Did she take good care of the animals?"

"I'll say. It's always the best for those guys. Prime dog food for Zip and only alfalfa and oats for the horses. Fed them way better than me, that's for sure."

"Did she ever forget to feed or water them?" Mike asked.

"Do you forget to eat?" Ron responded. "She would have forgotten to eat herself before she'd forget to feed her animals. And do those horses look like they ever missed a meal to you? There just ain't no way. What difference does that make, anyway? Ya think that those PETA people killed her because she was mistreating her horses?"

Mike shook his head and stood up and stood in front of a window looking out at the yard. "Nah, I'm just tryin' to get a complete picture of the situation. Right now we don't have a motive, and very few leads concerning her death. If you think of anything, please let me know. Right now, I'll get outta your hair and go see how the guys are doing outside. Thanks for the coffee." He laid one of his business cards on the counter, set the mug beside it, and headed out for the door.

Ron followed Mike outside. "I really want you guys to catch the creep what killed Jodie. I know a lot of folks think that 'cause we weren't married that it is no big deal to me. But we were together for over eight years. I was married to a woman for fifteen years that I wasn't anywhere as close to as I was to Jodie. I loved her, and I want to see the killer pay for what he did."

15

It took Mike most of half an hour to find Ted and Tony. They hadn't gone that far, but he missed them on the first two passes because the brush was so thick.

When he did find them, they were about two hundred yards behind the Shear property, on National Forest land. The big men were standing over a patch of ground that didn't take a woodsman to realize had been recently disturbed.

"What'da ya guys think happened here?" Mike asked, walking up to them.

"Judgin' from the look of these clods and roots, I'd say something got buried here, and whoever buried it didn't think anyone would ever come a-looking," Ted answered, "but we're gonna need a shovel to find out what it is." The hole appeared to have been a roughly rectangle shape about two feet by three feet.

"Before we arm wrestle to see who is gonna go back to the rigs to get a shovel," Mike joked, "did you find anything else that's interestin'?"

"Well, before we tear the arms off you, we'll be glad to give you the details," Tony quipped. "We found a real well-worn horse trail that goes from the makeshift corral out to the public land. It looks like someone from here has spent a lot of time on horseback. From the size of the trail, it appears that the rider went on and off the property on a trail that is over to the west of us almost every trip. I think that the routine may have occasionally been altered when the rider followed one of the dozens of game trails that crisscross this area. We were following one of those trails when we ran across this hole."

Ted started back toward the Shear property and said, "We found one other thing that may be significant. Come on, I'll show you." When they were back within sight of the house and corral, Ted stopped. "Ya see this spot? From here ya got a view of both the door of the house and the corral. You can tell that someone clipped a couple of branches off of this small pine tree, probably so they could have a clear view of the driveway. We found a halfway-buried cigarette butt and a candy bar wrapper here too. Someone spent some time watchin' Shear's place from here."

Mike could just make out the butt and a corner of the candy paper that Ted was pointing at. "How long ago do you think this stuff was buried?"

"Not long. The brand on the butt that's stickin' out of the ground hasn't even started to fade."

"Good work, you guys. I don't know what any of this stuff means, but it gives us a lot more to think about. And since ya did such good work, I won't hurt your arms by wrastlin' you. I'll go get the shovel, and we'll see what's buried back there. I'll get the camera too, so we can take some photos before we start ripping stuff up. Why don't cha see if you can find anything else while I'm gone?"

Mike had bought the digital camera a couple of years earlier with his personal funds. The county budget was always an issue, and some modern tools were necessary. The shovel was standard emergency equipment in East Lake County that an officer on a city police force might think was funny, but out here, where a winter storm could leave four feet of snow on the ground, they were a necessity.

"Find anything else that's interesting?" Mike asked when he got back with the camera and shovel.

"Nah," the deputies answered in unison.

"Okay. Let's take some shots of the cigarette butt and that candy wrapper. Once we have those photos, you can bag that trash as evidence, and we'll go see what's in the hole," Mike instructed.

Mike took several photos of the area that they assumed had been disturbed when something was buried. Then he began to gently dig. About a foot down, the shovel hit something spongy, and Mike used the point of the shovel to slowly scrape an opening in the soil. A patch of black hair became visible, and the pungent odor of rotting flesh filled the air.

"Well, it looks like we found Zip the dog," Mike said. "He doesn't smell too healthy. I'm glad he wasn't in here another week. At least the skin hasn't started to slip. Ted, you go back to your rig and grab one of those big garbage bags. We'll use it for an evidence bag. Tony, start taking pics every couple of minutes while I finish uncovering the dog."

By the time Ted got back with the bag, Mike and Tony had the dog uncovered and out of the hole. "Can you tell what killed 'em?" Tony asked as he opened the bag.

"Judgin' by the hole behind his left ear, I'd guess old Zip died of lead poison," Ted replied.

"Why da ya s'pose someone plugged the mutt?" Tony wanted to know. "Do ya think the fur ball may have attacked the dude that was hidin' out here watchin' the house?"

"That'd be my first guess," Mike answered. "Once we get the dog bagged up, I want you two to scour the area here tryin' to locate the casing from the round that killed the pooch."

Fifteen minutes later Tony called out from his hands-and-knees position in the bitterbrush, "Hey, I think I have it." He stood up with a shiny silver shell casing on the end of his pen. "Looks like a nine-millimeter pistol round. I've seen enough of them on the range to recognize it."

Mike squinted, judging the distance between where the dog was dug up and the spot where Tony had made his find. "If the dog was buried right where he fell, then that shell casing was about the perfect distance to have been spit from an autoloader."

"Yeah," Tony agreed, holding his find up in the light and peering at it. "I think I can see where the ejector grabbed it," he said as he slid the casing into an evidence envelope.

"Let's get this stuff packed up so we can turn it over to the white coats at the Oregon State Police lab. I hope that something we find will provide a clue as to what went on out here a week ago," Mike said.

When they got back to their rigs, Tony and Ted loaded the evidence bags into the trunk of their car and turned to Mike for instructions. "What do ya want us to do with this stuff?" Ted asked.

"Radio dispatch and ask them to call over to Salem to the lab and see if anyone is there to accept the evidence. If there is, I want one of ya to drive it over there today. And I want both of you to write up a separate report detailing what we found and how we found it. And keep this stuff to yourselves. I don't want some reporter gettin' aholt of any of this and flashin' it all over the news. Meanwhile, I'm gonna go talk to Ron and let him know that he won't need to be worrying about Zip comin' 'round for dinner."

Ted and Tony pulled out of the driveway as Mike made his way to the house. He did not like having to relay bad news, and sometimes people got as upset about the loss of a pet as they do about the death of a person. He made his way slowly up the steps, and for some bizarre reason noticed for the first time that the house needed a coat of paint.

Ron came to the door before Mike had a chance to knock.

"What'd ya find out there?" he wanted to know. "I saw you packing stuff back and forth."

"Well, Ron, I hate to have to tell you, but we found Zip. He was buried in a shallow grave back there on the public land. It looks like a single shot to the head did him, so I know he didn't suffer."

"Man, oh man," Ron groaned. "This used to be a nice place to live. But I've 'bout had it now. Think I might just pack up and get out of here before someone croaks me."

"I'm sorry," Mike said sincerely. He paused for a minute and then asked, "Do you know anything about what might be south or east of here? Any reason that someone from out those directions might be snoopin' around your place?"

"There isn't anything back there that I know of. But I never have gone out that way much. Jodie rode her horses out there all the time, but I think it's just public forestland for miles. Why are you asking?"

"I'm just curious. We saw the trail that Jodie apparently used to access that land, and it got me thinkin' about what she may have run onto or seen back there. Anyway, I am sorry that you're havin' to go through all this. And we are doin' our best to figure out what all of this is about and who is involved. I'll probably be back out here tomorrow with a couple of ATVs so we can search further into the public land. Do you mind if we park our rigs here?"

"Ya know, normally I'd say sure, but the memorial service for Jodie is tomorrow, and there will be some people—you know, family and friends—out here after that. I don't think it'd be too cool to have your sheriff's department rigs sittin' around here during that. It'd be too stark a reminder."

"Okay. I understand. I'll work out another time or something. I'll be in touch." Then, almost as an afterthought, Mike added, "Will Jodie's sister show up? I'd sorta like to talk to her."

"Yeah, she's supposed to be here. I talked to her on the phone and she said she was drivin' over tomorrow. I offered to let her stay the night here tomorrow night, but she said that she'd either stay in a motel or drive right back. I'll give her your number."

"Thanks," Mike offered before he headed to his rig. While he walked, that something about Ron's attitude was still niggling at the corners of his intuition, but he didn't know what or why.

16

"Gail, this is Mike. Ted, Tony, and I were out in the south part of the county this morning. We found some kinda interesting stuff. I would like you to go out there with me so I can get your perspective on some evidence. I need you to clue me to the exact direction the horses were looking when you were out there. And I want to take a spin out on the National Forest Land behind the property, just to see what's out there. Ya think you might be able to break free tomorrow and head out there with me?"

"You bet," Gail answered. "What time you figurin' to be out there?"

"Well, I want to swing by the post office and talk to them about the address on your check before we go. I know the postmaster is always there when I check my post office box at six in the morning, so I'll stop by and try to talk to him then. Why don't ya meet me at Cindy's Kitchen about six thirty, and we'll go from there?"

"Sounds like a plan. I'll even spring for breakfast."

"Now you're talkin.' Oh, and dress for some ATV action. I'm gonna borrow a couple of the search-and-rescue crew's machines so we can cover a lot of ground without spendin' all day doin' it."

"Great. But what are ya gonna do at the post office?"

"I'll explain it tomorrow. Right now I'd better call OSP and bring them up to speed."

"Okay. I'll see ya tomorrow at six thirty at Cindy's."

"Don't forget your wallet."

Not wanting to get up early and make the long drive from Prineville to Rosland in the morning, Gail decided to call her parents and ask if she could come out and stay the night. Her mother answered her call on the second ring. "Hey Ma, how was church this morning?"

"Good. We heard an awesome sermon out of the Gospel of Luke. And the music was fantastic. A new kid was playin' the drums, and he could make 'em talk. How was yours?"

"Um, didn't make it this mornin.' You know, with my schedule, it is hard to keep in the habit. I was wonderin' if I could come out this evening and spend the night. I'm meetin' Mike in Rosland in the morning and would like to not have to make the drive that early."

"That sounds great. I'll have something ready to eat about seven, if ya want."

"Yeah, that sounds good."

Gail arrived at her parents' home at about five in the afternoon. After going in to say a quick hello to her mom and dad, she walked across the property to her grandparents' house to visit with them for a while. "Hello, Grandma. Howdy, Gramps," she said as she went in the door. "What kinda mischief have you two been up to? Sold any good DVDs lately?"

"Hi Gail, I didn't know you were coming out," her grandmother said, obviously pleased to see her. Visiting your grandparents is always good for your ego, Gail thought.

"Well, it was kind of a spur-of-the-moment decision. I've got some things to do out here early in the morning and thought it would be easier to drive out now than tomorrow. Besides, this way

I can con a meal outta Ma. I don't get that much home cookin,' ya know."

"What's wrong? Did they forget to put a kitchen in that fancy new house of yours?" her grandfather teased.

"Oh, there's a kitchen all right. But there isn't a chef."

"Hmm, is that right?" Gramps continued. "Thought a big shot like you'd have a cook, a maid, and a chauffeur by now. Maybe even a gardener."

"Yeah, I did, but the stinking chef burnt the biscuits, and I had to let 'im go. But if you're looking for a job, the pay is poor, but the hours are long to make up for it."

"Ah, even a high-roller like you couldn't afford an experienced and fabulous cook like me. Why, I even know how to boil beef tongue and make headcheese. Talent like that costs money!"

"That's too bad. I haven't had any good vittles like that for a long time."

"Anything new on that dead gal?" Gramps asked.

"Nothing. But that's the reason I'm out here. Mike and I are goin' out and snoopin' around the area tomorrow to see if we can turn up any new clues."

"Ya think that's a good idea? I mean, do ya think it's safe for you out there?" Gail's grandmother asked.

"Sure. Mike knows his stuff. And we'll be careful."

"Ya got any good cop stories for us?" Gail's grandfather asked, switching subjects, knowing that Jan did not need to hear about the goings-on out at south end of East Lake County.

"Oh, I do! I got to arrest a guy the other night that had just held up the Stop and Shop Market out on Greenwood. This hero went into the store at about three in the morning, waved a gun around, and told the clerk to open the register. There was less than a hundred bucks in the till, so the robber is all bummed and demands that the clerk 'open the safe.' The poor clerk is trying to explain that she doesn't have the combination to the safe when a would-be customer drives up, sees the guy with the gun through the front door, and calls us. I love cell phones!

"I was the closest unit to the scene when the call came in, so I sped over there and arrived just in time to see the perp run out the door of the store and jump in his car for the getaway. I pulled my patrol car right behind him at an angle so he couldn't pull out, putting my car's passenger side almost against his bumper so my car would be between him and me, 'cause I knew he had a gun. I rolled out of my car and pulled my weapon just as he threw his car into reverse and smacked right into the side of my patrol car and caved in the door. So the guy lurched his car forward, but it's one of those little tiny Fords, and it gets high centered on the curb.

"Meanwhile, I'm yellin' at him to come out of his car with his hands up and throw down his weapon, and anything else I can think up to yell.

"So, the store clerk was peeking out the door of the store, the guy who called the thing in was still sittin' in his car watching, like he's watchin' *COPS* on TV or somethin.' The suspect was in his car, stuck up on the curb, and I'm left wondering what to do next. I didn't know if the guy was waiting for me to come around my car so he could blast me, or what, so I just kept yellin' at him to get out of his car.

"About the time I started to think I might just have to shoot the guy right there, my backup arrived all lights and sirens and screeched into the parking lot practically on two wheels. When the suspect saw and heard all the commotion, he panicked, jumped outta his car and made like a rabbit. He ran around the side of the store, and I hotfoot it after him. But I stopped at the corner of the building, thinking he might be waiting to ambush me. I peeked around the corner just in time to see him run full-tilt right into the store's garbage dumpster 'cause he was looking over his shoulder while he was running. When he hit the dumpster, his gun went flyin' outta his hand, and he went down like a mallard hit by a load of twos. I was on him before he could get off the ground.

"The guy was floppin' and kickin' and cussin,' knocked half goofy from runnin' into the dumpster, meanwhile I've got my gun on him, and I was shoutin' stuff like, 'Stay down! Put your hands to the side where I can see 'em!' I guess I shoulda just tazed him and been done with it.

"But bottom line is, no one suffered any injuries except the suspect, who had a giant goose egg on his temple from where he collided with the dumpster."

Gail's grandmother's eyes were wide like an owl's when she asked, "Do you think he would have tried to shoot you if he hadn't crashed into the dumpster?"

"I don't think so, Grandma," Gail answered with a snicker. "When we gathered the evidence, the gun turned out to be a cap gun that the guy had cut the red end of the barrel off of to make it look real."

Concern still obvious on her face, her grandmother then asked, "Was your back okay after all that chasin'?"

"Yeah, it's fine."

"What was the guy's story?" Gramps wanted to know. "Why was he holdin' up the store?"

"I dunno," Gail answered, "out of work, on drugs, just stupid. Take your pick."

"That's just old-fashioned sad. Do you ever think about why these guys are bein' so dumb? Just seems like such a waste," Gramps said, shaking his head.

"No, I really don't think about that very much. Except sometimes when I have to testify in court and the family of the suspect is there listening to testimony that almost always shows what idiots their child or spouse or sibling has been. But I can't really think about it. I just gotta do my job."

"I know. It just makes me sad," Gramps said quietly. "I always wonder what little choices, what small decisions made differently would have completely changed the course of their lives. Makes me wonder if there would've been someone there for them at those crucial times, would things have been different?"

"Ya can't save everybody, Gramps."

"Sure would like to, though. And Jesus could, if they'd let him."

Gail broke the pursuing silence to go back to her parents' to help with dinner.

"I worry about that girl," Jake said after his granddaughter was gone.

"Yeah, me too," Jan responded. "She could get hurt fighting with men all the time. Guns and knives and who knows what."

"I was thinking more of the spiritual war she's in. She's just seein' the physical. And she's getting hard and calloused from always lookin' at the bad, the ugly side of life all the time. I know she can't be thinking about the souls of the bad guys when she's in the middle of the fight, but I wish there was a way for her to see their need for salvation when she wasn't fighting with 'em. The police department has done a great job of preparing her for those physical fights. I just don't think we have done the same at fitting her for the spiritual battle that she's in. And it is every bit as real, ya know."

"Yeah, Jake, I know. But it's not as evident to everyone as it is to you. In fact, I don't even see the spiritual battle in quite as concrete a way as you. Please be patient with the rest of us: Patient and understanding. Remember, you haven't always seen it quite so clearly either."

"And I sure don't like her goin' out there tomorrow. That is a very dark place. It is absolutely crawlin' with the enemy. I'm not sure that she's properly equipped for the job," Jake continued.

"We'll just have to pray and trust the Lord to protect her," Jan said emphatically.

That night, after about four hours of sleep, first Jan, and then Jake, were awakened out of their rest. Neither of them had heard a strange noise or had any reason to become alert. But both knew why sleep would elude them in the hours to come. God was calling them to pray for their precious granddaughter Gail. And pray they did, until the pitch black of the Central Oregon night began to soften to gray on the eastern horizon.

> *Neither Eliab nor Yanoa were surprised by the pillars of light that shone up through the ponderosa pine trees whose limbs covered the little cottage housing those they were assigned to protect. But they were encouraged when they saw two more pillars shining brightly from the house next door. Each of these warriors had four faces, and from the ones that looked toward the King, shouts of praise resounded to their Lord. "Holy, Holy, Holy is the Lord God Almighty," they sang. And from the west they heard the voices of their comrades saying, "Worthy art Thou our Lord and our God."*
> *A battle was brewing!*

"How are your grandparents this afternoon?" Nate asked Gail.

"Oh, they seem fine, I guess. Gramps seems to get more caught up in the spiritual side of life every time I see him, though. Is he all right? I mean, there isn't anything physically wrong with him, is there? He's not dying or something?"

"He's okay, as far as I know. But I know what you mean. Ever since he had his heart attack three years ago, he sees the kingdom of God in increasingly real terms. I guess when you come as close to goin' to heaven as he, did it changes your perspective. I wish it was so real to me—without the heart attack of course."

"It just seems weird to me. It's like he's lost touch with reality or something. Really, we're in the physical, right? Won't there be time for all that spiritual stuff when we get to the other side?"

"I don't know, Gail. I read my Bible, and it's very clear that God expects us to live our lives in the here and now with a clear view of his kingdom, remembering that what we do here is impacting that other reality: That whole 'laying up treasures in heaven' thing. But I'll be the first to admit that it's almost impossible to do."

Gail sat quietly, thinking for several minutes, before saying, "I wish I could see it like that. But the here and now just seems like… the here and now to me. I'm caught up in doing my job and paying my bills and enjoying my days off. All of that is the 'real' to me. And, man, that's about all the reality I can cope with at one time. I believe in God and am thankful that Jesus came to die for my sins, and I want to go to heaven and all that, but if God wanted us to be always thinking of him and working for him, why doesn't he just end this and take us to that?"

"Isaiah 55:8 and 9 tell us that God's ways are not our ways, and his thoughts are so much higher than ours that our thoughts cannot even be like his. We have to believe that he knows what he is doing and act on that belief by being obedient to those things that he has instructed us to do."

Amy called from the kitchen, which had become the source of some very tantalizing smells. "Nate, could you set the table? And, Gail, would you mind putting a pitcher of water on? Then we should be ready to eat. It's nothing too fancy, just a taco salad and some homemade rolls. But we have some of your sister Erin's peach jam to go with the rolls, so I think we should be able to survive."

"It all smells delicious, and anyway, I think I could survive on Erin's peach jam all by itself," Gail said, laughing.

As they enjoyed their meal, they talked about Gail's sisters and their children. Amy and Nate had never enjoyed a role more than of that being grandparents to the two little boys and two little girls that their younger two daughters had given them. And Gail could never have imagined how much she was enjoying being an aunt. This was safe ground for conversation, since Amy did not like to be reminded of the dangerous aspects of Gail's job, and Gail was left feeling defensive about spiritual matters. So they laughed about something they could all relate to and enjoy, like the latest antics of the four children.

Amy told Nate and Gail the latest from Erin's three-year-old boy, whose father was a pastor: "Erin heard little Joel in the bathroom, talking to himself, so she looked in to see what was going on. Joel had his favorite teddy bear—Gail, that one that you gave him for his first Christmas—over the toilet, and he said, 'I gonna 'tize you in da name of da fadder and da ghost.' She stopped him just as he was getting ready to dunk his bear into the toilet bowl."

Nate chuckled and said, "I hope that bear gave the good confession."

Gail added, "Erin should be glad that Joel was saving his bear, and not his little sister. She'd have been givin' all kinda confessions if Joel had been tryin' to dunk her in the toilet bowl, but I doubt many of them would have been good!"

"Oh, I think he was just practicing on the bear," Amy countered. "Little Liz will probably be next."

17

Monday morning at a few minutes before six o'clock, Mike parked in the loading area of the Rosland Post Office and rang the buzzer by the back door. He was not a stranger here. He often came calling when he needed information about the change of address of someone he was hunting or for knowledge about individuals at an address he was interested in. Bart, the postmaster, always made him bring the proper paperwork with him, and dot the i's and cross the t's, but would then cooperate to the best of his abilities.

"Hey, Sue, is the big guy around today?" Mike asked when a clerk answered the door, already knowing that Bart was there because his rig was parked out back.

"Yeah, come on in. I'll get 'im for ya."

Bart Thompson looked a little harried when he came hurrying around the corner of the sorting cases to meet Mike. "Hey, Mike, what's goin' on?" the postmaster asked, in an obvious hurry.

"Not too much. This a busy day?"

"Ah, it's just a typical Monday. Too much mail, too few employees, but we'll get 'er done. Who ya huntin' for today?"

"More like fishin,'" Mike answered. "Does the address of 16173 North Bonanza Road mean anything to you?"

"What was it? 16173 North Bonanza Road? That's just about on the county line isn't it? Seems to ring a bell, but I can't think why. Ya got a name to go with it?"

"Yeah, in fact there are a couple of 'em." Mike checked his notebook and said, "Jodie Caddell and Joanie Craddock."

"Jodie Caddell? She's the gal that you guys found dead out there, isn't she?"

"Well, we didn't find her, but yeah, she's the one."

"But Joanie Craddock…I seem to recall somethin' about that name too. Let's go talk to the mail carrier that delivers out there, she might remember somethin'."

"Hey, Rose. Officer Divetti here is askin' about a Joanie Craddock at 16173 North Bonanza. You know anything about her?"

Mike pulled out the letter that Ron Shear had given him and handed it to the mail carrier. "Here, this might help you remember."

She looked at the letter and puzzled over it for a minute before saying, "I can't ever get this straight. I get a couple of pieces a month addressed like this, and I can't ever remember if I'm supposed to deliver it there or not. I hate to return it because it always looks like important mail. Bank statements and stuff like that. It seems like they accept most of it, but then sometimes they give a piece back marked 'not here.' So if I deliver it, and it isn't supposed to be there, I'm in trouble, but if I send it back, and they want it, I'm in even more trouble.

"But wait a minute, don't tell me they called the cops because I delivered mail to their address that doesn't belong there!"

"No," Mike stated. "But it doesn't go there. It's kinda strange, though, isn't it, mail coming to an address that the people aren't at?"

"No, it's not strange at all," Bart explained. "Banks and credit card companies require a physical address for their customers. It's not unusual for people on the dodge or people living out of their cars or under a bridge or whatever to randomly choose an address and use it. Sometimes they even put up a mailbox and receive mail at the address of a vacant lot. It makes things real interesting at times."

Mike scratched his scalp and said, "So you think that this Joanie Craddock has never lived at this Bonanza Road address and has just given it to the bank to satisfy their requirement for a physical address."

"Yep, that's my best guess, but I don't know. We'll return this piece of mail to the sender and they can go from there."

Rose was back to putting mail in delivery order in her mail case but added over her shoulder, "I'll put a note on the address to help me remember to return any mail for this Joanie Craddock that comes in the future. I sure don't want you or your ugly men to arrest me for something like that!"

"Oh, I'm sure they'll get ya for somethin' better'n that," Bart snickered. "Probably somethin' like impersonatin' a mail carrier."

Bart escorted Mike to the back door, obviously anxious to get back to the routine business of the day. Mike went through the door and turned and thanked Bart for his time.

"No problem, Mike. Anytime we can help. Good luck with your fishin,'" Bart responded as he closed and locked the door behind Mike.

Gail was waiting in her pickup in the parking lot of Cindy's Kitchen when Mike pulled in to park. She climbed out of her rig and waited on the sidewalk as he got out of his truck and walked back to the trailer, checking the straps on the two quads he was pulling.

"Morning, Gail," he grunted as he did his inspection. "You think your back is healed enough to stand the bouncin' around that this machine will provide?"

"Oh, I'll be fine, as long as I'm ridin' something with wheels and not hoofs," she replied.

"Great. Let's get inside and see what's new on the menu. It looks like a good day for a quad ride through the woods."

"I dunno. The weather report on the eleven o'clock news last night said we had a good chance of thunderstorms this afternoon," Gail offered.

"You and I both know how often those guys get it right. Look at that blue sky up there. Not a cloud in sight. Naw, it's gonna be a perfect day. Besides, we should be done by early afternoon. Those summer thunderstorms almost always hold off till late afternoon," Mike said confidently.

"Who are you trying to convince with that statement, me or you?" Gail asked.

"Probably me. But even if we do get caught in a storm, it'll be warm enough to not be an issue, right?"

"Yeah, I've always kinda enjoyed a good summer storm."

Inside, they claimed a booth toward the back of the restaurant. A gal that they been a couple years behind them in school brought them each a glass of water and a menu and asked if they would like coffee.

Gail smiled at her, checked the nametag to be certain, and said, "Hi, Sandy, what's new with you?"

"Oh, there's never anything new. It's the same old stuff just a different day. You know how it is, grumpy kids, too many bills, and sore feet. What's up with you guys? Are you guys a couple now?" Sandy asked, fishing for gossip.

"No. This is all business," Mike stated. "And yes I'd like some coffee. Black, please."

"'At's right," Sandy said. "You guys are both cops, aren't ya? That's strange, ain't it. Two cops from the same class in our little school. No, actually there are three of you. I heard Jimmy Scoggins is a cop over in the valley someplace."

Gail smiled and said, "I guess it musta been something they

taught us in history class. Could I have coffee too, with cream and sugar?"

"Sure thing, be right back," Sandy said headed back to the kitchen.

When Sandy was out of earshot Gail said, "I thought that was Sandy, but I wasn't sure. Life has not been good to her, has it?"

Mike fiddled with his silverware before answering. "No, she's had it rough. She has three kids by a guy who's now over in Salem in the state's big house. I think she has had a bit of a drug problem from time to time. It's sad to see, she had so much potential in school. She was smart and pretty, from a good family, but she made a couple of bad choices, and bam, here she is ten years later."

"Man, does anyone ever escape?" Gail asked rhetorically.

"Some do, but not many. And most of those that do have so much baggage they're pullin' behind them, things will never be easy.

"The only real success stories that I have known to come out of that downward spiral are a few that get crazy about religion. In fact, the church that your dad, mom, and grandparents attend has a couple of amazing success stories. But those folks have just traded drug and alcohol dependence for God dependence, so have they gained anything?"

Gail thought about it for a second and smiled. "I don't remember ever having to arrest someone who was high on God."

Mike chuckled and said, "Guess you got a point there."

Sandy brought their coffee and asked for their orders. Gail opted for the house special of eggs, bacon, toast, and hash browns. Mike went right to the biscuits and gravy.

While they waited for the food, Gail turned back to the case at hand. "So, what were you doin' at the post office?"

Mike explained what he had found out about Joanie Craddock's little address scam. "It's sounds crazy till you think about it," Mike said. "But ya know, you can get the balance of your checking account and even pay your bills right online. There's really no reason that you would need to get real mail connected to your account."

Gail was making a face that was not pleasant when she replied, "You mean to tell me that when I started my involvement in this spider-web of a case of yours, I was at an address that has no connection to the person I was looking for? That's just perfect! Joanie Caddell was never at the address?"

Before Mike could answer, he realized that Sandy was at their booth with the food. She interrupted their conversation by saying, "Joanie Caddell is a semi-regular here, lousy tipper, too. She comes in about once every other week. Not really on a schedule but often enough that we all know who she is. Nobody ever wants to wait on her. She's mean. Why you guys looking for her? I'd love to see her get her chops busted."

Mike replied before Gail had the chance, "We're not really looking for her, just talking. But what kind of mean is she?"

"Oh, you know, just real bossy," Sandy said as she set down the food. "She's like, never satisfied with her food or the service. It's always too cold or too salty, or takes too long to get to the table. She always gripes about the booth bein' dirty or the prices are too high. Crap like that. And then leaves a fifty-cent tip. She's real prime piece of work, that one. Are ya sure ya can't haul her skinny little butt off to jail? Charge her with unnecessary ugliness or something? I'd be more 'n happy to provide a lack of character witness."

"We aren't gonna arrest her for anything. But I'd like to talk to her," Gail said. "You have any idea where she lives?"

"Somewheres down near the county line, I think. But I'm not sure. She ain't real talkative when she's in here, 'less you count complainin,' and I sure don't hang around her table to make chitchat."

"That's okay. No big deal. It's really not important," Gail said.

"Okay. You guys enjoy. Holler if you need anything. And I think you oughta be a couple," Sandy said with a wink as she went off to her next table.

Mike dug into his biscuits and gravy as if he hadn't eaten for three days, but he did manage to say between bites, "I doubt that your Joanie Craddock has anything to do with the murder of Jodie Caddell, but coincidences drive me crazy. Like the detectives on TV always say…there really isn't any such thing as a coincidence."

"I don't know if there is a connection or not, but I sure wish that Joanie Craddock had never gone to that stupid garage sale. And I wish even more that I had never gone out to try to retrieve those movies."

"Hey, what's done is done," Mike said as he finished mopping up the last of his gravy. "There is no way you could've known it was gonna turn into this kinda can of worms when you went out there."

Gail had hardly made a dent in her breakfast when Sandy came by with the check. "Is everything all right?" Sandy asked when she looked at Gail's plate.

"Yeah, fine, I just really don't feel much like eating," Gail replied.

"Well, at least it doesn't look like our hometown Bubba is havin' that problem any day of the week," the waitress said as she patted Mike on the shoulder.

When Sandy had left, Gail turned to Mike and asked, "You ready to get out there and see what we can find out?"

"Yeah, as much as I'm enjoyin' the ambiance of this place, we have us a job to get done."

"What?" Gail laughed. "You aren't gettin' touchy about your size in your old age are you?"

Mike just shook his head and stood up without answering.

Gail left a hefty tip on the table and started to slide out of the booth.

Mike glanced at the ten lying on the table, gave Gail a funny look, and said, "You feelin' that generous, or has your eyesight failed you? That's almost as much as the check must be."

"Yeah, well, I can't help thinkin' about how hard is must be for Sandy to be raisin' those kids all by herself."

"Okay, it's your money, but the dime bag or case a beer that your ten spot is gonna buy ain't gonna do those rug rats any good."

"Come on, at least let me think that I'm buyin' eggs and milk and bread. Man, you didn't used to be so stinkin' cynical."

Mike scowled and headed for the door. "And I didn't used to see what was goin' on in these people's lives every lousy day either. You see it too. Don't tell me it doesn't get to ya."

"Yeah, I know what you mean, but somehow it's different when it's someone I know," Gail admitted.

"Well, if you were with the county instead of the elite force in Bend, half the people whose sorry butts you'd be draggin' to lock up would be people you used to know. It gets to where they're no different than the strangers after awhile."

"Hey, Cindy," Mike shouted through the pass through. "It all right if we leave Gail's Toyota in your lot for awhile? We got some business down south and don't wanna hafta take both rigs."

"It's the blue pickup," Gail added.

"No problem," Cindy replied. "Mondays are never too busy around here anyway."

"Thanks," Mike shouted as he headed out the door.

Gail settled up for the meal, and by the time she got to the parking lot, Mike was behind the wheel of his Ford, with its big diesel engine rattling loud enough to wake the dead. She climbed up into the cab, and they headed south, neither of them saying a word, lost in their own thoughts, as they rolled south on Highway 197.

18

"Hey, you missed the turn," Gail said when she realized they had blown right past Bonanza Road.

"Yeah, I know," Mike replied. "Shear is having the memorial service for Jodie today, and he didn't think it would be too cool for us to be parked in his yard when the friends and relatives arrived. So I got to studyin' the map, and I think I've found a Forest Service road that will take us right behind the property."

"Okay, but aren't we gonna be in Chiloquin County?"

"Probably. But I put in a call to the Chiloquin county sheriff, and he doesn't have a problem with us sneakin' onto his turf. He said that they rarely have opportunity to get that far north anyway. Oh, I think that's the turn," Mike grunted as he braked hard to get the truck and trailer slowed down enough to make the turn onto a road that was little more than a cow path.

They drove west on Forest Service Road 172 for a couple of miles, with a huge cloud of dust marking their progress. "I'd guess we're about due south of the Shear property here. What'd ya think?" Mike asked.

"I guess," Gail answered, "but I've only been out there once, and you know how it is when you're huntin' for an address. You never pay much attention to how far you've gone."

"Well, I think this is about right. Let's park on that spur road and ride the quads north, see what we run into," Mike said, pulling the rig off the road at a spot just wide enough for another rig to get by, should someone happen along.

They spent fifteen minutes undoing straps and unloading the ATVs. Then Mike gave Gail five minutes of instruction on how the machine worked before they put on their helmets and started the machines up. "This is goin' to stir up a sight of dust, even at a slow pace," Mike said, tapping his machine with his knuckles. "You'll probably want to hang back until the worst of the dust settles before followin' me. I'm just goin' to follow this trail north until I get my bearings and figure out if we're in about the right spot," he said, taking off.

He was right about the dust, Gail thought as she watched him disappear into the brush. She waited until the worst of it thinned out before following. At least it wouldn't be hard to keep track of him; the ATVs left great tracks in the soft ground, and the cloud of dust hanging in the air was a dead giveaway of his direction.

The trail they were on narrowed as they got farther and farther away from the Forest Service Road, but it was still a distinct trail twenty minutes later when Gail rode around a corner and found Mike standing by his machine, concentrating on something to the northwest of them.

"See those buildings through the trees?" Mike asked Gail when she came up beside him and shut down her machine.

"Yeah, I can see something. Is that Shear's house?"

"I'm pretty sure that it is. We'll move a little closer on foot and find out."

"How'd you do that?" Gail wanted to know.

"Do what?" Mike asked innocently.

"Land us right on the spot, that's what."

Mike laughed and held up a piece of electronics about the size of a cell phone. "Old Indian trick," he said. "I programmed the spot into my GPS unit when I was out here yesterday."

"Oh you are such a turkey. I was gettin' really impressed. I thought you were a master woodsman or somethin.'"

"Well, you should be impressed. Master woodsmen use the latest technology, don't they?"

"Okay. So what do you think we should do now?" Gail asked to change the subject.

"Well," Mike replied, "I think we should walk down to where Ted and Tony found the dog's grave, so you can see if it is in the vicinity of where those horses were staring when you were out here."

"That sounds good. Let's go," Gail said, taking off her helmet and setting it on the handlebars of the ATV.

As they were weaving their way through the thick pines and bitterbrush, both of them were on the alert. Neither of them had seen anything at all to make them uneasy, but the hair on the backs of their necks was sticking up. Both were putting on the bravado, not wanting the other to think they were on edge, when a big jack rabbit broke from its hiding place in the undergrowth and went bounding across the trail. Both of them were grabbing for their firearms before they realized what was happening, and then they sheepishly grinned at each other and shrugged, knowing that they had been frightened enough by a rabbit to go for their guns. The comedy of the situation put them both at ease, and they continued toward the building with a little more confidence.

The horses whinnied and nickered, telling them that they had been spotted.

When they got within about fifty yards of the house, they realized that there were only two cars in the driveway of the Shear home. Glad that they would not be in danger of interrupting a group of mourners, they held a quick conference and decided that they could proceed, but with stealth.

"Head over by the corral, and I'll move back to where we found the dog. When I'm in place, I'll wave. You see if you think that is where the horses were looking when you were out here the other day," Mike instructed, and he headed back through the brush while Gail moved toward the corral.

Gail was concentrating on the horses as she moved forward. She hoped that they would not put up too much of a ruckus when she got closer to them. The last thing she wanted was for someone to come out of the house and ask her what she was doing sneaking around their property. The big brutes were milling in their enclosure, shaking their manes and snapping their tails, but so far it did not appear that anyone in the house had noticed.

She decided not to press her luck by getting any closer to the horses until Mike had gotten into position. She was staring at the area where she expected him to appear when she heard a door slam shut at the house. Instinctively Gail stepped behind a couple of thick pines and turned toward the house. A small middle-aged woman with snow-white hair down to the middle of her back had come out the back door of the house and appeared to be heading for the corral. The woman walked with confidence and perfect posture and went straight to the horses' water trough and turned on the water. The horses forgot about Gail and went for the water. While the water trough was filling, the woman went into the shed and brought out a couple of flakes of hay that she put into the manger, much to the delight of the horses.

While the animals were enjoying their meal, the white-haired lady climbed the rails of the corral and dropped down inside the enclosure with practiced ease. Retrieving a currycomb from a niche between the shed wall and the corral, she began currying one of the horses, to the obvious delight of the animal, whose muscles rippled under the skin when the comb was stroked across it. It took no guessing to decide that these animals were accustomed to this treatment.

The horses had slicked up every scrap of hay by the time the grooming session was complete. The woman then put the comb away, turned off the water, and produced a rope lead from another hiding spot. She clipped the snap of the rope lead onto the halter of one of the horses. She snubbed the gelding to a rail in the corral and went to work on his hoofs with a hoof pick. The big animal was as gentle as a puppy throughout the process and when the woman led it to a small gate at the side of the corral. She opened the gate and brought the horse from the enclosure and tied it to the corral near the shed door. She then went into the shed and returned with a saddle, reins, and saddle blanket; moving with practiced ease, she soon had the horse outfitted for the trail. The woman swung easily into the saddle, and the horse and rider headed down the trail that would take them within feet of where Gail was hiding.

Without really knowing why, Gail slipped a little farther into the thicket of young pine trees that was behind her. Holding still, she watched as the big animal and its rider walked by. When the horse was almost even with Gail, it rolled its eyes and started to rear, but the woman in the saddle was in command and quickly gained control of the beast. The two of them went on up the well-used trail and disappeared into the dense trees.

When horse and rider were out of sight, Gail went back to the trail and began to scan the area where Mike had headed. After a few minutes of studying the area she thought he should be in she caught a glimpse of him as he stepped into a small clearing and waved. She waved back, and then looked back to the horse that was left standing, somewhat forlorn, in the corral. The horse was staring intently at Mike, with almost exactly the same stance as it and its partner had had the last time Gail had been to this property.

When Gail rejoined Mike, she asked, "Did you see the woman on the horse?"

"Yeah, I did. I'm kinda wonderin' who she is and where she's headed. She looked like a woman on a mission."

"I'll say. And did you see how she handled that horse? This ain't the first day her butt's been in that saddle."

"No. And it's not the first trip that pair has made up that trail." Mike took off the baseball cap he was wearing; *East Lake County Sheriff's Department* was embroidered across the front. He scratched the coarse stubble on his head. "I don't think that was Jodie Craddock's sister. According to Shear, she was drivin' over from Portland today—and I'd really like to interview her before she goes home. I'd also like to have a talk with that lady."

"Maybe this horse-lover is Shear's sister," Gail said. "Or maybe she's just a friend of the dead woman. But I'd like to know how she has gotten so well acquainted with those horses. Those nags were not the least inclined to show any friendliness toward me."

Mike laughed and said, "I've always heard that horses were good at judgin' character. And they sure ain't nags. If I don't miss my guess, that nag as you called it, was some expensive horse flesh."

"Expensive or not, they're all nags to me. They are ornery, stinkin' critters. When I was growin' up I always wanted a horse. But my dad always told me that they were too expensive and weren't good for anythin' but eatin' anyhow. It used to make me mad, but I'm beginning to believe that he was right."

"You're just ticked at 'em cause you couldn't keep your butt in the saddle. It twernt the horse's fault you got unloaded and broke your back. Anyway, what did ya think?" Mike said, getting them back on track. "When you were out here last week, were the horses, looking in the direction of where the dog was buried?"

Gail looked back over her shoulder to the corral. "Yeah, I'm sure they were. For some reason they were fixated on something right in this area."

"Well," Mike responded, "I can't prove it, but I think someone was watchin' you while you were snoopin' around down there. And I think that someone saw you pick up and toss that beer can, and later they planted the can in the house by the body in hopes of throwing our investigation off the track. If I'm right in those suspicions, we're dealin' with some smart and experienced bad guys, the type of bad guys that have a lot to lose if they get caught; the kind of bad guys that will do most anything to keep from gettin' caught. And I don't mind admittin' that it scares the bejeebees outta me, because my experience in murder investigations isn't worth enough to make a down payment on a baloney sandwich."

Gail stood there in the dust, staring off in the direction that she had watched the horse and rider disappear, and said, "Well, I don't have even that much experience with this stuff. But I do have something that is gonna help, and I know you well enough to know you got it too. And that something is stubbornness. We're gonna worry this thing like a hound dog on a fresh venison bone."

Mike nodded, smiled, and said, "Well, we best start worryin,' then. Let's get back on those machines and see if we can find anything interesting out here!"

"What'da we do if we run into Ms. Horse rider?" Gail asked.

"I'm hopin' we do run across her. And iffen we do, we'll talk to her like we would anyone that we find around a crime scene: Nice, polite, and stupid. A third of that comes pretty natural to me, and a lot of times that approach gets me some good information. So let's go huntin.'"

19

They rode slowly through the Central Oregon countryside, not really knowing what they were looking for, but looking hard all the same. But as hard as they were looking, neither of them saw the horse and rider tucked away in a pole pine thicket. The rider saw them, however, and tracked their progress until they were out of sight. A few minutes later the rider kicked her horse into action and rode hard back to the corral, and a phone.

Aside from an occasional covey of quail, a few mule deer, and a whole bunch of jackrabbits, they didn't see anything interesting for the next hour and a half. Then they broke over a hill and found themselves looking at a completely different landscape spread out before them.

The barren land of bitterbrush and juniper trees was sliced by a quarter-mile swath of green. Willows and aspens and lush grass lined the banks of a winding stream. The presence of water changed everything. The sight was so unexpected that it almost seemed like a mirage. Mike and Gail were both surprised, and they just turned off their machines and sat staring.

"Did you know this was here?" Gail asked after a few minutes.

Mike shook his head and replied, "Well, I should have. I looked the map over before we came out, and I saw that the Little Deschutes River ran through here, but I didn't imagine it would look like this. It's so green, it almost hurts my eyes."

"After all the brown dusty country we've ridden through, this just seems impossible," Gail said.

"Yeah, but I don't think it has any connection to our case, so I guess it's just incidental information."

Gail laughed, "It won't be incidental information to my dad and grandpa when I tell them. They're always looking for spots like this."

"What for?"

"For fishin'! I bet that stream is full of fat and lazy brook and brown trout."

"That doesn't mean anything to me. I hate fishin'!" Mike said.

"Dad and Gramps always say that they wish more people felt that way. More fish for them!"

"'At's okay by me," Mike said in a distracted tone as he watched the sky. "They can have 'em. But look at those thunderheads building up in the southwest. I've been watchin' 'em for the past half hour, and they're getting darker and darker by the minute. And they're headin' our way. I think we better find some cover. I don't wanna be out it the open if a hailstorms hits."

"What happened to all that toughness of this mornin'? But I'm with ya. Do you have any ideas as to where we might find good shelter?"

Mike pointed to the northwest and indicated a stand of giant old-growth ponderosa pine trees. "That stand of pondies would break the force of any hail and wind. But then, they might attract the lightning. What'da you think?"

Gail nodded to a jack pine thicket about a hundred yards to the south, "I vote for takin' our chances in that stand of small stuff. It won't be as good a cover from hailstones, but the trees are probably too small to invite a strike."

"Well, let's check it out," Mike said as he started his ATV.

They parked their machines and pushed their way into the trees just as the first rolls of thunder echoed across the forest. The wind was whipping the pine trees, and needles and dust filled the sky. The sound of the wind through the limbs of the trees sounded like crashing surf. The clouds in the approaching storm were nearly black in the center, while the edges were silver. Their leading edge looked like sheetrock mud feathered out with a trowel, but on the trailing side they were piling up on each other like cars in a chain-reaction accident. The first big drops of rain splattered into the dust as they searched for good cover under the thirty-foot-tall trees. They found a likely spot and settled in for the show.

The time between the flashes of lightning and the boom of the thunder got shorter and shorter as the storm moved toward them. The sound of the wind would have drowned out a locomotive. The big drops of rain were increasing in volume too. Within minutes, the storm was right over them, and the sky was alive with lightning bolts, and the earth shook from the thunder. The dry ground refused to absorb the onslaught of water from the rain, causing puddles to form in every low spot. Pine needles floated in these puddles like kelp over a tide pool, and the oversized drops splashed in like bombs.

The riot of noise from the storm made conversation impossible, so the pair of cops just sat and watched the display. The warmth of the summer day was forgotten as they were quickly soaked to the skin by the rain, but at least they were spared any hail, and their helmets kept their heads dry.

The storm moved over them and away as rapidly as it had arrived. They remained slightly awed as they watched it move away. The sun came out, and as the air warmed, steam rose from the puddles. The wind was stilled to a breeze. The air held that strange aroma of stirred dust and ions that only follows a good thunderstorm.

Gail moved out of the thicket into a clearing. She sat down

on a log in a clearing where the sun could hit her to dry out her drenched clothing. Mike followed and found his own perch about ten feet away from her. He broke the silence by saying, "A storm like that would almost make a fella believe that there was a God."

"Mike, you've known me long enough to know I'm a believer. Are you baitin' me?"

"No, Gail, I'm not tryin' to get to ya. I'm serious. I've never spent much time thinking about God or any of that stuff, but once in a while, I remember something your dad said at our baccalaureate service when we graduated high school. You remember him givin' that speech?"

"Yeah, I remember that he spoke, but I sure couldn't tell you anything he said."

Mike turned his face up toward the sun and looked thoughtful, almost embarrassed. "I remember him telling us that the most important thing that any of us could do in life was to take advantage of God's offer of making us part of his family. You know, I had kind of a rough childhood. My dad left when I was just a little squirt, and Ma had to work two jobs to pay the rent and keep us in beans. There were lots of times when I daydreamed of being part of a real family. That family thing your dad talked about sounded real good. Do you feel like you're part of God's family?"

"Yeah, I guess so. I mean, I don't feel it like Dad does, and sure not like my grandfather. He acts like he thinks he's in heaven already. Actually walks around talking out loud to God when he doesn't think anyone is listening.

"Me? I dunno. I mean, I wanna go to heaven and all that, but there's a lot of life in the here and now that needs livin.'" Gail thought she almost sounded like she was apologizing, and she found that irritating. How did we get on this subject, she wondered?

"Yeah, well duh. Who doesn't wanna go to heaven? The only alternative I've ever heard of isn't too inviting. But man, how can anyone ever be good enough to get into God's family, or into heaven?"

"Man, Mike. You should be talkin' to my dad or a preacher or something. All I know is that if we admit to God that we are sinners, ask him to forgive us, and commit our lives to him, we're in his family and headed for heaven."

"That sounds way too simple. If it is that easy, why do we have all of these other religions that are searching for the truth? And why isn't everybody in God's family?"

"Well, from my angle, it's simple enough. But that don't make it easy. Who wants to admit that they're a sinner? But the really hard part is that committing our lives to him. That's the part I'm havin' a problem with. He asks some things sometimes that are pretty durn hard to do."

Mike sat thoughtfully, stirring the dirt with a stick. Down an inch below the surface, the dust was still powder dry, despite the downpour that had just occurred. After a few minutes, he said, "Well, I've got no issue with admittin' that I've messed my life up. I got a divorce, a truckload of debt, and a bit of a drinkin' problem to prove it. That's why I like my job so much. When I'm at work I seem to have everything under control. But at home, that's a whole different ball game. As fer committing my life to God, I'm not sure what that means. But if it would help me untangle my mess, I might be for it."

Gail stood up and stretched before she responded. "You need to sit down and talk to Dad."

"I don't wanna bother him."

"Oh, don't you worry. Talkin' about stuff like this is the only thing he enjoys more than eatin,' huntin,' and fishin'—in that order. Gettin' him to shut up once you got 'im started would be the hard part. Don't cha think we oughta start hunting again?" she said, wanting to get the conversation to safer ground.

"Yeah, I suppose. Sorry to go off like that. I guess that storm just knocked the tough guy right outta me."

"Hey, it's no problem. But I do think I'll sic the old geezer onto ya."

"That'd be fine by me. In fact, I hope ya do. I'm serious about wantin' to be a part of God's family. I used ta think that the P.D. was gonna be the family I missed out on. But it's all backstabbin' and political—just about like most of the dysfunctional families that provide our job security. There's gotta be something more." With that, he walked over and wiped the beaded water off the seat of the ATV he had been riding.

Mike pointed across the hundred yards of green that was irrigated by the stream and said, "I'm gonna find a place to ford the crick, and then I'll ride upstream on the far side. Why don't you wait till I get across, and then ride parallel to me on this side? We'll see what we can find."

"Okay. But ya know, I been thinking. Where da ya suppose our horse and rider went? You'd think we would have run across them out here."

"It's a big country. She could be most anywhere."

By the time they were back on their machines and moving, Gail was a little stunned at the way the conversation had gone. Mike had always been the picture of independence. She couldn't believe that he had put down his macho cover to be so real. At the same time, she could not remember when she had felt more alive than when she had been telling Mike about Christianity. And she was definitely going to sic her dad onto Mike.

Mike was regretting having been so honest before his four-wheeler had moved fifty yards. He certainly hoped that none of this talk would make its way back to the department. The guys would laugh him off the force. He worked hard at building and maintaining his tough-guy persona. But at the same time, he hoped that Gail would arrange for her dad to give him a call.

Gail waited, watching, as Mike looked for a place to cross the stream. Once he found a ford and crossed, he waved and they started out. There were old logging roads on both sides of the stream, so progress was relatively easy. They rode slowly for about a mile, looking for anything unusual or suspicious.

An old dead ponderosa snag caught Gail's attention. Not because it was unusual; there were dozens of snags in the area, the remnants of lightning strikes, bugs, disease, old age, or whatever kills big trees. But this old tree skeleton was serving as a perch for eight vultures and about twice that many ravens. Where there were vultures and ravens together in these types of numbers it could only mean one thing. Something was dead and ripe. She stopped her machine, and when Mike noticed, she gestured toward the scavenger-filled tree. Then she parked the ATV, got off, and walked toward the tree to get a better look.

Always cautious, the shiny black ravens took to the air with a raucous cawing as soon as they realized that Gail was headed in their direction. The vultures stayed in the snag until she was within thirty yards of them, then they only moved to another nearby tree with an awkward beating of their massive wings. Several more of both types of birds startled her when they rose from the ground amid a cacophony of bird noises from just beyond the dead tree. That was when the stench assaulted her senses. It was the distinct thick smell of death and deterioration. It was an odor that her job had forced her to become accustomed to, and this was not strong compared to an enclosed area, but it was never good. She literally followed her nose.

The scavenger magnet, and the source of the odor, was the carcass of a Black Angus heifer. Gail walked around the bird buffet at a distance of about twenty feet. Observing the dead animal was especially ominous with a tree full of buzzards diligently observing from only fifty yards away. They made no attempts to appear polite but stared sullenly, intent on getting back to their meal, as she made a circuit around the corpse.

Mike took some time getting back across the river. The stream took a giant bend and formed a deep pool right at this spot. But he joined her by the time that Gail had completed the first circle of the dead animal. "What 'ave you got?" he asked.

"Sun-baked buzzard barbeque."

"Smells delicious."

They were slowly scanning the ground around their corpse when Mike said, "Some rancher is gonna find this real curious. Come take a look at this."

When Gail looked over, Mike was pointing a small digital camera at a print left by the toe of a hiking boot. It had been protected from the rain beneath a dense sagebrush bush. The edges of the print had crumbled and were rounded, so it was not a fresh print, but it was fairly distinct, so it was not very old either.

"Huh," Gail grunted. "I'm no expert, but I'd guess that print was made pretty close to the same time that this heifer quit breathing."

"Ya think maybe this critter didn't expire from natural causes?"

"I'd guess, but I dunno. Let's take a closer look."

"Okay," Mike agreed. "Just let me mark this boot print first so we don't trample it." He tore six inches of orange surveyor's tape from a roll he took from his pocket and tied the tape to the sagebrush above the print.

They scanned the ground for more clues as they moved closer to the animal. When they were almost to the carcass, Mike bent down and studied something on the ground. "Hmm," he said, "This is gettin' curiouser and curiouser."

"What'd you find now?" Gail asked.

"The butt of a Winston cigarette. Smoked right down to the filter, then half buried. Just like the one we picked up from behind Shear's property."

Gail was looking intently at the dead animal while Mike placed the remains of the cigarette into a bag. She tilted her head to one side and moved closer before she said, "Well, unless coyotes and buzzards have started carrying knives, some other varmint was on this critter before those scavengers. The hide was split down the backbone in a jagged line."

Mike came up beside her and examined the animal's hide. "That's exactly how a poacher takes the back strap off a buck. Only most poachers do a neater job. Looks like this guy's knife could stand to be sharper. But you're right. A critter uglier than these birds was after this animal first."

"I dunno how this ties in with the death of Jodie Caddell, but that cigarette butt tells me that there's some kinda connection," Gail said.

"It's a far leap from a murdered lady to a rustled cow," Mike said, "but I don't doubt that you're right. On the other hand, I know the foreman of the YZ is gonna be mighty interested in this business."

"How'd ya know this is a YZ animal?"

Mike flipped the hide over and pointed to the brand, a y and a z laced together, forming what looked like an hourglass. "Ya don't have to be a detective to figure out that brand in this country. The YZ owns three-quarters of the livestock in Central Oregon. But before we notify the ranch, I think I'd better give our buddies at the OSP a heads up on this. I imagine that they're gonna want a look at our heifer."

20

Mike took one last look around the area where the dead animal lay before turning to Gail and saying, "I don't think we're gonna find anything else around here. We better head back to the rig and get outta here. I wanna talk to a couple of my friends over in the game division, see if they're havin' a fresh rash of poaching in this area. And I'll let the detective at OSP know the GPS coordinates of this animal in case they want to come out and look her over.

"That thunderstorm dropped enough rain to hold down the dust so you should be able to follow right behind me on the way out, so we should make good time gettin' outta here."

Gail looked off in the direction of the waiting birds and answered, "I got a little business to take care of here. You go ahead and take off, I'll catch up. Your tracks should be easy to follow." In Gail's mind, this was embarrassing. She worked very hard at being as good, or better, at every task that a police officer faced, as a man; but, no matter how you stacked it, relieving your bladder was harder for a woman than a man.

"No problem. I'll talk to you at the rig," Mike said. He fired up his ATV and took off.

Three minutes later Gail picked up her helmet, preparing to

follow Mike, when she heard the sharp, distinct report of a high-powered rifle. The first report was quickly followed by a second, then a third. The echoes were still reverberating through the trees while Gail was calculating. There were no big game seasons open, and the shots were too close together to be target practice. She had a very bad feeling about those shots, and her instincts and training kicked into high gear.

Instead of following Mike's exit trail as she had planned to do, she went north about two hundred yards and then took a course that she thought would run parallel to his. Once on her course, she rode for approximately the three minutes that she judged were the time between his leaving and the shots. Riding at about the same speed that she had expected him to ride, this should put her about two hundred yards north of where he should have been when the shots were fired.

She parked her machine in a thicket of jack pines, slipped her nine-millimeter Sig Sauer from its holster and began stalking what she thought would be Mike's position if he had been the target of the shots. It seemed too quiet as she crept through the stunted pines, twisted junipers, and tangled sagebrush. There were no jays squawking, no chipmunks chirping, not even the whistle of a hawk to break the silence. She did hear the distant groaning of a motor and strained to discern whether it was a truck motor or a distant airplane. When she decided it was a plane, she started forward again, inching and looking, pausing and listening, making progress the way that her father had taught her to stalk elk in the archery season. She had slipped forward like this for about ten minutes when her nose picked up an odor that was out of place. It took only a second for her to realize that the odor was gasoline.

She sniffed to determine the direction the smell was coming from and decided that she needed to turn east. She had spent a few more minutes moving silently through the brush when she spotted Mike's machine lying on its side about seventy yards away. There was no sign of Mike, and every nerve in her wanted to sprint over to the ATV and find him. But she had no idea where the shooter was, and she did not want to give away her location before she knew what she was up against.

So Gail crouched behind a young juniper and waited, watching for movement or a sound, or anything that would give away the position of her prey. Minutes ticked by. Sweat began drying on her forehead. She fought to keep her emotions in check. And she worried that Mike was up there, alone in the brush beside his machine, bleeding out.

She had just decided that the shooter had taken off when a pine squirrel began scolding something off to the south. She stared in that direction until her eyes began to burn and water. She frantically wiped her eyes and forced them to focus. And she saw movement. A rifle barrel materialized from behind a log, then a man's head and torso. The shooter was getting up from his position of ambush. He had expected Gail to charge in to give aid to her partner and was waiting to pick her off when she did.

Gail watched as the sniper crept from his hiding place and began stalking her. After a few minutes she realized that he had heard her park the ATV and was heading toward it in search of her. She contemplated her next move, knowing that her handgun was no match for the high-powered rifle that he was carrying. He moved slowly, but even from her distant position she could hear him break an occasional limb under his feet. Good, she thought. He was not a woodsman.

She weighed her options. She could wait until he snuck past her hiding spot and then fall in behind him and try to get close enough to take him from behind, or she could take the opportunity to go check on Mike. Visions of him helplessly lying in his own blood, his life pumping out, made her decision for her. She had to find out if Mike was hit, and how badly. So, when the shooter had passed out of sight, Gail used her hunter's stealth to get to where she had seen Mike's machine.

When she got to the machine it took a minute for her to locate Mike, and panic welled up inside her. Then she saw him motionless in a clump of yellow rabbit brush just a yard from the ATV. He wasn't moving, and there was no sign of blood. He was laying facedown, and her training told her not to move him in case of head or back injury. She quickly reached under him and felt his carotid artery for a pulse. Her excitement at discovering a strong pulse in his neck was dashed by the sight of a round hole, about a quarter of an inch diameter, in the side of his helmet.

Her mind was spinning in a hundred directions when the nearby blast of a rifle, then another, nearly stopped her heart. The deafening report reminded her that she was still being stalked, and she quickly moved away from Mike, knowing that the shooter would come back here after discovering that she was not with the machine. She assumed that the shots were used to disable her ATV.

She took up a position in a thick patch of sagebrush about fifteen yards from Mike, thinking that the culprit would check to see if she was with the down man. As she waited, she listened and heard a rock roll and brush snap, then a chipmunk cheeping. All this was to the north of her position. While the shooter was no woodsman, he was no imbecile, either. He had guessed that Gail was waiting to ambush him, and he was avoiding that ambush by circling the location at a distance.

So now it had become a game of cat and mouse. But which of them was the cat, and which the mouse, she wondered? For the moment, Gail thought, she had the advantage. She could hear the shooter as he moved. Soon, though, he was going to be out of earshot, and then he and his long gun would have the advantage. She decided to move away from him while she still knew his approximate location. He would expect her to stay near Mike or return to her ATV. She knew that he had disabled her machine with his last shot. And there wasn't anything she could do for Mike while the sniper was at hand, so she moved quickly toward the position that her opponent had been in when she first saw him.

She moved quickly but silently down the decline and across the slight swale to the spot she suspected that the shots that had taken Mike out had come from. When she got there her suspicions were confirmed by boot tracks in the rain-dampened soil and a single half-buried Winston cigarette butt. She would bet her whole next paycheck that these boot prints were a match for the print they had discovered by the dead heifer.

Thinking that the sniper might return to this location to watch for her to check on Mike, she moved back into thick cover about fifteen yards away, hoping to ambush the ambusher. And she waited. And waited. And waited. The wildlife in the area began to return to their normal routines. A pair of towhees was hunting seeds among the yellow flowers of the rabbit brush. A little lizard with his cobalt-blue belly did pushups on a sun soaked rock. A brood of golden mantels played tag on a nearby rock pile. But there was no sign of Mr. Camouflage.

She considered using the cell phone that was in her fanny pack, but she was afraid that the beep that it emitted when opened would attract her attacker's attention. She knew she should call in some backup, but who to call? They were in Chiloquin County territory, and she did not know anyone in that department. Besides, she was not at all sure that she could direct anyone to within five miles of their position. While she debated she checked the phone. There was no signal, so the decision was made for her.

Gail checked her watch and was surprised to see that it was mid-afternoon. It had been eleven thirty when she had left the dead cow's location. No wonder her legs were cramping from being coiled beneath her. She had been playing this deadly game of hide-and-seek for over four hours, and it had been a least two hours since she had last heard her attacker change position. Logic told her that he had left the scene. After all, what would he gain by staying, other than the possibility of being killed? And he obviously was not a woodsman, so she thought it unlikely that he had the patience to stay silently hidden for this long.

Besides, she needed to check on Mike again and try to determine how badly he had been injured. And she needed to get out of this brush before dark, or she would not be able to get out before morning.

With this rationalization, she cautiously moved from her hiding spot. She moved an inch at a time at first, then, emboldened by success, she started moving faster. She was a third of the way back to Mike's location when a slight movement caught her eye. Something like instinct told her that the motion was the rifle being brought to bear on her. She immediately leapt to her right and hit the ground in a shoulder roll when a blast from a high-powered rifle destroyed the quiet of the forest. She felt the air displacement caused by the bullet, and then she was firing her Sig and rolling farther to her right. When she came to rest behind a huge ponderosa log, her fifteen round clip was empty. She would have sworn that she had pulled the trigger no more than five times. The odds of her hitting anything at the distance of over a hundred yards, especially when she hadn't even seen her target, were astronomical, but her spray had kept the sniper from squeezing off another round.

Gail was frantically wrestling with her fanny pack, trying to get to one of her two spare clips of ammo, when she saw her assailant leave his position above where Mike lay. She involuntarily held her breath while she watched the man move in a manner calculated to put him in position to get a clear shot at her. Her hands found a full clip and locked it home while she watched the killer angle to her right, where a small knoll would provide adequate elevation for him to see over the log she was using for cover. The casual way that he moved suggested that he knew she was watching and did not care. He was completely confident that he was outside of the effective range of her handgun, and he was confident that she was unable to escape. Watching the man's confidence chilled Gail to the core. She had to make a move before he got into position!

Her mind raced as she considered her options; at his current casual pace he would be in position in about three minutes. She could try a shot, but hitting anything at a hundred and fifty yards with her nine-millimeter was impossible. She could charge his position, but he would calmly shoot her through. She could scramble for a new hiding spot, but the nearest cover was twenty yards away, allowing plenty of time for the sniper to take aim and fire as she scrambled through the open. None of the options seemed to offer the opportunity of a positive outcome.

She needed a miracle, so she cried out to God.

In a calmer moment she would have been the first to acknowledge that this was against her principles. Not that she believed that God was unable or unwilling to help. It was just that a person should not cry out to God when they are in trouble, when they have rarely talked to him at any other time. That was a mark of the worst type of hypocrite. But when you have been pushed to the brink of the cliff, and the goad is at your back, principles are jettisoned.

Without further thought she began moving, without the benefit of cover. As she headed for a new position with a lot of cover, she watched her attacker. He was looking right at her as he moved, but he did not seem to see her, and he made no move to take aim. It was as if she was invisible.

She was a good fifty yards away and in some good cover when the sniper attained the high ground that allowed him to see behind the log that a moment before she had been hiding behind. He shouldered the rifle and pulled the scope to his eye with practiced ease. Even at the distance that separated them, Gail could see the expression of confusion on his face when he let the firearm down. His head rotated as he checked to make sure that he was looking behind the right log. Satisfied that he was, he mounted the rifle again. And again he could not find his target.

As she watched, Gail could tell he was perplexed; but, for that matter, so was she. Taking advantage of his confusion, Gail quickly began moving east. She used every bit of the available cover, not believing that her invisibility was more than momentary. Choosing routes that were rocky to leave less sign, she continued in a generally eastern direction. When she estimated that she had moved about a half-mile she climbed a small rise. From this position she could see for miles in every direction. And as far as she could see there was nothing but rolling acres of timber, sage, and rabbit brush.

Gail sat on a flat rock with her back against a juniper tree to break her silhouette and watched her back trail. She tried to formulate a plan, but not knowing what the shooter was doing made planning nearly impossible. If she knew for sure that he was hunting her she would circle back to check on Mike; leaving him wounded was eating at her. But the killer might still be staking out Mike's position, waiting for her to return. If he was using Mike for bait, going back was nearly guaranteed to get her killed.

As she attempted to concentrate and come up with the best course of action, the circumstances of her escaping from behind the log back there kept crowding out the rest of her thinking. What exactly had happened? There was no way that the sniper was unable to see her. But could it have been a miracle? She had been asking God to intervene. Or was it just some trick of the lighting in the woods? She had read about what hunters called early-morning blindness. That is when a hunter will mistake a doe for a buck, or a shooter will put a round into a fire-blackened log, believing they are shooting at a bear. She remembered a case that took place in the Oregon coastal mountains years ago. An elk hunter accidentally shot a little girl who was wearing a yellow raincoat as she waited in the fog and rain for the school bus. That hunter had thought the child was an elk. She had been in the shadows, and the sun had been behind her. But even as she rationalized, she knew deep down that her escape was not a product of lighting. But what had happened, she wondered?

21

Gail was concentrating on watching for the sniper and trying to figure out how she had escaped an almost sure ambush when her cell phone rang. The sound startled her so badly that when she jerked alert and grabbed for her pistol, it felt like she pulled a muscle in her neck. She had forgotten all about the phone, having ruled out the possibility of it receiving a signal way out here in the pucker brush. She rooted through her fanny pack, but it took until the third ring to find the phone and snap it open. Then she frantically scanned the area for movement, hoping that the guy stalking her had not been within earshot. Satisfied that she had not been discovered, she whispered, "What?" into the phone.

"Whatever happened to a friendly 'hello' or 'howdy,' girl?" her dad growled back through the static.

That crackling noise told Gail she'd better say what she needed to say in a hurry; the connection was apt to evaporate at any second. "Dad, Mike is down, and I'm being hunted by a guy with a rifle. Get a hold of the state police and get them on the move!"

Nate was completely baffled. Gail was talking quietly and fast, and his hearing was marginal at best. And what he thought he was hearing made no sense at all. He hit the "loud" button on his phone until it was at max volume and said, "Slow down and speak up, girl. You're not makin' very good sense."

Gail's voice got a little more desperate when she continued, "Call the state police and the East Lake County Sheriff's Department. Tell them that Mike has been shot, and the shooter is after me."

"Okay, okay. Now I'm gettin' it. Where are you?"

"We parked on the forest service road just south of Bonanza Road in Northern Chiloquin County. From there we rode ATVs west till we hit the Little Deschutes River. There is a huge bend in the river, with a really deep hole, where we found a dead heifer—rustled, I think. We were headed back to the east, probably less than a mile from the river when we were ambushed. That's where Mike is down. I'm about another half-mile away from the river. Get some help here quick. I don't know how bad Mike is hit, and I don't know when this dirt bag is gonna find me." Then Gail realized with a sickening dread that her phone had gone dead. She had no idea of how much of what she had said had been heard. She felt like smashing the phone on the rocks when she checked the little graph of bars and none were lit. The screen read "no service." She wrestled with her emotions and tucked the phone back into her pack.

Nate checked his topographical map of northern Chiloquin County. He had fished the Little Deschutes River through the stretch of water that he thought was near the spot that Gail had described. But he had always gone in from the west side. Roads went within a mile of the river from the west. He lined Bonanza Road with the logging roads that he was familiar with and came up with a plan. But since the roads on the west side of the river were private logging company roads they were not numbered or marked the way the roads on the east side of the river were. He would be flying by the seat of his pants, but being able to drive within a mile of the river was worth the gamble.

He jotted down a few brief notes about what Gail had told him then tracked Amy down in the backyard where she was doing some weeding. He gave her a brief summary of what was going on, and watched the color drain from her face as he talked. "Please call the Oregon State Police and East Lake County and relay this information to them," Nate quietly requested.

"What do you think you're gonna do?" Amy asked quickly.

"I'm goin' down there and see if I can find 'em. You know that the cops 'ill take all night getting set to go in. Those kids might not have that kinda time," Nate replied.

After thirty-five years of being married to this stubborn man, Amy knew it was futile, but she could not resist arguing. "You'll end up getting shot or hurt or something. Can't you just leave this to the police?"

"You call 'em and tell 'em what's up, then call next door and ask my parents to get on their knees over there. We're gonna need the cover, and that's a fact."

Nate did not take the time to engage in further discussion. Instead he trotted back to the house and changed into his warm-weather camo gear. In the garage he spun the dial on his gun safe until it clicked open. Looking inside the safe, he considered his options. The Ruger 10/22 was light and quiet, but too small to be effective. The .300 WinMag was too awkward and heavy. The Winchester .243 would be a great choice, but his twelve-gauge Browning Gold was the gun he felt most comfortable with. He spent literally hundreds of hours a year with it, and burned through two or three cases of shells. He loved to hunt ducks and upland game birds, and he loved to do both with this gun. He grabbed the gun and the two boxes of double-ought buckshot he had bought for coyote hunting and threw them onto the passenger side seat of his Dodge pickup truck.

Fifteen minutes after his call to Gail had terminated, he was headed down the road. He stuffed the shells for the shotgun into his pockets as he steered with one hand. Then he fished under the truck seat, found his flashlight, and put it into his jacket pocket.

Out of the glove box he grabbed half a dozen granola bars, a lighter, and a compass, all of which he stuffed into another pocket. With practiced ease he pulled the fore stock off the Browning and popped out the plug that limited its magazine capacity to two, the legal limit for shells when hunting birds. Now the scattergun would hold five rounds.

Normally he drove like the old grandpa he was. This night, however, he was pushing the Dodge's Cummins diesel engine to the limit. The big pickup did not corner as good as he would have liked on this particular trip, but it more than made up for it on the straight stretches when Nate pulled onto the Highway 197 and headed south. The speedometer in this old rig had never seen three digits before, but the needle was visiting the top end of the circle on this trip. Traffic was uncharacteristically light, which made excessive speed that much easier. The few cars that were on the road would just have to excuse his dust. If any troopers took exception to his driving, he would be glad to take them with him on his hunt, but they best not try to stop him.

Minutes after turning south onto Highway 197, Nate turned off on to what was more of a goat path than a road. It was nothing more than a couple of tire ruts off through the brush. Pine boughs scraped the cab of the pickup on both sides, and bitterbrush rubbed the undercarriage. Nate was glad that the thunderstorm had damped everything down so that he did not have to worry about his exhaust system starting a fire. He had used this road a couple of times and thought that it would bring him within a mile of the big bend in the river that Gail had described, if it was the same big bend. The deep hole was usually good for a couple of nice brown trout and a sack full of pan-size brookies. But he was not planning on any fishing today. He was picturing the trail from the road end to the stream and planning the best way to get there.

He rounded a turn in the road and had to slam on the brakes to avoid a herd of Black Angus cow-and-calf pairs in the road.

The cattle scattered like bucks in deer season, which was a little unusual. Most times they would just stand in the road and stare at you, bellowing, but this bunch went off through the brush sounding like a freight train that had left the tracks.

Shortly after the near cow collision, Nate came suddenly to the end of this trail he was using for a road. He was not expecting the end so soon since he usually traveled this road at about a quarter the speed that he was moving today. He slid to a rough stop beside a couple of boulders that dissuaded people from driving any farther. Jumping out of the truck, he grabbed the Browning off the seat and dragged it out behind him. As he fed shells into the shotgun, he was jogging down a trail that led to the river before the Dodge quit rocking.

By the time he was out of breath and needed to stop to give his old lungs a break, he was within two hundred yards of the river. He knew he needed to slow down and start using some stealth, even if his lungs could stand the run. He used the time he needed to catch his breath to study the layout between the timber that he was in, and the river. He had to cross the two hundred yards with very little cover, and he did not like it.

22

Gail continued to scan her back trail for any sign of movement. She also kept watch to the north and south of her location in case her adversary was attempting to flank her. Movement to the south, less than a hundred yards away, caught her attention. She watched intently as four mule deer snuck out of the timber and stopped. A doe, two fawns, and a yearling were concentrating on something in the direction they had come from; their big ears swiveled on their heads, and they held their heads high, nostrils flaring, as they attempted to catch wind of whatever was behind them. Satisfied that whatever had chased them from their cover was indeed a threat, they bounced to the west on stiff legs.

Figuring that what had startled the deer and what was hunting her were one in the same, Gail went on the offensive and started moving into a position that would allow her to intercept him when he came out of the timber on the deer trail. She had just gotten into position behind a boulder when a man armed with a rifle came into view fifty yards from her. He was moving on a course that would bring him within twenty feet. As she watched from her place of concealment, Gail realized that this was not the man that she had been playing cat and mouse with most of the afternoon. This man was much shorter and stockier than the guy that she had eluded earlier.

Not knowing how this new player figured in to her predicament, Gail stayed hidden and waited for him to come to her. She studied him carefully as he moved closer. He, like the other man, moved with confidence, comfortable with himself. His firearm fit him well, like an extension of his body. It was obvious that this was not the first day that he had carried the rifle. But it was also obvious that he was not used to moving through this type of terrain. His feet sent an occasional rock clattering away and broke a twig every few strides. He kept alert, scanning the trail ahead as he walked. He was not out for a casual stroll.

Gail let him draw even to her, and then slightly past before she spoke. She had her Sig Sauer locked and loaded and aimed at the center of his back when she ordered, "Throw the rifle to the side and get down on your face."

The man didn't show a sign of the surprise she expected when she spoke. Nor did he comply. He simply quit moving and stood completely still. She gave the command, a little louder and rougher, "Police! Lose the gun and get down. Now!"

Still the man stood motionless, and all the steel that her training had instilled in her spine began to melt. Her gun began to shake, and when she gave the command, "Hit the dirt or I'll shoot!" her voice cracked. And he continued to stand like a statue. It wasn't supposed to work like this. Not one of her training drills prepared her for this. Her mind was racing. Should she shoot, should she approach, or should she repeat her command?

Before she was forced to make a choice between those poor alternatives, the man spoke. "Lady, you and I both know that you are not going to shoot me in the back. How would that look, you hiding out here in the wilderness and shooting some poor unsuspecting antelope hunter from behind? I'm all legal, you know. Antelope tag is in my wallet, license is all up to date, my firearm is legal, and I'm on public property. What say I turn around and we talk this over in a proper fashion?"

His voice was calm and reasonable. What if he was an antelope hunter? Gail knew that there was an open season in the summer, but she thought that it was later—in August. "No! How about you just throw down that rifle, get on your stomach, and then we'll talk." Her confidence was coming back as she talked. There were no antelope in this particular area!

"Okay," the man said. "I guess it's not worth getting shot over. But do you mind if I don't throw the rifle down? How about I just lay it down and then step away from it? It's a very expensive weapon—a gift from my father—and I would very much hate for it to be damaged."

It seemed like a reasonable request, politely made, and it was indeed a beautiful weapon, so Gail agreed, "All right, but slowly. Just lay it across that sagebrush bush over there. Then step slowly away from it, and get on the ground."

He complied, laying the rifle exactly where Gail had indicated, and then stepped back. Gail's attention focused for an instant on the rifle, and in that instant the man was in motion. He leapt to his left and hit the ground in a practiced roll. When he came up he was bringing a handgun to bear on Gail. She reacted almost instantly, but the man was moving so fast that her first shot went wide. She saw her adversary flinch at the next two shots, but then he was returning fire. Chunks of rock sprayed her face when a round hit the boulder in front of her, but she continued to pull the trigger on the Sig. Suddenly the man went down in a heap. Gail looked down and saw the slide on her weapon locked back. She had burned through the clip.

With a sickening realization she recognized that her weapon was out of ammo. A split second later, she was struck by the fact that she had just shot a man. She watched him for any sign of life but did not approach. She felt sick. And she felt helpless. Through the haze in her mind, she realized that shock was setting in. She was trying to get into her fanny pack to get the last clip of ammunition when she realized that her left hand wasn't working very well. She looked down and saw the blossom of blood on her jacket at her left shoulder. She stared at the spreading stain for a moment before the fact that she had been hit registered.

She glanced back at the man on the ground. He had not moved. Then she reached her right hand inside her coat and found a hole just beneath her collarbone. Blood was oozing, not gushing, so she concluded that the bullet had missed her lung and any major arteries. Still, she knew she should stay put and not risk more serious blood loss, but she was not sure that the man on the ground would not regain consciousness. And she was afraid that the shooting would bring the first gunman to her position.

She managed to get the full clip out of the pack, extracted the empty clip from the butt of her gun, and rammed the full one home. She gave the man on the ground one last look and started moving.

23

Nate was kneeling on one knee watching the clearing that separated him from the river. He had been studying the area carefully and saw nothing threatening. After about five minutes his breathing had returned to normal. Then, just as he started to stand to move forward, he faintly heard gunfire, a lot of gunfire, in the distance. The shots were too close together and too far away for him to be able to accurately tell how many shots were fired or how many weapons were involved. Forcing himself to not speculate about what it meant, he reined in his emotions. He had to remain calm if he was going to be of any assistance. With a jaw set with determination he set out in the direction of the gunfire in a landscape-eating gait.

Just before reaching the river, Nate noticed where a four-wheeler had flattened the grass. The machine had been through here since the rain had fallen earlier in the day. That meant the tracks were no more than six hours old. Nate prayed that they had been made by Mike or Gail and not by some buckaroo from the YZ, as he started to follow them. He had been on the tracks for less than a quarter mile when he came to the big bend in the river, and one of his favorite fishing spots. He did not as much as look at the hole. His attention was all on his surroundings. The last thing he wanted was to walk into an ambush. His nerves were strung tight. He wanted to hurry, but he needed to move with caution. When a covey of about twenty-five quail exploded from beneath his feet, the shotgun was on his shoulder, safety off before the source of the racket had a chance to register in his mind. He stood shaking, trying to get his heart rate down and his nerves under control.

Nate no more than got past the deep pool than the tracks he was following forded the river at a shallow spot, so he crossed too. He normally would have hated the fact that he was going to have wet feet for the rest of the walk, but today he did not even consider taking time to find his way across on a log or something. It might take an hour or more to find a natural bridge on which to cross, and he did not think he had even a minute to waste.

Following the tracks of the quad, Nate spotted a tree filled with buzzards and ravens as soon as he got out of the river. His feet sloshed in his boots as he headed in the direction of the snag where the big birds were congregating. The tracks he was following headed the same direction and led directly to the carcass that was attracting the attention of the carrion eaters.

While Nate studied the dead beef he noticed the tracks of a second ATV. That bolstered his suspicion he was on the right track, the trail of Gail and Mike. It was further confirmed by the boot tracks around the dead animal. One pair was much larger than the other and the larger pair sunk considerably farther into the soft soil, evidence that one of the people was considerably larger than the other; an apt description of Gail and Mike.

Nate started off on the trail of the ATVs with renewed enthusiasm and caution. He was anxious to find his daughter and her friend, but he was not at all eager to meet their trigger-happy attacker. For the past fifteen minutes he had been making progress on the tracks of the quad he guessed was ridden by Gail, judging from the boot tracks around where it had been parked, when the sharp smell of gasoline hit his nostrils. He stopped next to a small juniper and carefully observed the area. Seeing nothing out of place, he moved forward twenty yards and stopped to scan the area again. Again, nothing caught his attention. Advancing another ten yards, he spotted an ATV with a camouflage paint job.

Before he went to the machine he scrutinized the landscape for possible spots for a sniper to hide. There were several, and he studied each of them carefully, making sure that he wasn't turning himself into a target. When he was satisfied that no one was using this machine for bait, he went in for a good look. The bullet hole through the gas tank was instantly obvious. The one that had gone into the block was less noticeable. Someone had made sure that no one was going to be able to ride out of here on this machine. Across the back was stenciled, "Property of East Lake County Search and Rescue." The county comptroller was going to be none too happy about buying a replacement.

The obvious question was, where did he go from here? He searched for tracks and was quickly rewarded with a set that he took to be Gail's, so he set off after them, moving as slowly as he could force himself to go. Inching forward, when the heart of a father that was beating in his chest was urging him to hurry, was a challenge. But he realized that he would not be any help to anyone if he went blundering into an ambush. So he moved at a turtle's pace. He scrutinized every hiding place, judged every bit of cover, and took half an hour to cover a hundred yards. In those hundred yards he reached the crest of a hill that gave him a vantage point into the next draw.

The slightly higher elevation provided opportunity to seriously study the area ahead. Nate scanned the near slope first, not wanting to be surprised by an enemy at his very feet. He looked under every bush and tree and beside every rock. He checked for movement and unnatural angles. He was methodically sweeping his eyes down the near slope, intending to then perform the same sweep up the far slope, but when his eyes were scanning the bottom they hit the black grip of a quad's handlebar. Because of the brush the machine was in, he could make out only a rough outline but it was enough for Nate to be positive that it was the second machine belonging to East Lake County Search and Rescue.

Assuming that Mike was with the machine, every ounce of Nate's considerable weight wanted to rush down the slope and assess Mike's condition. Instead he continued his methodical scan up the far slope. Once he was reasonably convinced that no one was staking out this location, he moved quickly to where he believed he would find Mike. As he got closer he could see a huge arm of a man stretched out beside the quad. That sight motivated him to move quicker. By the time he reached the downed officer, his heart was pounding as if he had just completed the first two legs of an iron man triathlon.

A jolt, half of shock and half of relief, hit Nate when he knelt beside Mike to feel for a pulse. As Nate gently placed his hand on the big man's neck, Mike's eyes sprang open.

"Whoa, big fella, I'm here to help," Nate quickly assured him.

"'At was my first guess," was Mike's reply.

"Ya know who I am?" Nate asked.

"Sure. Just because I'm lyin' out here in the brush like some kinda road kill don't mean I been struck stupid. Have you seen any sign of Gail?"

"No. Do you have any idea where she might be?"

"I been driftin' in an out of consciousness for the past couple of hours, but maybe an hour and fifteen or twenty minutes ago, I heard a serious firefight taking place somewhere uphill from here. I imagine that she was part of that."

"Yeah, I heard that too. Before I head out to try and find her, tell me about you. Where you hit?"

"Not sure. I've tried to move, but nothin' seems to wanna work. I don't mind tellin' you, I'm scared to death."

"Got any ideas as to how to get outta this jam?" Nate asked the downed man.

"Well, I ain't been able to use my radio. Maybe ya could get aholt of dispatch and tell them what's goin' on. My GPS is in my left cargo pocket. Fish it out, and it'll give you our coordinates so you can tell them exactly where to find me."

Nate was amazed at how calm the big man was, considering his situation. He appeared to be unable to move anything below his neck, but here he was calmly giving instructions. Afraid that he might hurt Mike, Nate gently began feeling for the GPS device. It was exactly where Mike told him. Once he found it, however, he had no idea how to operate it. But Mike patiently explained what buttons to push, and in seconds the little electronic marvel gave their coordinates.

"Now," Mike instructed, "push the button on the top of the radio that is on my left shoulder. Then hold the receiver a little closer to my mouth, there ya go."

"Dispatch," Mike spoke in the radio. "This is Sergeant Mike Divetti. I've been shot and am unable to move. I need a helicopter or rescue crew to pick me up ASAP." Mike calmly gave the coordinates provided by the GPS, answered a few questions that Nate couldn't understand because of the squawk of the radio, and then he terminated the call.

"Okay, they should be here before too long. You'd better go see what you can do 'bout finding Gail," Mike said.

"Are you all right here by yourself?" Nate asked.

"No. I don't know if I'll ever be all right again. But there is nothing you can do about that. And you might be able to give Gail a hand, if you can find her."

Nate wasn't inclined to argue. He was worried sick about Gail. And it would be dark in a little more than an hour. Still, he was apprehensive about leaving Mike, not knowing where the gunman might be. "You sure you're all right with me leavin' you? What if the shooter comes back?"

"I'm pretty sure that he thinks my ticket has been punched. He hasn't shown any real interest in me since he put that round through my helmet. You go on and make sure that Gail is okay. Search and Rescue will be here for me within the hour. Just promise me one thing."

"What's that?" Nate asked.

"Come by and play sky pilot when all this is hashed out."

"What'da ya mean?" Nate asked, puzzled.

"I need to talk to ya about gettin' right with the man upstairs. I've seen some strange goings-on today. And I'm fairly sure that you can fill me in on the particulars."

"Deal," Nate said, standing up. "Did ya get a read on the gunfire?"

"Bein' down on the ground like this kinda distorts things, but I'm pretty sure that the shots came from almost due east of here. If I was you, I'd follow this draw up to the top and then head east from there. But stay off the trail. If my buddy is still out here waiting for some more target practice, he might be bunkered in watching the trail."

"Okay," Nate answered, already moving. "If I don't run into anything, I'll head back here in 'bout an hour. I don't wanna be wanderin' around out here after the sun goes down. A man could get plugged by his own kinfolk in the dark."

"Sounds like a plan. Good luck."

"It's not luck that I'm in need of, it is prayer. If ya know how, start prayin.'"

Mike was glad that Nate was moving out of earshot at that last comment. He really did not want to admit that he had no clue how to pray.

24

Gail did not want to be standing around here if the other gunman showed up. Escaping by some weird miracle was fine, great in fact, but she did not want to place herself in the position of trying a repeat performance. She could feel every heartbeat throb through the hole in her shoulder, and every step earned a shot of pain, but she knew she could not stop to assess her injury until she got some distance between her and the downed man.

She headed south and west, hoping to cut the trail of the man she had shot. She wanted some idea as to where he had come from. Moving as fast as possible while remaining alert, Gail picked up the trail easily enough, and followed it for something like a hundred and fifty yards. It looked like he had come in from the east. Once she felt that she was a safe distance away from where the shooting had taken place, she sat down on a log and tried to figure out how badly she had been hit.

The entry wound was relatively small. Probably a .38, she thought. She flinched as she reached back, trying to find the exit, and was relieved to find that there was no hole in her back. She did, however, find a lump where the bullet lay just beneath her skin. So she only had to worry about blood coming out one side, and of course about how much blood was seeping inside her. But her lungs felt clear, so she didn't think that she needed to be too concerned about internal bleeding. The blood flow from where the bullet had entered had nearly stopped.

Once she had determined that she wasn't apt to bleed to death, she started trying to decide what her next move should be. After a little internal debate and deliberation, she concluded that she needed to go back and check on Mike, regardless of the consequences. If she ran into the other gunman, she'd just have to play it by ear, but she could not justify leaving her friend lie unattended any longer. Gail wondered about her sudden lack of caution and thought it might have something to do with the close range shootout and her resulting wound. Had escaping two close encounters of a deadly kind given her a false sense of immortality?

It had been too strange of a day to waste thought on those abstract philosophies. She just needed to get moving, to get back to Mike and find out how badly he was hurt, or worse. But she wasn't going to let herself think about that either. She merely wanted and needed to keep moving. She'd react to whatever situation was presented as it happened.

As bold as she was feeling, she still used all the stealth she could conjure as she headed back toward the spot where she'd left Mike. Using the lengthening evening shadows and all the available cover to conceal her movements, and protecting her wound, she made slow but steady progress. The flitting of every bird, the twitch of every chipmunk tail, and every other movement caught her eye, and she studied each until she was satisfied that it represented no threat. It was amazing how many birds and small animals had their homes in areas that would have appeared void of life when you were tearing through on an ATV, Gail thought. With evening closing in, a lot of critters were looking for their last calories of the day.

She was studying a Rufus-sided towhee whose sudden flight had caught her attention when she noticed other movement. A man's leg materialized, and in an instant she saw the entire person, seated on the ridge to her northwest. It was the gunman from whom she had made the great escape. He was about sixty yards from her, and she could tell he was intent on something or someone coming from the west. As she watched the man, trying to discern what course of action she should take, he raised a rifle to his shoulder and began sighting through the scope. She didn't know who he was taking aim at, but she figured that whoever it was would most apt to be on her side if this scuzbag was fixing to shoot them.

She knew she had to keep the creep from taking the shot. She didn't want to waste any of her ammo when she knew she was way out of range, and doubting that she had time to get into shooting distance before it was too late, she gave her best imitation of an Indian war hoop and ran for cover. She headed in the general direction of whoever had been about to be shot, half expecting to be shot herself.

Five quick blasts sounded like thunder as she ran. Gail had covered about a hundred yards when she was so out of breath that she knew she needed to find a place to stop and rest. The wound in her shoulder was obviously taking its toll on her endurance. She found good cover among some boulders and juniper trees, stopped, and started watching her back trail.

Fifteen minutes passed with the silence being interrupted only by the chirping of chipmunks, peeping of birds, and other normal forest sounds. She knew that she was being stalked and that her only hope was to see her adversary before he saw her. Her nerves were strung to the breaking point, and she was straining her eyes so hard that they were blurring and watering. She wondered if this day was ever going to end.

The shots had been close. She had her Sig pointed in the direction that they had come from, expecting to be overrun by the shooter at any second. Her heart was pounding so hard that she knew she wouldn't have been able to hear a herd of elephants approaching at a dead run, even though she was doing her best to bring her emotions into control. She waited there in the fading light thinking that she did not want this to be her last day. She had too many things left to do. Too many things left undone.

She began to pray for the second time today.

Her heart rate began to come under control. Her thoughts began to slow down. The panic that had filled her chest was loosening. That is when she heard the rock clatter. Close. Right there, off to her left. While she had chosen this spot for its cover, so she would not be seen, the distinct disadvantage was that she could only see any distance in about a ninety-degree arc to the northwest. This noise, which she would wager had been the result of a boot hitting a loose rock, came from the south.

She slowly pivoted to face that direction, squatted down to make herself the smallest possible target, and lined her nine-millimeter in a two-handed grip with the location of that rock. The wound in her shoulder was forgotten. She heard a branch rub over clothes, and everything else was gone from her mind. The sound had come from what she estimated to be fifteen feet. She corrected her aim to cover this new sound. At the sound of a footstep she began to tighten her finger on the trigger. The barrel of a long gun came into sight from behind a thick juniper, and then the outline of a man became visible through the branches. She centered her sights on the main body mass, and her finger tightened a little more. She would have liked to fire through the tree, before her target had a chance to get into the clear and have a shot at her. But she couldn't risk having a tree limb deflect or absorb the shot.

So she waited, forcing herself to breathe in a slow, deliberate cadence.

25

Jake was on his knees in front of his recliner, his face buried in his big callused hands, as he pleaded with his King for intervention. He didn't know the details, but he knew that a battle was raging, and both his son and granddaughter were in the thick of it. He wasn't even sure what he should be asking for, so he prayed that God's kingdom would triumph. Groans came from his lips, and sweat ran off the thin hair on the back of his head and soaked the collar of his well-worn plaid-flannel shirt.

Jan, knees crippled with arthritis, couldn't kneel in front of her chair as she had in days gone by, but in her heart she knelt in front of the throne of heaven just the same. She was begging her King for the safety of her family. She never knew the details like Jake did, but she knew that darkness was trying to drown out the light, and she asked over and over that Satan and his forces would be bound. Tears trickled down the creases in the skin on her face, but in her intensity she didn't feel them or even taste their salt when they touched her lips.

Eliab and Yanoa were at the heart of the battle and were delighted to see warriors with them that they had not seen released for battle for a very long time. While their adversaries were loud and bold, they could make no real advancements on their position. With the reinforcements that the King had sent, the safety of their charges was not in doubt.

As exhausted as if he had spent the past two hours shoveling snow, Jake crawled up into his chair. He was spent. But it felt good. He was confident that the battle that he had glimpsed was going the right way. His groans turned to murmurs of praise.

Although she didn't see it even as clearly as Jake's blurry vision of the battle, Jan felt the tension leaving her shoulders with the awareness that her God was in complete control. For fifty-plus years, she had found him always faithful. Not that everything worked out the way she thought it should. No. But he was always faithful to his promises. And she felt a sense of peace with the realization that God was no different today than he had been in all those other days.

The two old prayer partners looked at each other; Jake nodded and said, "There's a ferocious war goin' on out there this evening. Wish I could git me a clearer glimpse. All I'm seein' is a clash of darkness and light. But the light is winnin,' and that's fer shore."

Jan gave him a tired smile and replied, "Ya know, I think you're better off with the blurry view. I 'spect that yer ole ticker might not be able to tolerate a clear picture."

"Yep. You're probably right. But when my old worn-out heart does give in, that's the same time I'm goin' see the clear picture. Some days I can't wait."

"Ya know, you always talkin' about gettin' to the other side kind of hurts my feelings. Am I so bad to live with?"

"Nah. But it's gonna be that much better over yonder."

"Well, I'm not quite ready to leave my kids and grandkids. And apparently the good Lord ain't ready for you to go home either. Else you wouldn't still be here givin' me grief."

Jake smiled, knowing he was going to get the last word in on this. "I think I hear them angels practicing their scales. Time's gettin' short. We'll all of us, you, me, the kids and grandkids, we're all gonna be goin' home real soon."

This bit of banter had been going on for years, and both of them seemed to derive a certain pleasure from this verbal jousting, even though either of them could recite the lines of the other from memory.

26

Another step, and the target would be in the clear, and Gail would finish squeezing the trigger. The man was moving so slowly that she wondered if he may have realized that she was there. But he was looking away from her, so she didn't think he had discovered her. He took that step, and at the same time turned his head toward her. She applied that last half an ounce of pressure and she recognized that her target was her father at the instant the hammer fell.

Instead of the blast and buck that she anticipated there was… nothing. Some movement bred of her surprise sent her father/target into motion. His gun came to bear as he leapt to his right. Just as he lined the shotgun up with Gail, she was yelling, "Don't shoot! It's me, don't shoot."

Nate was close to turning inside out as the confusion of the situation began to clear. He stood speechless, trying to make sense of this scene. Gail blurted, "What are you doin' here?"

"Well, I thought I was rescuing you. But now I'm not sure you haven't killed me with a heart attack!"

"You have no idea how close I was to killing you. But not just from fright. I nearly shot you through and through. I thought you were one of the crazies that are runnin' around out here trying to kill me. I don't know why this thing didn't drill a big old crater right through your chest," she said, waving her handgun in the air.

"I'm a crazy, all right. But I ain't one of them that are trying to kill ya."

Gail stood up, and Nate took another step toward her. Her voice shook when she said, "Yeah. I figured that out, too late. This weapon has never misfired before." She racked the slide and her mouth dropped open when nothing came out of the chamber. She had dropped the hammer on an empty barrel.

Nate grinned sheepishly and said, "I thought I taught you to be sure your weapon was loaded. I guess that was another lesson that you didn't learn. Good thing for me!"

Gail popped the clip out of the Sig. It was full. She looked at the gun through squinted eyes and worked the slide. Everything seemed to work the way it was supposed to. "I know I jacked a round into the chamber after my little shootout," she said quietly to herself as she holstered her pistol. Nate reached out and hugged her with the arm not holding the Browning. They stood for a moment in an awkward sideways hug. It was an unusual event. Their family was not much on the touchy-feely stuff. "I don't know what happened," he said, "but whatever it was, I'm mighty thankful."

It was during that embrace that Nate noticed the blood on her coat and sweatshirt.

"Are you all right? Have you been hit?"

"Yeah, but I think I'm okay. I got in a bit of a firefight with a guy back there, and I got stung. I don't think it hit anything vital, though. I can still move my arm, and I'm breathing all right. Just flesh, I guess. And it hurts like crazy."

"How 'bout blood? Are you still bleedin'?"

"I don't think so. I've got some clothes kinda stuck in the hole, and it isn't soaking through. I am feelin' a bit wrung-out though. I was trying to drag myself back to Mike when I ran into our buddy. He was taking aim on something, probably you, so I let out a war whoop and took off runnin.' Then I heard some serious shooting. What was that about?"

"I saw a guy over there who was obviously stalkin' something. He had a rifle in his hands, bent over at the waist, scannin' the country like a bull hunter on opening day of the elk season. I was watchin' him tryin' to figure out what he was up to when I lost sight of him. He musta spotted me, 'cause when I heard your rebel yell, I looked up just in time to see him jerk his rifle off me and try to get a bead on you. The Browning here just kinda started barkin' about then. He was close to a hundred yards away, so my buckshot wasn't too effective—too spread out—but it musta been whistlin' around him pretty good 'cause he dropped his rifle and lit out of there like a gut shot cat. I found the rifle. One of those double-ought pellets managed to pretty much ruin the scope. Guess that's why he dropped it. I found a couple of spots of blood too. Not much, so I'm guessin' that one of those pellets kinda grazed him.

"Mike told me you were up here, so I kept on looking for ya till ya found me."

"You saw Mike?"

"Yeah," Nate replied. I stopped and talked to him a minute before comin' up here."

"You talked to him? He's awake?"

"He's alert enough. But he can't move except to talk and blink. I couldn't see any sign of an injury, besides that bullet hole in his helmet, that is. There's no blood or anything. I think the jolt from that high-powered round hitting his helmet just broke his tweedle."

"Do you think he's gonna be okay?"

"Well, I ain't a doctor. I think so, but that bein' paralyzed can't be a good sign. We'd better get back down to him while there's still a little light. Ya think you're up to walkin'?"

"Sure. There's nothin' wrong with my legs, 'cept they're a mite weak. But I'll make it all right. You just lead the way. Oh, by the way, I knew you weren't a doctor. They don't usually use the highly technical term 'tweedle when speaking to laypeople. What is a tweedle anyway?

"I'll explain later. We don't have time for in-depth medical explanations now."

Nate filled Gail in on using Mike's radio to call for help as they stumbled down the trail to where Mike was waiting. By the time they got back to the downed man, it was completely dark, and visibility was about zero. Nate might have stepped on the injured cop had Mike not heard him coming and said, "Hey, you plannin' on stompin' on me? What, you don't think I'm not bad enough hurt already?"

"Sorry, Mike," Nate said. "My night vision ain't the greatest. Guess I shoulda been using my Maglite, 'cept I don't really wanna draw too much attention. Where's your rescue team? They figure out who was down out here and decide not to come to fetch ya? If ya weren't always givin' everybody a hard time, they might be more willin' to come save your sorry hide."

"Oh, I imagine that the cavalry is on the way," Mike replied. "But it takes a while to scramble search and rescue, especially during fire season. And when a chopper is involved, it takes even longer. Why don't ya try my radio again and see if you can find out what's up?"

Nate turned to Gail and said, "You're used to talkin' on those stupid radios, why don't you see what you can find out?"

"Sure," Gail said, moving closer to Mike. "Let me give it a try." Within minutes, Gail was able to make contact and find out that the team on the ground was headed down the highway with a trailer full of ATVs. Their ETA was about twenty minutes out. The helicopter should arrive within five minutes of the ground crew.

While the trio waited in the dark, Gail filled the two men in on her shootout with the gunman. "It was bizarre," she said. "We were exchanging shots like in a wild west movie. He went down hard, I think maybe for good. I didn't even realize I was hit till it was all over."

"You're hit?" Mike asked.

"Yeah. Just a flesh wound, I think. Nothin' seems to be broke, and I haven't bled much."

"Well, I guess you'll get a free helicopter ride too, courtesy of the county."

"I dunno," Gail responded. "I'd kinda like to go with the team so I can show them where the downed man is. Just in case he's still alive. If we can get him out, we should, if only to try to get him to give us some details of what in the world is goin' on out here."

"I dunno," Nate interjected. "We'll let the medics decide whether or not you're up to that. Meanwhile, in case they decide you need to go in, why don't you fill me in on where you were so I can take the team to the guy?"

"Once the dad, always the dad, hey Pops? You're just a civilian. You shouldn't even be out here."

"Well, girl, I'd say you and this big oaf that's pretendin' to be hurt were pretty durn lucky that this old civilian found ya. You'd be shot to Swiss cheese, and he would be studying the stars and waitin' for the coyotes to come eat 'im if I hadn't showed up."

"Hey, hey, you two," Mike chimed in, "We got 'nough enemies out here without you two startin' in chewin' on each other. Anyway, I betcha they'll have dogs with 'em, so finding the guys that you two shot up shouldn't be too tough. So," Mike continued, changing tones and subjects, "I wanna know what happened out here. Gail, how in the world did you get away from the guy that plugged me? I know he had the drop on ya. And him with a rifle and you with nothin' but your Sig."

In the dark, the cop and the dad could not see Gail flush, but she could feel the heat rise up her neck and set her face on fire. She couldn't begin to understand what had happened, so how was she supposed to explain it to these guys, or to all the guys that were going to quiz her on it later? After a couple of minutes of quiet, she said, "I dunno. It was totally weird. It was like the guy couldn't see me, and I just walked away."

The hairs on the back of Nate's neck stood up when he heard this brief description of Gail's escape from the sniper. How close his daughter had come to being killed had not really come home to him until she was relating her escape.

"Man, that is crazy," Mike said. "I have definitely seen some strange goings-on today. I think maybe that bullet to my head did more than just paralyze my body, it rattled my brain too."

Nate whispered, "Oh, I think God's hand was protectin' the two of you out here today."

The conversation was put on hold by the sound of quads approaching from the west.

"All right, here come the troops!" Mike blurted. "Turn the key to aux and flip the quad's lights on. If the guys get on a high point they'll spot us from a mile away."

It worked just like Mike predicted. Within fifteen minutes Ted and Tony, two state troopers, and half a dozen volunteers on the search and rescue team were on the scene. The surreal quiet of the desert was instantly turned into controlled chaos. The volunteers immediately went to work locating a spot adequate for a helicopter landing. Once they found a suitable location they went to work with pulaskies and made a clearing, which they then doused with water; they then lit flares and placed them and some portable spotlights in the clearing to mark the point for the helicopter crew. Within minutes the area was lit up like a movie set.

The two state police officers went right to work too, one questioning Nate, and the other interrogating Gail. Ted and Tony, big and hard as they were, forgot their tough-guy images and hovered over their sergeant like a couple of old brood hens.

Five minutes after the arrival of the first wave of rescuers, two more quads arrived, carrying a county deputy each. Behind these machines were trailers, each loaded with a portable dog kennel. One of the kennels held an aging German shepherd and the other a young black lab.

There was just enough time before the medical evacuation helicopter arrived for Mike to give directions to the dog handlers so they could get the dogs on the scent of the sniper. The canine cops should be able to track the criminal right to the spot of Gail's shootout. Once that location was found, Nate—who had volunteered to stay on site—would direct the troops to where the second shooter had discarded his rifle. With even the slight blood trail the dogs should be able to follow that scent easily.

By the time the helicopter arrived, the scene had turned from near chaos to military orderliness. Once on the ground, the medics wasted no time in beginning to assess Mike's condition. Once that it was determined that he was stable, they began strapping him to a backboard. When they went to lift the board they groaned and called for help. Ted and Tony bent to the task, making rude comments about diets and hernias. As they were carrying him to the helicopter, Mike yelled above the noise of the rotors, "You guys better check Gail. She took a round in the shoulder. She should probably be flying the friendly skies too."

"Okay, bubba, we'll check her," the flight nurse responded. "But unless her condition is dire, she won't be flying. With your weight, you're all the cargo our little ship can lift."

"Hey, enough with the weight jokes already. But you check her. She may need this flight worse than me."

"You just settle down," the nurse, who wouldn't tip the scales at more than 130 pounds, quipped. "We'll check her out. But you need to calm down before I stick a needle full of sedative into one of your oversize hams." Ted and Tony laughed so hard at the treatment their boss was receiving from this little woman that Mike was afraid they might drop him.

"You big galoots just shut yer traps and get me on that chopper," Mike ordered. "I ain't near as big as either one of you."

"Yeah boss, we know it," Tony said, "but we ain't the ones pretendin' to be hurt just to get a little attention from cute little Nancy Nurse here."

"Shut up and load me up so you can get goin' with the canines and run down the bad guys. This ain't a picnic, ya know. And you're on the clock, so quit your loafin.'"

"Aye, aye, boss," Ted answered. "You just lay back and relax. We don't want the nurse to have to give you a teeny weenie shot. That'd probably make you pass plumb out."

Once Mike was loaded on the aircraft, the nurse went back to take a look at Gail's bullet wound. "It's not gonna kill you," she concluded, "but you need to get to the hospital as soon as you can. That bullet needs to come out, and the wound needs to be cleaned and disinfected. Try not to jolt it around and restart the bleeding."

"Yeah, right," Gail answered sarcastically. "Like the ride out a here on the back of one of these ATVs is gonna be like ridin' in a limousine."

The nurse winked and said, "Oh I'm sure a tough, rough, and ready copper chick can stand a little bouncin' around. Maybe one of these hero types can find a stick of wood for you to chew on. I know they can't spare you a shot of medicinal Jack Daniels though. They've only enough for themselves, I'm sure."

27

"Well, well, well," the police department chaplain said from the doorway of Gail's hospital room. Chuck, one of the chaplains for the City of Bend P.D., was a retired officer and very well respected by officers in all the Central Oregon departments. "Looks like they need to call maintenance and have your name put on the door of this room if you're planning on bein' a regular guest here."

"Very funny. Haven't you got any real work to do? Ya gotta be hangin' around here harassing the sick and injured?"

"Between you and Divetti, I think I could about be justified in goin' on staff here."

"Hey, speaking of Mike," Gail said, her tone changing to serious, "have you seen him today? I haven't been able to get anyone to tell me a thing about his condition since the helicopter took him out of the woods."

"Yeah. I just came from his room. He seems to be doin' good. He's feeling some sensations in his feet and hands and can move them slightly. The white coats think that the whiplash from him taking that high-powered round in the helmet bruised his spinal cord, but they are pretty certain that he will make a full recovery."

"Wow! That is great news. I was really afraid for him."

"It was pretty scary, all right. But from what he tells me, you had a couple pretty good scares of your own yesterday."

"Man, it's all just a big blur. And to tell you the truth, I'm really not too sure what happened out there yesterday."

"What da ya mean?" Chuck asked. "Mike made the same comment, then he clammed up. What? Did you guys see a flying saucer, or a Sasquatch, maybe? What's the big mystery?"

"No. There weren't any spaceships, and Bigfoot didn't make an appearance. But some impossible stuff happened that I really don't know how to talk about. Stuff like out of the Bible; stuff that I don't understand. Maybe I'll tell you about it when I get it sorted out in my own head."

Chuck stared out the hospital window, shook his head, and said, "You guys are killin' me! I wanna hear about it!"

"Sorry, Chuck." Gail looked down at her hands and picked at an imaginary hangnail. "All I can tell you is that either I went invisible for a while yesterday, or the guy that was tryin' to shoot me went blind. Then, I swear, God took a live round right out of the chamber of my Sig. Saved me from cuttin' my dad to rag dolls. See? It's crazy, and I can't get my mind around it. And I sure don't need you or anyone else telling me that there has to be a logical explanation!"

"Whoa, girl, whoa. I'm not goin' try to argue you out of believing in miracles. I'm one of the guys that knows that God is still doin' 'em, remember?"

"Well, I'm not sure I am. Or at least wasn't. I dunno."

A tear started down Gail's cheek, and she quickly brushed it away. "I'm sorry. They've got me so doped up on pain meds, I don't know what I'm thinkin' or feelin.' They dug a nine-millimeter round outta my shoulder when I finally got here last night. That was after getting my teeth bounced out on a search and rescue quad; and after ridin' up Highway 197 in a county rig traveling at warp speed. Hasn't the county got enough money in their budget to put shocks on their rigs? Getting shot at was safer, and more fun, than the trip in!"

"Hey, they got ya here, didn't they? And no, they haven't got any funds in their budget. They're lucky to have enough money to buy gas for their rigs. You hotshots in the city don't know how good ya have it!"

"Anyway," Gail said, "Let's change the subject. Did you hear anything about whether they found the guy I shot?"

"Yeah, they found him."

"Is…was…did he make it?"

Chuck took a deep breath. "No. He was dead when they found him. He was wearin' a vest, believe it or not, but one of your rounds went in right under his left arm. Apparently the hits you were scoring to his main body mass turned him sideways to where you had just the right angle to put one in the gap. They think it killed him almost instantly."

Chuck didn't think that Gail could get any paler. But she did. She was quiet for quite a while, then asked, "Any idea who he was?"

"Well, he was carrying a driver's license. But nothing came up when he was run through the system. Not even a traffic ticket. He was probably carrying bogus ID. They're waiting for results from his fingerprint search through AFIS now."

"How 'bout the guy that Dad singed with his Browning? Did the dogs track him down?"

"That old German shepherd, Rudy, tracked that guy for what they say was better than a mile. But the guy had come in on ATV, and once he got to where it was parked, he was outta there. And you know what a spider-web of roads it is south of where all your excitement took place. There are a bazillion miles of interconnected logging roads. He could have gone anywhere once he got on his machine."

Chuck stood, stretched, and said, "I gotta get goin.' Just so you know, there's an officer outside your door. Until they can figure out what happened out there yesterday, I guess the brass feels like you need to be protected; or at least watched. They have someone on Divetti too."

"Great," Gail groaned. Who's out there?"

"It's Borchers right now. Danielson is on the next floor with Mike. They'll rotate different officers every four hours while you're here. Anyway, I'm outta here. Call me if there's anything I can do for ya."

"Thanks, Chuck. Hey, am I on admin leave or anything because of the shooting?"

"I don't know. There's some confusion about that since you weren't on duty. I'd guess that the chief or at least Captain Elliott will be by to fill you in on that stuff."

"Well, they'd better hurry. I'm plannin' on being discharged as soon as the doc comes by on his morning rounds."

28

After the chaplain had left, Gail lay there in the hospital bed and stared at the ceiling. The myriad of medications that were in her system had her mind in a fog, and no matter how hard she tried, she couldn't get herself to focus on any particular issue. She wanted details on Mike's condition. She wanted clarification on her status in connection to the shooting. She wanted to talk to her father about the strange things that had happened the day before. She wanted to get out of the hospital. She wanted her mother to come by and hold her hand. Instead of getting any of the many things she wanted, she slipped off to sleep, wanting.

When something in her subconscious told her that she needed to come back to the surface, she forced her eyes to open. Chief Yeager and Captain Elliott were standing at the foot of her hospital bed; they were looking down at her with what she took to be scowls. Oh, boy, she thought, here it comes. Simultaneously embarrassed and awash in panic, she fought to clear the cobwebs from her mind. She had spoken with Chief Yeager a grand total of six times in her seven years on the force, and each of those contacts had been quite formal. Her interaction with Captain Elliott was a little more frequent, but not much. She would feel far from comfortable in the presence of these two officials under the best of conditions; lying in bed, hair a snarling testimony to the events of the past twenty-four hours, arm in a sling from a gunshot taken off duty, were not the best of conditions.

Captain Elliott broke the awkward silence with, "Good morning, Officer O'Conner. Chief Yeager and I stopped by to check on your condition."

"Thank you," was all Gail could manage in reply.

"How are you feeling this morning?" Chief Yeager asked.

"Stiff, sore, and confused is the honest answer, sir," she managed.

"Well, we don't want to add to your discomfort any more than necessary," Captain Elliott said. "But we thought that it was important to stop and make sure that you are going to be all right, and to try to get some clarification as to what took place yesterday. Your involvement in a fatal shooting is going to draw considerable attention from the media, as I am sure you realize, and before we start giving details to the press or to the city council, we wanted to get your side of the story. Do you feel well enough to provide us with some details?"

"I guess so," Gail replied while she tried to adjust the head of the hospital bed. Her first attempt got her feet started up, and then the head of the bed went down. Finally she got the right button, and she was able to adjust herself into a sitting position. She had a fleeting thought that maybe she should request a representative from the union be present before she started talking, but quickly discarded the idea. Asking for a union official to be present would make her look guilty.

Her two superiors pulled chairs to her bedside, and the captain took out a pen and pad. "Could you give us some background as to what you were doing out in the wilds of Northern Chiloquin County with Sergeant Divetti, who was on duty—but in the wrong county?"

Gail did her best to explain the mix-up with the garage sale

DVDs and how her attempt to retrieve them got her involved in the investigation of a murder in East Lake County. By the time she got to the part of the narrative where yesterday's shooting started, she was feeling a little more relaxed, and she could tell that the two men were intrigued.

When she finished, Chief Yeager took a deep breath and said, "So. Do you have any idea if there is a connection between the dead woman and the men that were trying to kill you and the sergeant?"

"Minutes before Sergeant Divetti drew fire, we had discovered the remains of what appeared to be a cow that had been rustled and butchered. I think that the attack may have been connected to our finding the dead cow. The rustlers may have simply been out looking for another animal to butcher when they spotted the sheriff's department uniform and thought that they were about to be caught and started shooting."

Captain Elliott put his pen in his shirt pocket, pulled on his chin with his left hand—a trademark habit of the captain—and asked, "Wouldn't it be a bit extreme for a rustler to shoot an officer over a couple of cows?"

"Maybe," Gail replied, "but I grew up down in the south end of the county, and I know how rough and irrational some of the people down there can be. If they thought that the choice was between being caught—even for something as minor as rustling—or killing a cop, they'd choose the killing every time."

"Oh, I don't doubt but what you are right. I've had my share of experiences with the type of people that you're talking about. I haven't always spent my time behind a desk, you know. I was an officer for a long time, and a detective longer still. That's why I don't believe in coincidence, and it just seems like an awfully large and strange coincidence that you and Sergeant Divetti were out looking for clues to a murder and ended up as ducks in a shooting gallery."

Gail answered, "You may be right. But I don't see what a woman with a broken neck has to do with a couple of guys with high-powered rifles running around out in the woods shooting at cops."

"Well, you were out in those woods looking for clues connected to that strangled woman. And I've a feeling you were closer to finding something than you know," Chief Yeager pointed out, standing up. "Please do not talk about any of this with the press. Direct any inquiries to our public relations department. And concentrate on recovering."

As the two men prepared to make their exit, Gail blurted out what was foremost on her mind throughout their short visit. "So am I in trouble over this?"

It was the captain who answered with a shrug. "You know we can't discuss that with you. The State of Oregon and the two counties involved will be investigating. Our review committee will look at the findings of those investigations before we reach any conclusions. Meanwhile, you need to concentrate on getting that shoulder healed up."

29

When Nate awoke, sunlight was streaming into his bedroom. It took him a few seconds to remember why he was in bed so late in the morning. His habit was to be up and about early. He had been up most of the night working with the canine unit that was trying to find the man he had wounded. Most of the little bit of night that was left when he finally got home had been used bringing Amy up to date on what had taken place. Still, he had a twinge of guilt about wasting the best part of this day. He loved mornings, and it felt like he had squandered a thing of great value when he spent one in bed. That was part of growing up on a farm and having to be up and about early to get the chores done, he surmised. But, he thought, people pack a lot of baggage from their childhoods that are worse than that.

When he sat up, his lower back let him know that it wasn't happy about the previous night's adventure, and his knees informed him that they didn't approve either. When he got up and headed for the shower, his whole body chimed in with a complaining chorus. Man, it was tough being old, fat, and out of shape. Looking in the mirror and seeing bloodshot eyes beneath a bald head didn't do anything to bolster his ego, either. Man, who was the wise guy that invented the mirror? The guy ought to be horse whipped. Depressed as he felt, he knew he needed to get up to the hospital to check on Gail. Anyway, trying to do something for someone else almost always brought him out of the funk.

The hot shower loosed his joints, and he felt almost as if he might survive by the time he got down the stairs to where Amy was at work in the kitchen. She was busy kneading a batch of bread. He sat down at the island counter and said, "Mornin,' beautiful. Sorry I kept you awake half the night."

She turned, smiled, and returned his greeting. "Mornin.' I can't believe you are up and about already. You need more 'n three hours sleep. When you gonna realize that you're not twenty years old anymore?"

"Oh, believe me, I realize it, all right. I feel at least one hundred and twenty this mornin.' And if there had been any room for doubt, it would have been dashed when I tried to put on one of my button-down shirts. The durn thing's been in the closet too long. Clothes shrink from bein' in the dark too long, ya know. And before you start tellin' me I'm crazy, I can prove my theory. See, the top of the shirt—the shoulders, chest, and arms—it gets some light, and that part didn't shrink as much. But the bottom, ya know, the belly and tail, they never get any light, and look at 'em. They're shrunk till they won't go 'round me."

Amy rolled her eyes and asked, "Why ya tryin' to get all duded up, anyway? I haven't seen you in a dress shirt since forever."

"I just thought it might be nice to look less like a hick when I go visit Gail in the hospital. Those folks that work in that place think that those of us that live down here in the south end of the county are a bunch of red-necked hillbillies. Though they're right, I like to keep 'em guessin.'"

"I called up there already and talked to one of the nurses that had been taking care of Gail. Apparently Gail is doing fine. She should be released today, soon as the doctor takes a look at her."

"Well, that's good news. She'll need a ride, though. Her rig's still down at Cindy's Kitchen. Why don't ya call her and find out if she wants us pick it up and drive it up to her? Or if she'd rather, we could bring her home so she can spend a few days here to convalesce."

During Amy's phone conversation with Gail, it was decided that it would be best if she stayed with her mom and dad for a few days. That would give her mom opportunity to spoil her by waiting on her hand and foot while her shoulder did its healing.

When Nate and Amy reached Gail's room an hour later, they were shocked and frightened when they found a police officer stationed outside. The fear drove Amy out of her normally easygoing manner. "What in the world is going on here?" Amy demanded of the man in uniform blocking her daughter's door.

The young officer answered, "Just following orders, ma'am."

"Don't you ma'am me, young man! I want to know what you're doing here!"

Nate gently took Amy's arm and said, "Now, let's calm down. I'm sure everything is fine. Give the officer a chance to explain."

The cop looked relieved to be saved from a mother's wrath and responded by explaining, "My orders are to not let anyone in this room without checking identification. So, if you'll just show me your driver's licenses I'll be glad to step aside."

"I'm sorry, officer, I'm just a bit undone," Amy said as she dug for her license. "Seeing you here just gave me such a fright, I lost myself for a moment."

"No harm, ma—eh…no problem," the red-faced cop stammered.

Inside the room, Gail was obviously about to lose herself. "The doctor still hasn't made an appearance," she complained. "And I am not interested in spending any longer in here than I have to."

"Come on, Gail, it's only noon. The doc will be here soon, I'm sure. But while you two tigers try to get your hormones in check,

I'm gonna go check on Mike," Nate said as he started backing out the door. There are times when even the bravest of men retreat.

Up a floor, Nate found a partner to the officer that had gotten sideways of Amy. This time Nate was not taken by surprise. He stepped up, ID in hand, and was quickly admitted to Mike's room.

Jake was mowing his lawn, enjoying the smell of the fresh cut grass being released into the warm morning air, when the urge hit him. He immediately shut down the mower, brushed the loose grass from his pant legs and headed into the house, pausing at the door only long enough to exchange his boots for his house slippers.

Jan took one look at the intent expression on his face and mumbled, "Oh, no. Now what?" as he slid by on his way to his recliner.

"I don't know," he answered. "Just know something important is happening up to the hospital, and I got orders to pray. I didn't get any details."

"Nate and Amy headed up there about an hour ago," Jan told him. "If anything had changed with Gail's condition, they'd have surely called to let us know."

"Don't think it has anything to do with Gail," Jake replied. "Just know that the battle's raging."

> *Eliab and Yanoa were ecstatic with their orders to head to the hospital. They could tell from the King's tone that this was going to be a good battle.*

"Hey, Mike, how ya doin,' big guy? I am sure lookin' forward to tellin' everybody at the gym that I can bench press more than Big Mike," Nate joked as he walked into Mike's room.

"Hi, Mr. O'Connor," Mike replied. "I'm doin' all right. I can move both my hands and feet," he said as he demonstrated. "I'm not gonna be runnin' any races right away, but the neurologist was by this morning and said there was no reason to think I shouldn't be back on duty within three to four weeks. So you'd better brag about your liftin' abilities quick. I'll be back sooner than you think!"

"Yeah, and you'll pass my feeble efforts on your first day back, ya big lout."

"I guess the real reason for surprise isn't my recovery, but how that bullet didn't go right through my skull. When they got me to the emergency room and took off my helmet, the slug just rolled out as harmless as could be. No one that looks at the helmet can figure out what kept the bullet from punchin' my ticket."

"That's amazing!" Nate agreed.

"How is Gail doin'? Is she gonna be okay?"

Nate laughed, "Yeah, she'll be fine, unless her doctor doesn't show up pretty soon and get her released. She does not want to spend another night in here. I'm afraid she might start hurtin' people if they don't kick her loose pretty soon."

"I hope, for the nurses' sakes, that she doesn't have any mace with her!"

"When do you think they'll cut you loose from here?"

"That depends on how quickly I regain full use of my arms and legs. "They're talkin' physical therapy starting tomorrow. Then we'll have to see how well I respond to that."

"Great. We'll be praying that God will grant you a complete recovery, and quickly."

"Mr. O'Connor…"

"Please call me Nate."

"Okay, Nate. I can't quit thinking about the stuff that happened out there yesterday. I mean, I was completely helpless. I'm not used to that. I don't mean to sound conceited, but ever since I was in first grade and beat up the third-grade bully, I've always felt like I could take pretty good care of myself. Yesterday, all that changed. I couldn't do anything. That was the worst feeling of my life. But lying there, seeing only glimpses of what was goin' on around me, and hoping that Gail would not get shot, wishing that something would happen to save us, for the first time in memory, I cried out for God's help. And Nate, crazy as it seems, God answered."

"Mike, what's so amazing or crazy or scary about that?"

"I've never really been sure that God even existed. I mean, I've wondered, and I was planning on asking you about your God thing even before the weird stuff started, 'cause I've got some tough things goin' on in my personal life. I even asked Gail if she thought you'd be willing to talk to me. But then I cried out for God's help when I was absolutely helpless, and he came through for me. Is that for real, or was I hallucinating?"

"Well, I gotta admit, I've been a follower of Christ for better than forty years, and I have never witnessed anything remotely close to the things that you and Gail claim that you lived through yesterday. I've cried out for miracles any number of times, but I have never seen an instantaneous miracle. Oh, I've seen some healings and things, but never anything that happened visibly and instantly. And I gotta tell ya, I am jealous. But I'm also absolutely positive that you were not hallucinating. Don't ask me why God chose to reveal his power to you yesterday, but he obviously had his reasons."

"So, what does he expect from me? I mean, I didn't make any deals like you hear about. No 'save me and I'll become a monk' or anything. So what does God want from me?"

"He doesn't need anything from you. He already owns everything. But what he wants from every person is worship. He wants you to commit your life to him."

Mike didn't say anything for what seemed to Nate like an eternity. Finally he looked directly in Nate's eyes and said, "I have absolutely no idea how to do that, Nate."

"You've already taken the first step. You've admitted that you are not in control of your life. Next, you have to agree with God when he says that you are a sinner. Can you do that?"

Mike gave a half laugh and said, "Man, that one's easy. I have made a mess of so much of my life with bad choices and crazy stunts. I'm a sinner, all right."

"Okay. Do you believe that Jesus died to save you from those sins?"

"I do, Nate, I really do."

"Are you willing to submit to the Lordship of Christ, to live your life for *him*?"

"Wow. Is that part of this deal?" Mike asked. "That seems pretty extreme. That would mean a complete change of lifestyle, wouldn't it? I'm not sure I can do that. I have way too many vices."

"Well, yeah, it is a complete change. In fact, the Bible puts it this way: '…the old is gone, the new has come…' The good news about that is that we're not left on our own to do it. God gives us his Holy Spirit to show us how, and to give us the ability, to change. An unbeatable deal, really. God made a way for us to escape sin, then he offers us an opportunity to be his children, then he gives us everything we need to live the way he wants us to live. All we gotta do is receive the gift. What'da ya think? If God was giving you the ability and desire to make the changes that he desires to see in you, do you think you'd be interested in changin'?"

Tears were running down the big tough guy's cheeks as he moved his head up and down in a barely perceptible nod and said, "Yeah. I am."

There was shouting and laughing and loud praising of God in the realms of heaven and Eliab and Yanoa were on the front wave of the celebration. "Glory and honor to King Jesus," they shouted with their huge angelic arms raised high in the air. "Another of the lost lambs of the kingdom is safely home." The two warriors could have received no greater reward than the look on the face of their master as he nodded his approval in their direction.

A strange sight greeted the officer who was guarding Mike's door. When he looked into the room to investigate the strange glow that seeped through the crack between the bottom of the door and the shiny linoleum floor, he saw Nate kneeling beside the hospital bed, the muscular hands of the two men locked in an overhand grip, and tears rolled down the faces of these burly manly guys. He wasn't too surprised to see Nate in that pose. Nate had been the teacher of a high school youth group that he had occasionally attended—so he knew that he was serious about the Christianity thing. But Mike? Mike had been one of the instructors in a tactical defense class he had taken as a new recruit. There had been no sign of any Christian love in that course—plenty of bruises and sweat, and some pretty colorful language, but no softness of any kind. Mike must be hurt really badly to be going all soft and fuzzy.

Nate got up off the floor and sat in the chair the hospital provided for patient's family and friends. "Mike, I gotta tell you a couple of things now that you are in the family."

"Family, eh? I think I like that. So what's the bad news?"

"It's not so much bad news as just fact, son. First, we need to get you dunked as soon as you're physically able."

"Dunked?" Mike asked.

"Baptized. It's the first step of obedience that God assigns to believers. The act paints a picture of you being identified with your new Master. You go down into the water—and that's a picture of death, then you come up—and it's a picture of resurrection."

"Okay, I can handle that, I think. But you said you needed to tell me a couple of things. What's the other one? I suppose I gotta start givin' money to the church."

"No, details about things like tithing…the money giving thing'll come later. But, well, a lot of folks think that once they enter the family of God, everything is just gonna naturally come up roses. They have the idea that all of life's problems will evaporate, and it is gonna be all health, wealth, and prosperity. Well, it doesn't exactly work like that. In fact, in a lot of ways, things get tougher."

"Oh, I guess I haven't thought that far out. But what'da ya mean, things are gonna get tougher?"

"For one thing, a lot of your friends, family, and coworkers are gonna think you've turned into some kind of a freak. You're gonna start acting different—they're not gonna like the changes—so they'll stop wanting you around.

"Then, the lifestyle changes that God will show you that he expects, when you study the Bible, are goin' to require more discipline than anything the police force has ever thrown at you. It is the best and toughest thing you've experienced in your life."

"Man, you ain't makin' this look easy. Is it too late to change my mind?"

Nate shook his head, "Nah, God doesn't force you to do anything. He encourages you, but it's always your choice. And I gotta tell ya, you are more than compensated for any hardship you are asked to go through."

"Now I'm completely confused. What'da ya mean, compensated? I thought you just said there wasn't anything to that health and wealth business."

"Compensated mighta been the wrong way to say it," Nate said. "What I mean is, whatever Christianity costs you, the relationship with God, and his people, that you gain is worth far more. There is just no comparison."

"I don't know about all that stuff, Nate. All I know is, my life is a loss. I mean, I've got a good job, some great friends, and I enjoy my hobbies. But everything else just seems so messed up. Ya know what I mean? There's got to be more to all this than goin' ta work, comin' home, goin' fishin.' Repeat. And the junk I deal with on the job—little kids abused by their parents, young people strung out on dope, married people beatin' up on each other, friends stealin' each other's stuff—man, it's job security, but it's such a downer. And

I'm no different. My wife took my son and left me because I was drinkin' too much, not spendin' any time with them 'cause I was usin' myself up at work, and then being totally selfish when I wasn't workin.' I just want to see something positive."

Nate was beaming when he replied, "Well, you're gonna see some positive, all right. We'll get you plugged in at church, and if you're willing to be obedient, you'll have enough good things goin' on in your life that you'll be able to deal with the negative. I can't wait to watch!"

"Well, I hope I don't disappoint you."

"Don't worry about that. I'm gonna be watchin' what God is doin,' not what you're doin,' and that is never a disappointment. But hey, I need to get back to Gail's room to see if that doctor ever showed up."

"Tell Gail I said 'hi,' and I'll be in touch with her soon. And Nate, thanks. I can't even begin to tell you how much I appreciate what you've done for me today."

Nate grinned like a kid who had just caught his first fish as he was heading out the door. "Mike, the pleasure has been all mine. You keep getting better. And, oh, is it all right if our pastor stops by to visit? If it is okay with you, I'll ask him to come by and meet you."

"You bet. I'd like that. I'll see you later."

By the time that Nate got back to Gail's room, the doctor had completed his visit, and she had been cleared to check out. They had an uneventful trip home, and once they were there, Amy kicked into full momma mode and got her daughter all nicely situated in the room that had once been her room ten years earlier. The ride had completely wrung Gail out, and she was more than willing to take Nurse Mom's advice and go straight to bed.

30

The first three days of Gail's convalescence went by quickly. Then, as her wound healed and she began to feel better and have more energy, time began to drag. She was worried about the outcome of the investigation surrounding her killing of the gunman. She was also concerned about the continuing investigation of the death of Jodie Caddell. Mike's recovery was on her mind, as well. When she began to pace and pester the dogs, though she didn't mention any of what was bothering her, Nate knew that it was time to divert his daughter's attention. He suggested that they have lunch at Cindy's and pick up the Toyota. He thought that the freedom that came with getting her wheels back might take some of the edge off her restlessness and aggravation.

Cindy was cleaning tables when Nate, Gail, and Amy walked into the restaurant. "Hey, Cindy," Nate hollered when the woman looked up, "I see that you haven't had that junker of a Toyota towed off yet. I hope it hasn't decreased the value of your property too much!"

"No," Cindy countered, grinning, "but a buyer is coming by in a couple a hours to pick it up. I should get enough out of it to pay the parking fees anyway."

"I hope it hasn't caused you too much trouble," Gail said.

"Naw," Cindy answered. "It hasn't bothered us at all. How're you doin,' girl? I heard that you had yourself a little excitement lately."

"Way more excitement than I needed, Cindy, that's for sure. But I'm on the mend now. Thanks for letting me leave my rig here."

"Don't mention it. Like I said, it hasn't hurt a thing. I'm just glad to hear you're doin' okay. Now, are you guys just here to harass me, or you gonna sit down and supplement my income?"

"Aw, we got a good buy on a case of Rolaids, so we're gonna eat," Nate quipped, "if you picked up any fresh road kill lately, that is."

"I might not have anything to your liking. I ain't picked up a skunk for a long time. But I might be able to come up with a crow or two if you're lucky."

Nate and Cindy continued to trade good-natured verbal jabs as he, Amy, and Gail ordered and enjoyed their lunch. A visiting tourist might think the two were about to come to blows, but the locals all recognized the dialogue as the friendly war of wits that it was. The battle was unofficially scored a draw when Nate paid the check. Gail again expressed her thanks, and Amy gave Cindy a sisterly hug and apologized for her husband's behavior.

"Don't go apologizing for the mouth of your big galoot," Cindy told Amy. "Being obnoxious is Nate's best attribute," she laughed. "And everybody's supposed to do what they're good at, aren't they?"

"And no doubt about it, you bring out his best in that category!" Amy replied.

Out in the parking lot, Gail told her parents that she was going to swing by the sheriff's department office and see if they'd had any success in sorting out the details of what took place down south.

Mike's temporary replacement was glad to fill Gail in on what had been learned about the shootout. "Yesterday morning we got the results from the fingerprint search on the guy you took out," the acting sergeant offered. "The guy had a sheet that went from here to Christmas. A lot of petty stuff, but a couple of big convictions added in. From drug running to assault, from car theft to tax evasion, you ended the career of a real loveable guy. Somebody may miss the guy, but it won't be anybody in law enforcement.

"We tracked down his residence, an ugly little singlewide rental out in the pucker brush. A couple of investigators from OSP went out there in the afternoon yesterday. They found some interesting stuff, including a length of hemp rope that they think may have been instrumental in the untimely demise of your friend Jodie Caddell. The lab is working on the rope, along with a bunch of other evidence from the house, trying to verify their suspicions. Anyway, it looks like you might be going from a suspect to a hero, all in one easy move. We'll know more once the lab gets done working their magic."

Gail hadn't realized how concerned she was about her involvement in the whole mess until she heard this encouraging news. She felt the weight lifting off her back even as the information was shared with her. "So, are there any theories as to why the killing took place? Or who his partner, the guy my dad tangled with, might have been? Or why they were so aggressive with me and Mike?"

"No, we are just getting goin' on this stuff. Hopefully they'll find some clues to all that as the investigation goes on."

"Okay. Say, what's the latest on Mike?"

"I talked to him this morning 'cause I needed to get his help on a couple of administrative details—I hope he gets back to work soon, this job is drivin' me crazy—and he seemed to be doin' really well. He thinks they might cut him loose from the hospital tomorrow. They've even had him up walkin' around a little."

"Man, I gotta stop by and talk to you more often. You are full of good news!"

"Stop by anytime, but don't count on me bein' in this job much longer. I can't wait to get back on patrol. I think I'd rather wrestle bears than fight with the dad-burned paperwork and all the political crap that comes with this job. Mike can keep it."

Gail laughed and said, "I wish you'd tell me how you really feel. But thanks for the information." She quickly headed for her pickup, left town, and started for her parents' home. She felt a hundred pounds lighter and ten years younger than she had two hours earlier, and she was anxious to get home and share the good news with her parents.

Amy and Nate were happy to hear that Mike was healing quickly, and they were ecstatic when they found out that the suspicions concerning Gail were probably being cleared. At Nate's suggestion, the family held an impromptu prayer meeting to thank God for his intervention and healing. Even as she listened to her parents talk with their God, Gail was struck with their apparent familiarity. She prayed, and more since witnessing the miracle of her escape from the gunman then ever before, but she wondered if she would ever be able to talk with God as easily as if he were sitting in a chair across the room from her, like they seemed to be able to do. Too often it felt like her prayers never got higher than the ceiling. God just seemed so big, so far away and—she used to think—so far removed from the details of her everyday life. Now she wasn't so sure. She was still trying to process the events of the past week. Thinking about it made her head hurt. When the "amen" was tacked onto the end of this prayer session, she decided to drive to the hospital to visit Mike.

31

The guard was gone from in front of the door of the hospital room and the door was open, so Gail walked right in. "Hey, big guy. I can't believe they haven't thrown you out of this place yet," she teased as she walked into Mike's hospital room. "Nurses must be very tolerant people."

"Oh, my amazingly winsome personality has them eating out of my hand," Mike replied. "In fact, several of the nurses have brought their daughters in to meet me. They're unashamedly trying to get me into their families."

"Yeah, right, and the FBI have been by tryin' to recruit you. The poor girls would probably need some time in the psych ward if they so much as looked at you," Gail jabbed. "Anyway, I hope you are better physically than you are mentally. Your brain is obviously still swollen. But I hear that they have had you up walking."

"If you want to count shuffling along behind a walker, I took a few steps. Man, I can't believe how weak I am, or how hard it is to get my limbs to do what my mind is telling them. It's frustrating."

"You sure you aren't just milking this thing to get out of work, or maybe to keep the nurses fluttering around you?"

"Oh, I should have known that you'd catch on to my tricks. I learned the technique from you."

Gail turned serious and said, "So, they think the guy I shot out there was somehow involved in the killing of Jodie Caddell?"

"That's what I hear. Strange, ain't it? I've been lying here tryin' to tie all this together. What do ya suppose he was doin' out there, and why do you think he tried to take us out?"

"Well, I been spendin' a lot of time thinkin' about it myself, and I think that someone told him we were out there, someone involved. Someone who knew we were investigating the murder and thought we were gettin' too close."

"If they thought that, they were sure wrong. We didn't have hardly a clue."

"I know that, but they apparently didn't. I think that someone was watching me the first time I was out at that house trying to collect those stinkin' DVDs, and I wouldn't be surprised if that same person saw us nosing around and called in the hit team."

Mike scratched his head. Even that simple movement seemed exaggerated since his arms still weren't working properly. "Well, that's an interesting theory," he said, "but we don't have a shred of evidence to back it up. It is nice that there is a suspect in the murder other than you, though. And it's nice to know that the guy you shot had a long history. That should really help your cause when the shooting review team meets."

"Yeah, all that's a huge relief, but now I just wanna know what was goin' on out there. The whole thing is just hinkey."

"I know what ya mean. I'm curious too. But you know how this stuff goes. Now that the killer has been identified, and there is no need for a trial, the whole thing will be forgotten. There're too many other, hotter cases to spend taxpayer money on."

"How 'bout the guy my dad scratched with his Browning? Isn't anyone interested in tryin' to track him down?"

"Oh, a lot of folks would love to ask that dude some questions, but we don't have a decent description, or any leads. Unless they find something at the house of the guy you took out, we're never gonna know who that guy is."

"Has anybody checked hospitals and medical clinics? He may have been hit bad enough to require treatment."

"Faxes went out to all those places. Nothing surfaced."

Gail took a deep breath and exhaled slowly and audibly, "And what about the woman we saw out at the house? The one who disappeared on horseback? Who the heck was she?"

"That's a really good question. But once again, I don't have an answer. I sent the tiny twins out there to ask her some questions, and she was gone. The horses are gone too."

"What? Did Tony or Ted talk to Ron Shear about that?"

"Yeah, they did. But Ron said he didn't know what they were talkin' about. He claimed that no one but Jodie Caddell ever rode those horses." Mike stopped talking and struggled to reach up and scratch his head again, and then he continued, "There aren't many folks that stiff-arm Tony or Ted. Almost nobody when the two are together."

"So what happened to the horses?"

"According to Shear, he had to get rid of them because they reminded him too much of Jodie."

"Didn't waste much time gettin' 'em outta there, did he?"

"'At's not exactly a crime, is it?"

"No, but I find it a mite curious. But enough shop talk. When ya gonna get out of here?"

"I'm hopin' tomorrow. The docs and the physical terrorists have to get together and work up a plan for my rehabilitation, then once they're satisfied that I have been sufficiently punished, and that I should be capable of taking care of myself at home, they'll cut me loose."

"Good," Gail said, standing up to leave. "Please keep me posted on what the investigators come up with."

She had started out the door when Mike called her back to ask, "Did your dad mention what happened when he was here talkin' to me the other day?"

"No, what happened?"

"I asked Jesus to save me."

"Mike, that's fantastic!"

"I think so. But your dad made it sound kinda scary. Is it really hard?"

Gail took a deep breath before answering, "Well, I'm afraid I don't do a very good job of being a Christian, so I guess it hasn't been that tough for me. Though if you make your beliefs obvious, you're probably gonna take some heat."

"Oh, I think I can take the heat. What I mean is, how hard is it to live your life the way that God wants you to?"

"I don't do that good of a job of that either, I'm afraid. I've been praying that I can change that, though. I think the weird thing that happened when the shooter was struck blind was God's way of getting my attention. The hard part, for me at least, is accepting that God provides the whole deal. I don't want to be in debt to anybody. You know what I mean? I wanna pay my own way. With God that just ain't gonna happen. He provides the whole deal. That bothers me. I want to do something. But I can't. Just like I couldn't get away from the sniper, really I can't do anything in life that pays God back."

Mike's eyes sparkled when he replied, "Sounds like a sweet deal to me. I like free. But you can't be for real. I don't gotta do anything? I mean, I hafta go to church and stuff, don't I?"

"I'll be honest: I'm confused about that myself. It seems like you should have to do something, like give your money at least. But Dad keeps tellin' me that being one of God's people makes you want to do those things, but doin' 'em doesn't pay God back. I dunno. You need to talk to Dad about that stuff. But I gotta tell ya,

I'm glad you've taken the first step. It'll give me someone to talk to about this stuff."

"I'm glad too. I don't understand anything about the whole deal, but I do know that even stuck here in this hospital bed, I feel better about my future than I have since I don't remember when."

Gail shook her head and started for the door again, "I guess we're both nothin' but nuts. Anyway, I hope you get released tomorrow. Let me know, will ya?"

32

The evidence gathered from the rental trailer house that had been the home of the man killed during Gail's shootout had initially sparked a lot of interest. The rope had proven to carry Jodie Caddell's DNA. But it carried the DNA of several other unknown individuals as well. That fascinating fact had several agencies scrambling, hoping to clear up open files. But the fervor died quickly when no correlation was made to any known cases.

Nearly $50,000 in cash discovered in the house had stirred up a good bit of speculation as well. But the source of the money was as elusive as the identities of the people who had left their DNA on the rope. So, as Mike had predicted, within a few weeks the case was buried by new, more pressing matters.

The evidence may not have helped solve any other cases, but it, along with the rap sheet that came back on the dead man, did clear Gail of any suspicions concerning the death of Jodie Caddell. With outstanding warrants in three western states, he wasn't the type of guy that had made a lot of close friends in the criminal justice community. It also made the investigation of the shooting a mere formality. The shooting was quickly deemed to be justified.

So, as soon as her shoulder was adequately healed, Gail was back on the job in her normal capacity. On her first day back, Chief Yeager and Captain Elliott had even come by to congratulate her on the "volunteer" work she had performed. They did take the opportunity, however, to warn her to avoid becoming involved in cases outside the jurisdiction of the City of Bend in the future.

Mike did not recover quite as quickly as everyone had hoped, but physical therapy was continuing, and progress toward a full recovery was being made. He was well enough to be on light duty and was helping to work the phones at the East Lake County Sheriff's Department. One of the first calls that he had made was to the YZ ranch. The foreman, Zip Hallcraft, was very interested to hear about the cow that he and Gail had found the day of the shooting.

"I'm sorry to take so long getting the information to you," Mike apologized to the rancher. "I've been laid up. You probably heard or read some of the details of what took place the day we found your cow. Anyway, I wanted you to know, even if it is two months later."

"No cause to apologize. I understand there were a lot more pressin' issues to attend to. I did hear about the whole episode. We been hopin' there wouldn't be no liability issues raised since y'all were on property of the Z. Been kickin' myself for not havin' posted that stretch with 'No Trespassing' signs.

"We did find the heifer you and that gal cop found to start all the fun. We found another carcass upstream from there about a mile, too, about two weeks after your big adventure. Pretty much the same scenario, 'cept it was a steer. Throat had been cut, back straps and one ham removed."

"Have you had a lot of this type of thing this summer?" Mike asked.

"Anytime you have animals out on range you have some shrinkage. I don't recollect anything quite like this before, though."

"What was different about this?"

"Well," drawled Zip, "I can't figure how the owl hoots got close enough to these animals to cut they throats. Range animals like this are about as wild as deer. 'Taint easy to get close enough to throw a loop over 'em, let alone slit a throat. This is the first time I've seen an outlaw be so particular about the cuts of meat he takes, too. Normally they'll take most of the animal.

"And another oddity, usually the rustler will take an animal near a loggin' road. Somewhere that they can drive to and make a quick get-away. The heifer was near a quad trail, so they could have used a machine to get in and get the meat out, but the steer, it was quite a ways off any trail you could drive to. Why, it was even kinda hard to reach on horseback."

Mike was really curious now and continued the questioning. "Any idea of who might have been involved?"

"None." The foreman's voice, like gravel at best, dropped a little lower. "We don't take kindly to losin' stock. Bad 'nough we have the losses from the cougars this pansy state protects without havin' to lose valuable stock to someone who's just interested in the finest cuts of meat. Iffen the boys and I catch 'em, we might be tempted to use the three S's."

"Okay," Mike bit, "what're the three S's?"

"Shoot, shovel, and shut up," Zip replied.

"Hold it now, Zip. This isn't 1870, ya know," Mike said.

"Yeah, and it ain't liberal minded Portland or Eugene either," Zip countered, sounding peeved.

"That's true, but ya still can't take matters into your own hands, even if we do live in redneckville."

"Shucks, I know it. I's just blowin' off steam. But it does seem to me that the girl cop you were with did a little 'takin' matters into her hands' with the one fella. We heard he was shot to smithereens."

Mike tried to keep from sighing out loud when he answered, "Well, that guy was laying down a lot of lead. She took a round, as a matter of fact. Self defense is still permissible."

"Well, me an' the boys will just make sure that they fire first, then we'll defend ourselves. 'Sides, we're not in your county anyways, are we?"

"No, you're not. But I'm on pretty good terms with them whose county you are in. But enough arguing about things that are hypothetical, let me ask a question. Did you happen to find anything that might have been considered evidence anywhere around the steer carcass? Or have you found any carcasses like this anywhere else?"

"What kind of 'evidence' you talkin' 'bout?"

Mike hedged, not wanting to plant any ideas, "Oh, anything that might give us a clue. Things like trash, footprints, anything like that."

"Naw, nothin' that anyone mentioned. We're just a bunch a old buckaroos, though. We wasn't really lookin' for evidence. We was lookin' for culprits. And no, like I told ya, I haven't seen anything quite like this anywhere before, and I been makin' my livin' off the back of a horse for the best part of five decades.

"Oh, wait a minute, there was one strange thing one of my buckaroos found when we were pokin' round that steer. He found an obsidian knife."

"Ya mean, like an Indian artifact?"

"Well, I'm no archeologist or nothin,' but I'm not sure it was old. In fact it kinda looked like the rustlers may have busted it when they kilt the steer."

"You still have the knife?"

"Hey, you know it's agin' the law to disturb anythin' that may be historic. I'm sure the boys left that thing right where they found it."

"Okay, I get it," Mike said, getting ready to wrap up the call. "But if you stumble across that artifact, or anything else interesting, I'd appreciate your givin' me a call."

"We've moved our stock off the range and onto the feedlots for winter now, so whoever was helpin' themselves is gonna have a little harder time until next spring, but if anything comes up I'll let ya know."

Mike sat staring at the phone after the call had ended. It was strange that rustlers had set up shop in the same area where he and Gail had been bushwhacked. He thought he might make calls to some of the other large ranches in the area and see if any of them had found anything similar.

He didn't have much luck with the calls. Cowboys hadn't much taken to cell phones yet, and most of them were outside working their herds. He left messages on a couple of machines asking for a call if their ranches had suffered from any unusual rustling in the past year. Then on his last call, he got an answer. The foreman of the Silver Lake branch of the Bell Cattle Company happened to be in his office cleaning up some paperwork from a bull sale the ranch had conducted the weekend before.

After introducing himself and explaining the nature of the call and expressing his surprise over getting an answer, Mike asked, "Did you have any rustling on your ranch this past summer?"

"I don't get astride a horse much these days. I turned eighty-seven this past spring, so I use any excuse to give my ole bones a break from the saddle. Fact is, I ain't been on a horse, 'cept for the Fourth of July parade, for over a year. Spend most of my time in this chair. The owner only keeps me on 'cause I'm kinda like a bad habit. Been workin' this ranch, 'cept for a four year-hitch in the army, since 1937. Her granddaddy hired me, then I worked for her ma till she retired and gave the place over to 'lizbeth to run. Anyways that's why you caught me. As far as rustlin,' there's been no more than the usual. We came up a couple of cow/calf pairs short at round up, and we were missin' a few head of young stuff, 'bout an average year. Why you askin'?"

Mike explained the unusual form of theft that had occurred on the YZ ranch.

"Well, now," the old cowhand said, "that puts me in mind of the type of rustlin' that went on back in the Depression. We called 'em stewpot rustlers. Folks that were starvin' would kill an animal to feed their family, but with no vehicles and freezers or refrigeration, they'd only take as much of the animal as a couple of them could carry and only as much as they could eat or dry before it spoiled. If I was you, I'd be lookin' for someone with a family that's fallen on hard times. Course, I thought the gov'ment took care of folks like that these days. T'weren't so easy back in the day."

Mike thanked the man for his help and hung up, trying to mesh what the old man said to the facts of the rustling that had take place on the YZ. He didn't have much time to think about it as the phones started ringing with the day's ration of crises now that it was past eight in the morning, and the general populace was awakening to the day.

33

Nate woke to the sound of coyotes yapping and howling somewhere to the west of the house. He lay in the dark listening to the eerie calls that were half music, half frightening. He spent a few minutes enjoying the sound of the song dogs with goose bumps on his arms, but knew that his labs were going to join in at any moment. The contribution of the big dogs was neither musical nor frightening, just irritating. Nate got up to go down the stairs and shut his mutts up before they woke the neighbors. An hour before dawn; it was Nate's favorite time of day. He fed the boys, a guaranteed way to keep them quiet, and went to the kitchen to start his own breakfast. As bacon was frying, he thawed some bread from the freezer for toast and started a pot of coffee, a beverage that he detested, but he knew the aroma would bring Amy to the kitchen, and he wanted the company. And the plan worked. He heard her slippers on the hardwood floor just as he was taking the bacon from the frying pan.

"Hey, beautiful," he said without turning around. Want to join me for breakfast?"

"Who are you expecting? After all these years you can't be calling me beautiful."

"That's why God designed for our eyesight to fail as we age. By the time gravity makes everything droop, our eyes are too weak to see it."

Amy laughed, "Now that's a real romantic line. So gravity has made everything sag, has it?"

"Oh, boy, my smart mouth got the best of me this time, didn't it?"

"Just like it usually does, but I'll forgive you for a cup of that coffee."

"What do I get for bacon, toast, and coffee?"

"For all that, I'll promise you the rest of my life."

"Now that's a deal I'd make every day!"

"I know better than that. There's no way you're gonna cook this type of breakfast every day. So what's on your agenda today, since it's Saturday and you don't have to work?"

Nate jammed a slice of bacon in his mouth and talked around it. "I was just talkin' to the dogs about that very thing. They were complainin' that they haven't gotten out much this fall, and they think that it is high time for a quail hunt."

"Oh, so now you're takin' advice from the dogs," Amy answered.

"I only listen to them when they give really good advice. I don't listen to them when they tell me to dig in the lawn or bite the meter reader."

"Hmm...how come I'm surprised? So where are ya goin'?"

"I was remembering a big flock of birds that I kicked up when I went in lookin' for Gail and Mike that day last summer. If no one has gone in there and shot 'em up, I should be able to bring enough of the tasty little critters home for a good meal."

Amy turned serious. "Do you think it's safe to go back down there? They never did find the second guy, did they?"

"No. But I'd bet that guy is twelve states away by now. That whole deal was just a fluke, anyway. I think we just wandered into something we didn't understand, and we were lucky to make it out with as little damage as we suffered."

"I dunno. I hate you going back in there alone. What if you're wrong? That crazy guy could come out on top this time."

"There is nothing to worry about, but if it'd make you feel better, when I call down to the YZ to ask permission to hunt on that section of their ranch, I'll ask if they have noticed any more strange events in that area."

Amy was up cleaning up the dishes from the breakfast bar when she said, "Okay. But be careful. If I was you I wouldn't want to go anywhere near that place. You, Gail, and Mike almost all got killed out there!"

"Amy, it wasn't the place. It was the people. And one of them is dead, and the other is undoubtedly as far away from that spot as he can get."

Nate's call to the YZ confirmed what he had told Amy. The ranch hands had rounded up the cattle from that area during the last week of September and hadn't experienced anything unusual. The buckaroo that Nate talked to thanked him for calling for permission to trespass and asked him to be easy on the fences, saying that they'd had some of them cut lately on other parts of the spread. He also requested that Nate let someone on the ranch know if he saw any stray cattle. They came up a few head short when they had made the roundup.

The dogs showed nothing but enthusiasm when Nate got his shotgun from the gun safe and loaded it and his vest into the pickup. They whined and howled and generally made a nuisance of themselves as he put on his hunting boots. When he opened the truck's tailgate, they loaded up without having to be told. They might not know where they were headed, but they were more than ready for an adventure, especially an adventure that involved a shotgun.

Traffic was light as Nate turned the Dodge onto the highway

and headed south. Deer season was over, kids were in school, and a lot of the snowbirds from the area had already headed south for the winter. If you didn't mind cold nights, fall was a great time to be in Central Oregon. When he had driven to the end of the dirt road that gave access to the YZ, the same spot he had parked when he came out to rescue Gail and Mike, he sat in his rig and enjoyed the view.

Off in the distance, the aspens along the river had been turned brilliant yellow by the fall frosts. Their bright color against the dark green of the pine forest was spectacular. Add to the scene the unbelievable blue of the cloudless sky, and you had a feast of color that no artist could adequately or accurately capture. Nate would have spent a lot more time drinking in the view, but his partners in the bed of the pickup were not here to enjoy the scenery. They were impatient to get out and tear up the underbrush. They made a series of short anxious barks and snorts until Nate got out and let down the tailgate. As soon as they were on the ground they ripped and galloped in seven directions at once. He knew that they would be worthless for hunting until they got the initial burst of energy burned off of their enthusiasm; Nate let the dogs tear around while he pulled on his hunting vest and retrieved the Browning from behind the seat of the pickup and slammed a round of eight shot into the chamber and slid two more into the magazine. By the time he was set to hunt, the boys were also.

It was unlikely that they would encounter any game birds before they reached the willow thickets that lined the river, but Nate still enjoyed watching the big dogs cast through the sparse underbrush. They kept their noses to the ground and sucked in every smell. The power of the big black and the speed of the smaller younger yellow lab was a combination that was almost poetic. By the time they reached the river, they had settled into a businesslike routine. The black was intently working the landscape fifty feet ahead of Nate; the yellow was investigating the cover just outside that range.

Once near the river, among the willows, where quail or grouse were more apt to be encountered, Nate slowed his pace and got the dogs in closer to him. The birds they were hunting were explosive, erratic fliers. When they came off the ground, they spun and dove and flew among the trees like bees. To have any hope of success in bagging them, you had to be close to the flush.

They hunted upstream, staying on the west side of the river. They would cover the east side on the return trip. The day was perfect; cool enough for a good long walk, but warm enough to allow you to stop and enjoy the sights without freezing. Nate loved the fall. And he loved to be out in the wild with his dogs. Getting into a covey of birds would just be an enjoyable bonus.

His mind was in neutral when the dogs kicked up a group of a half dozen quail. Nate barely brought himself back to reality in time to squeeze off a quick shot at the slowest bird before the flock disappeared into a thicket. Surprisingly, the quail went down in a puff of feathers, and Luke brought it to his master with a proud strut in his walk. Nate accepted the bird from the dog and rewarded him with half a dog biscuit. Once the bird was in Nate's vest, the trio got serious about the hunt. Within an hour and a half of the first flush, five more birds were added to the game bag, both dogs had made impressive retrieves, and it was time to think about crossing the stream, turning around, and heading back toward the truck.

First though, Nate found a log that allowed him to cross the stream without getting his feet wet, then he sat down on a convenient boulder and pulled out the lunch he had prepared from his leftover breakfast. The dogs had been intent on the hunt until they heard the crinkle of the lunch sack and saw their master preparing to eat. Once they realized that it was lunchtime, the hunt was forgotten, and they were focused on a new mission: claiming part of that lunch. They watched every move of Nate's hands as if they were hypnotized, sure that each of the bites was supposed to be theirs—and many were—until the lunch sack was empty and stowed back in the vest.

The dogs were getting tired and slowing down, but still working hard, as they made their way down the east side of the stream. Nate was satisfied with the game they had taken, but would like to have added a grouse or two to his harvest. Amy loved fried grouse, and he was always pleased to have a couple of them for her enjoyment. He was thinking about the possibility of a pair of ruffled grouse, watching his dogs for any sign of them catching a scent of game, and enjoying the day, when Barney hit a scent and headed down hill toward the water.

The dog wasn't acting like he was on a grouse or quail; those kinds of birds didn't usually run this far. This looked more like pheasant, but Nate had never seen a pheasant in this part of the state. As Barney headed to the river, Luke caught his excitement and joined him. The two dogs cast about on the edge of the stream, then went back up the scent past where Barney had first hit the mark. They ran in circles, acting confused, and then they ran back to the river where Luke jumped in and swam across. Now Nate was really curious. He'd never seen his boys act like this before. He called them off the scent, thinking that they might be after a porcupine, and he didn't need one, or both, of them ending up with a nose full of quills.

Once he had the dogs calmed down, Nate tried to find any tracks or signs that might give him a clue as to what kind of scent the dogs had encountered. He searched the ground carefully, but if there had been anything to indicate what had gotten the dogs riled up, they had destroyed it. He worked his way down the hill to the stream without finding anything that would explain the mystery. He stood on the stream bank, shotgun resting across the top of his shoulders, thinking and looking, a dog on their haunches on either side of him. Then something in the crystal clear, swift, water caught his attention. Across the stream, willow sticks were pushed into the streambed. They were arranged in an "M" shape, the bottom of the "M" against the far bank. The letter, if that's what it was, was about a yard square.

Nate's first thought was that some kids had been playing in the water. But why would kids be down here? And what kids would have a long enough attention span to stick a couple hundred sticks into the mud just to form a letter? Nate ordered the dogs to sit and, forgetting all about keeping his feet dry, waded out into the stream to get a better look at this weird sight. Once he was close enough to see it, Nate noticed the offal from a couple of trout inside the "M"; this made the curiosity even more curious.

Nate's mind was struggling to make sense of what his eyes were telling him. Then it came to him. He'd seen it on *Survivor Man* on the television. This was a fish trap. But why on earth would anybody go to the trouble of constructing a fish trap in a stream where trout practically fought over any fly cast toward them? It wasn't going to make sense to Nate, no matter how long he looked at it.

Just before he waded back across the stream, something in the mud at the edge of the water above the trap caught his eye. Moving closer, he saw that it was a footprint. A perfect human footprint, barefoot, short but wide, was imprinted in the mud. So maybe it was the work of children. No, the print was too big for a kid. But who else would be wading in these ice-cold waters barefoot?

He crossed back to where the dogs waited, sat down on a rock beside the stream, removed his boots, wrung out his socks, and dried his feet as well as possible with his handkerchief. His stiff frigid feet reiterated the question of who in the world would be wading barefoot in this frigid water, making ineffective fish traps? Once his boots and socks where back on his feet, he headed toward the truck, double time. Finding the fish trap made Nate completely forget about bagging a grouse. He was eager to talk to a game warden about what he had found.

An hour later, Luke and Barney hit a scent that had them tearing through the willows beside the stream. Instinct took over, and Nate scrambled so that he would be in position for a shot when the birds exploded from the cover. Thirty seconds later, no birds appeared, and the dogs started barking and whining; another unusual event for Nate's dogs.

As Nate moved in to see what had the dogs so fired up, he heard the sound of wings, but no birds emerged from the brush. The undergrowth was so thick that he had to get down on his hands and knees and push through to where Luke and Barney were whining and running in circles in a small opening in the thick brush. They were running around and around a large box woven from long willow branches. Inside the box, four quail were frantic to escape. In his frenzy to get at the captive birds, Luke rammed the makeshift box, flipping it over, and allowed the little balls of feathers to make their escape.

So, Nate now had a bird trap, complete with a very simple but effective figure-four trigger, to go with the fish trap. There wasn't a scrape of vegetation on the ground inside the trap. The birds had been in there long enough to have eaten every stitch of anything that was edible. It was bad enough to poach quail, but to trap them and then leave them to starve to death was unconscionable. Next, he thought, he'd be finding deer snares, or deadfall traps for squirrels. This was way beyond weird. The sooner he could get out of here and make a report to the Oregon State Fish and Wildlife Department, the better he would like it. Maybe they could make sense out of this whole trap business. He was going to have to hustle, however. Unless he really covered ground, the offices would be closed before he was able to get to a phone.

34

"Gail," Nate said when his daughter answered her phone, "what's up with the Oregon State Police?" The irritation in his voice was obvious when he continued. "I called and talked to the folks at the regional office in Bend three days ago. They didn't seem that excited about what I think is some extremely bizarre stuff. But they said they'd have a game officer get in touch with me. And I haven't heard a thing! Don't they care that somebody is out there poaching game?"

"Dad," Gail responded, "I'm sure they've got a lot bigger fish to fry. I know it has you all kinds of fired up, but a few fish and a couple of quail is not that big a deal."

"Well, who knows what else they're up to? I'm tellin' ya, it's pretty durn peculiar that someone would go to all the trouble of makin' those traps. There is a lot more to this deal than a handful a fish and a pair of quail. If I can't get anyone else to take a look, I'm gonna go back out there myself. Somebody's gotta find out what's goin' on."

"I'm sure it's just some kids playin' Daniel Boone. You used to tell me about how you set traps and stuff when you were a kid. Was that so weird?"

"Yeah, I've always been weird, but this ain't kids. It is miles to the nearest house. Where would any kids come from?"

"I dunno, but I sure don't think it's some kinda alien invasion or conspiracy or anything. And sure not anything big enough to expect the state police to drop everything and go after it like there was a kidnapping or bank robbery or murder."

"Okay, I get the picture. I know that the state police are understaffed and overworked. But there is something really, really strange goin' on out there, and I wanna know what it is."

"Would you please just wait for the police to take a look? What difference is a couple of days gonna make, anyway?"

"What makes ya think that the cops are goin' be more interested in a few fish and a couple of quail in a few more days, or a few more weeks for that matter? No, if they were gonna get back to me, they'd a done it by now. And you're the one said it was likely just some kids foolin' around, anyway. Maybe I'll run across the little hay shakers, catch the little varmints right in the act. That'd at least put my mind to ease."

"Yeah, I gotta feein' that the state po po have you lumped together with those guys that keep spottin' Big Foot. But if you're gonna go down there nosin' around, at least give Mike a call and let him know. Maybe he could call down to his counterpart in Chiloquin County and let them know what's goin' on, just in case you're right and it's more than just some brats goofin' around."

"That's not a bad idea. By the way, he was at church again Sunday. It looks like he's takin' his decision of being a follower of Jesus really seriously. And it appears that he's recovering really well too. He's movin' around like nothing ever happened to him. He told me that he was workin' his regular shift again and should be back to full strength in a couple more months. In fact, I've seen him in the gym a couple of times in the past week. I wish I could lift half of what he puts up. And he claims he's still only about a third of the way recovered."

"Yeah, he told me that he's doin' a lot better. It's great. He also told me that some of his friends think he's lost his mind. He's changing his lifestyle, ya know. He's been sorta rough, and his buddies are thinkin' the blow he took to the head rattled his brains."

"I warned 'im that he'd hafta deal with some of that. But he's tough, he can handle it. And if his buddies keep seein' that he's changed, some of them will start askin' him what happened to make him different. He's gonna have some great opportunities to tell people about God's kingdom."

"Great. Anyway, give him a call before you go off playin' lone ranger, will ya?"

"I will. I'd kinda like to talk to him anyway, see if I can recommend any good books for him to read, or anything."

Nate sat thinking about the phone conversation with his daughter. Part of him wanted to believe that she was right, that the traps he had found were no big deal. But there was another part of him that was quite sure that there was something going on down in those woods that needed to be uncovered. He would call Mike first thing in the morning and then head out on another quail hunt.

For now, he thought he'd better go and check on his parents and see if they needed anything.

When Nate went into his parents' home, Jake was watching the Discovery Channel, a program about whale migration or something. Jan was reading a Phillip Yancey book on prayer. He thought she should more likely be writing a book on that subject as reading one, but he didn't say that, knowing that it would only earn him a snort.

Jake turned off the TV, and after exchanging the typical good-natured insults, Nate told his dad about the traps he had found.

"I never had no call to make a fish trap," Jake said. "But we use ta make crawdad traps when I was a boy. Outta hardware cloth, could we get aholt of any. I can see how a big 'M' shape might work to catch fish, though. It seems like it'd be easier to use a hook and line, especially in that stretch of water. 'Less you didn't have no hooks, but hooks is cheap.

"We used figure-four triggers in our rabbit snares all the time. I didn't know anyone still knew how to make one of those. But when I was a boy, meat was a rarity and catchin' a cottontail or jackrabbit provided a treat. My older brother made a quail trap out a willows once. It had a figure-four trigger in it. He caught a whole covey a quail in it too. But one of our sisters let 'em go before he had a chance to harvest any of 'em. Boy, was he mad!

"Sounds ta me like you got somebody hungry livin' down in those woods. Somebody that knows how to make due with the things God provides."

"I dunno what's goin' on, but I aim to try to find out some more about it tomorrow. I'm gonna go out there and do a little more huntin,' but this time without the dogs. Maybe I can find some sign if I don't have those knot heads tearin' everything up."

"Gonna take your fishing pole?"

"No. I think I'd better take the Browning. Don't know what I might run into, but I think I'd feel better with some firepower."

Jan had been being quiet, but the firepower statement drew her attention away from the book she was reading. "You don't think it's dangerous down there, do you?"

"No. But I just wanna be careful."

"If you wanted to be careful, you'd just keep away from down there! And since when have you ever tried to be careful, anyway? I don't understand why you don't leave it to the police."

"Ma," Nate interjected, trying to diffuse the tirade. "Take it easy. I was all over that country just four days ago, and nothin' happened."

"Then why do ya need to go back? What makes you think you're gonna find anything now that ya didn't see then?"

"Well, for one thing, I'm not gonna have the dogs with me, so they won't be erasing every track within five miles of me."

"Oh, good thinkin.' Go out there into who knows what, and leave your best protection at home. I didn't notice that you were so stupid when you were growin' up. Must be that all that Mountain Dew soda pop you drink is poisonin' your brain."

"Or," Nate said under his breath, "it could be genetic."

35

The next morning Nate was feeding the dogs before the sun had cleared the horizon. An overnight breeze had cleared out the smoke from the pine-needle fires, and the air was brisk and clean. It was a perfect day for a Central Oregon adventure. Almost any other day, Nate would be debating with himself about how he should spend such an awesome day, but today the choice was already made. He was going hunting. Hunting for whoever was trapping game down on the Little Deschutes River. He wasn't happy about the consequences to the wildlife, but be was more interested in why someone felt it was necessary to use traps instead of the normal methods of fair chase.

While the dogs were speed feeding, Nate spun the dial on the door of his gun safe. He pulled the battered Browning Gold out of the safe at the same time that the dogs finished their feeding frenzy. Luke and Barney noticed the gun and went crazy. Since the gun being put in the pickup almost always meant a hunting trip, the two dogs had every reason to expect an outing, but this time they were disappointed. The labs escorted Nate out the driveway, one on either side of the rig, obviously expecting him to remember that he needed them and stop to pick them up. When the pickup reached the end of the driveway and turned onto the road, the dogs stopped and watched, incredulous, as their opportunity for an outing evaporated.

Jake and Jan were both reading their Bibles when the Dodge rumbled past. They looked up, glanced at each other, nodded, and went back to their reading. Without even speaking they had agreed that they would be spending a little extra time in prayer this morning.

When Nate reached the highway, he had to wait for several motor homes to pass before he could pull out and head south. The annual snowbird migration was at full strength, undoubtedly spurred by a weather forecast of overnight temperatures dipping into the low teens by the end of the week. Many Central Oregon homeowners chose to escape the harsh winters by migrating to Arizona or California. That suited Nate. In his opinion, the area was getting too populated. Having a few people leave for the winter just made things a little more pleasant. The folks from the church that spent their winters in the warm climates would be missed, though. Their areas of ministry in the church were hard to cover during their absences, as was their spending at the local retailers. But it was all just part of the facts of life in the area.

Nate parked the pickup in what was becoming his regular spot in front of the boulders at the end of the dirt road. He put on his shell vest, stuffed his lunch and water bottle into the pouch, and took the Browning from behind the seat. He shoved three game loads into the gun and set off for the river. He wasn't sure what he was looking for, but his plan was to just poke around and see if he could find anything to help explain the whys and whos behind the traps he had discovered.

He hadn't walked far when a pair of quail exploded from a patch of weeds just ahead of him. The bird on the left made a hard curve toward the river, but the other one flew straight away, presenting a perfect shot. Perfect shot opportunity or not, Nate didn't clip a feather when he sent a load of eights after the bird. A second blast had the same effect. Oh, boy, he thought as the bird made its escape, it's gonna be a long day if I'm shootin' like that. He stuffed a couple more shells into the magazine of the gun and kept walking, thinking that as much time as he had spent with a shotgun in his hands, and as much shooting as he had done in his life, he should never miss. Somehow, however, it just didn't work that way for him. He knew people who rarely missed, some of them with a lot less experience than him. It was kind of depressing when he thought about it. His shooting skills pretty much mirrored everything in his life. Success didn't come easy in anything. Whatever he accomplished came more through stubbornness than skill. He wondered what it felt like to be one of those people who had everything fall into place without trying.

When Nate reached the river, he stood looking around the countryside. The willows that lined the river couldn't really be called trees. They were actually no more than shrubs. The tallest stood less than fifteen feet, slender branches growing out of a common root wad reaching ineffectually for the sky. But they formed a dense thicket along the river and provided shelter for a host of wildlife and were the primary food source for beaver, muskrat, and deer. In the spring they would supply the necessary cover for nesting waterfowl, quail, grouse, and a variety of songbirds. They were stark in the fall, though. Leafless, they had a stark lonely appearance, like skeletal fingers making accusing gestures aimed at winter. The meadow grass was cropped short after a summer and fall of beef cattle licking up almost every succulent spear. All that remained was a tan mat, less than half an inch tall, cut by cow trails and littered with cow flaps and gopher mounds. The grass ended where the ground sloped up away from the river. The absence of water necessary for the more succulent plants gave the pines and bitterbrush opportunity. Mixed in throughout the lowland willows, grasses, and pines were the white-barked aspens, their naked branches beseeching the sky, where leaves of blazing yellow had lent color just days before. The band of mixed pines was, at best, a mere quarter mile wide. Up in elevation from them, where the land was nearly void of moisture, the gray-green junipers and sagebrush took over; the gnarled vegetation always made Nate think of the old people in the area, those people that were left over from when Central Oregon was populated by hardy, hard-working, hard-living folks.

Those loggers, mill workers, and ranchers had fought this harsh country to eke out a meager living. They had successfully battled the brutal winters in order to enjoy short summers. Now, however, they were losing out to the deep-pocketed retirement crowd that had discovered the recreational activities the area had to offer in the summer and could escape to the south in the winter. This new group was driving the price of land ever higher, and at the same time changing the politics of the region. As Nate surveyed the beauty of this remarkable stretch of river bottom, he wondered how long it would be before it was lost to some rich developer's scheme and dreams. His contemplation made him momentarily forget the mission he was on. The noisy calling of a flock of migrating white-fronted geese, their lopsided "V" formation stretched across the sky, brought him back to reality.

He left off his musings about the landscape and headed upstream, not knowing what he was looking for, but trying to be observant for anything out of the ordinary. Judging from the abundance of deer tracks, it appeared that the fall migration of mule deer was well underway. Every fall the deer left the snow zone and headed for the desert areas where food was readily available through the winter. The trip took a good number of them right through this area. It seemed to Nate that it was early for the migration to have begun, and he hoped that it wasn't a sign that snow was coming early on the high desert. Winters were long enough without it getting started ahead of the normal schedule.

A large deer, an old buck by the look of its tracks, had walked up the trail that Nate was using to parallel the river. The edges of the tracks cut sharp in the dust of the trail, which indicated that the tracks were fresh. Hoping to catch sight of the animal, Nate slowed his movement. He would take a step or two, stop and scan the willows through his binoculars, wait a few seconds, and then take another step. It was a method known as still-hunting, and sometimes it worked. This happened to be one of them.

The old buck was feeding on tender willow branches and didn't appear to have a clue that he was being watched. He had a massive rack, a good thirty-two inches wide, and perfectly symmetrical, with four points and long eye guards on each side. Nate found it both humorous and humiliating that this old boy had managed to avoid becoming a wall ornament and table fare. Deer season had ended only two weeks earlier and though any hunter would have been pleased to put a tag on this animal, here he was alive and well. By instinct, luck, or skill, he had managed to avoid the hunters and live through another season.

While Nate watched and admired the magnificent animal, the buck threw his head up; his nostrils flared, and his ears pivoted. All the deer's attention was focused on something on the other side of it, something near, or in, the river. Suddenly the deer spun around and started running right at Nate. The big animal was within ten yards of the man when it realized it was on a course that would take it within an arm's reach of its most feared predator. The buck dug in its hooves like a racehorse on the backstretch. It veered hard left and was out of sight in seconds.

Nate was left wondering what had spooked the buck. He scanned the area beyond where the animal had been feeding, expecting to see a man, or coyote, or perhaps even a cougar. But he couldn't see movement or anything unusual. He glassed the area with his binoculars for approximately five minutes, and then moved slowly forward, carefully listening and watching. When he reached the spot where the deer had been feeding, he stopped and waited. After a few seconds he was startled by thrashing, splashing, and a low growling noise coming from direction of the river. He stood trying to sort out the odd sounds. Running the facts through his catalog of experience he couldn't find a match to what he was hearing. Advancing toward the sound, every sensory on full alert, Nate's mind was in overdrive as he struggled to understand what was happening.

When he had worked his way through the thick willow bushes to a place where he could see the river, he noticed the brush on the riverbank shaking and jerking. Something was in the thick bushes causing a considerable commotion, but Nate was still unable to determine what it was, so he inched closer. Then he saw to his relief that it was only a river otter. But why was it acting so strange, with all this rolling and jerking and growling and hissing? Oh—then he saw it. The critter's hind leg was caught in a leg-hold trap.

Now this is all kinds of weird, Nate thought. First, it was too early in the year for trapping. The pelts wouldn't be in prime condition until the weather got a lot colder. Besides, the furbearer season didn't open until the middle of November. Second, no one who knew how to trap would make a set that was not situated in such a way as to make sure the animal quickly drowned. And this trap didn't look like an ordinary trap; the jaws appeared to be rubber. Leg-hold traps had steel jaws.

Nate sat down in the willows, about fifteen feet from the trapped animal, to watch and to contemplate what he should do. His first instinct was to release the animal. Not that he had any real love for river otters. They were quite abundant in this river, and they were ferocious feeders. Their main prey was trout. Reducing their numbers would only make fishing that much better. But something about seeing this beautiful animal struggle against the trap bothered Nate. The otter's slick black coat, thick tail, and cute rounded ears just made you want to like him. The animal's legs were short and stout, ending at wide webbed feet. He was obviously built for work in the water. Nate had watched a number of these animals fishing over the years; they always impressed him with their skill, playfulness, and the look of intelligence in their eyes.

The look in this twenty-pound fellow's eyes was a lot closer to panic than it was intelligence, however. It was obvious that he wanted nothing more than to be free from the spring jaws that held his foot. The large member of the weasel family would alternate between pulling against the trap and its line and doing belly rolls in the shallow water at the streams edge. When neither of those techniques worked, he tried gnawing on the trap and the cable that held the trap to a stake driven deep into the riverbank. When that too proved futile, the otter attacked the willows and other brush within reach on the riverbank. Then there was more growling.

Technically, it was illegal to release an animal from another person's trap, but that was exactly what Nate decided to do. He just needed to think of a way to accomplish that without being the victim of the critter's needle-sharp teeth. Nate had gotten one of his dogs out of a coyote trap by throwing his coat over the dog's head while he stepped on the trap's springs. The dog had been extremely aggressive, driven by the pain of having his foot in the trap, but Nate was sure that the dog had not been nearly as quick or attack-oriented as this wild animal was going to be. Maybe he could find a stick with which to reduce the tension of the trap's jaws enough for the animal to pull loose. He was looking for a suitable stick when he heard gravel crunching together upstream.

Nate froze in place and watched as a man in black knee-high rubber boots, Carhart bibs, and woolen jacket waded into view. He had a backpack strapped on his back. The man was concentrating on the otter and didn't notice Nate half hidden in the streamside brush. He was carrying a catch loop with a sturdy handle that he was preparing to use on the otter. As the loop was slipped over the otter's head, Nate noticed that the brown baseball hat that the man was wearing was emblazoned with the Oregon Department of Fish and Wildlife logo on the front. Relieved that this was apparently an official operation, Nate stepped up to the stream side and hollered, "Hey, how ya doin'? Ya need any help?"

The otter was thrashing and writhing at the end of the loop, commanding all of the man's attention, so the sound of Nate's voice startled him severely. He jerked badly, lost his footing on the slick river rock, and nearly fell as he tried to locate the source of the voice. After some frantic searching, he found Nate and made eye contact. "Man, you scared me half ta death. Where'd you come from?"

"I've been sittin' here cipherin' how to cut that critter loose without losin' a limb," Nate replied. "And he'd have been gone if I'd come up with an answer."

"Well, I'm glad you didn't. These guys are too hard to catch to just set 'em loose."

"What are ya gonna do with the critter?"

"Help me get 'em in a sack, and I'll tell you all about it."

"What'da ya want me to do?"

"Come 'ere and hold this catchpole while I get a transport sack outta my pack."

Nate leaned the Browning against a clump of willows and moved into position. The trapper handed him the pole. The strength of the captured animal as it pulled against the catch loop was amazing. How could a twenty-pound animal pull that hard? Nate hoped that the trapper would get the sack out of the backpack before the squirming bundle of ferocity was able to escape. But he didn't need to worry; the man wasted no time in getting both a sack and some type of muzzle out of his pack. "Hold on," he instructed and started to slowly move toward the captured animal. The closer the man got, the more the otter pulled, growled, and thrashed. Apparently the guy had done this before, because he was all business and did not appear to be the least bit intimidated by the aggression displayed by the otter. In fact the trapper had the muzzle on the animal, and the animal in the sack in seconds.

"Okay," he said after he had placed the sacked critter on the stream bank and removed the catch loop from around its neck. "Thanks for your help."

Nate crawled out of the stream, and as he moved to retrieve his shotgun, he half expected the noose of the catch loop to slide into position over his head. He felt foolish for having had the thought as he picked up the Browning and turned back to see the trapper adjusting his pack to allow the otter to be carried in it.

"So," Nate said, "I helped you get the Tasmanian devil into your sack. Now what's the story? What'd ya gonna do with him?"

"I'm workin' for the Oregon DFW. They're payin' me to not trap these guys durin' the furbearer season, but instead to trap them now and in the late spring. They're usin' the otters in some kinda wildlife exchange program with states where the otter population has been completely depleted. Oregon is one of only a few states that enjoy a thriving population of the critters."

"No kidding," Nate responded, "there are states that want more otters? I thought they were nothin' but pests."

"I don't know nothin' 'bout the politics of the program, I just know that the state is paying me more to catch these guys alive than I could make trappin' them for their pelts. And I don't have to skin 'em out or flesh, stretch, or dry the hides. It's a good deal for me!"

"How far ya gotta carry 'em?"

"That 'eres the down side. I'm probably only a mile from my rig, which ain't too bad. If I get one at the far end of my string, I can have as far as seven miles to hike out. That furry varmint is startin' to get pretty durn heavy at the end of that hike."

"So you're parked somewhere upstream of here?" Nate asked.

"No. My rig is downstream. I made twenty sets on my way up the river. I was headed back when I found that this trap was already successful. It's only been here a couple of hours. I don't usually catch something that fast! Usually these critters are nocturnal, and I won't catch 'em till after dark."

"How come I didn't see your outfit when I parked?" Nate mused out loud.

"I dunno. Where you parked?"

"I'm at the end of the dirt road that comes off Highway 197. You know, where the big boulders are piled to keep you from drivin' down to the river."

"Oh, I'm south of you. There's a road—more like a goat path really—that takes you almost to the river. That's important when you're packin' traps in and critters out."

"Yeah, I think I know where you mean. That's the road that crosses the boulder patch, isn't it? I don't know how ya get through there without tearin' something from the underside of your rig!"

"Well, my old Ford is lifted a mite. And I just kinda pick my way through the rocks. It's worth it to save the extra mile or whatever."

"I haven't seen a trap quite like that one," Nate stated, changing the subject. "Is it some special type?"

"Yeah. It's got rubber jaws. The state supplies 'em for me. They're designed to minimize the damage to the animal's leg and foot. They want the otters to be completely healthy when they are released. In fact, the state wildlife honcho in Bend will transport this guy over to Oregon State University tomorrow where the biologists will examine him, rehabilitate him if necessary, and get him all ready to ship to his new home."

"So what's Oregon get in return? Wolves?"

"Nah, I think this fella is headed for Pennsylvania. I don't think they got any spare wolves. I think we're tradin' for some special kinda wild turkey, but I'm not sure. Like I said, I'm just tryin' to make a few bucks by trappin' 'em. I don't really care much what they do with 'em. If I wasn't catchin' 'em for them, I'd be catchin' 'em for some rich witch to wear 'round her neck when she goes to some fancy party."

"Well, it doesn't make much sense ta me," Nate replied. "I dunno why anybody would trade a turkey for a fish killin' machine. But it sounds like it's a good deal for you anyway. Say, you aren't doin' any other kinda weird trappin' in this stream, are ya?"

"Well, I don't know if it's weird or not, but I been trappin' beaver and muskrat, along with the otter, outta this stream for the past fifteen years. I take bobcat and coyote in this area too. I'll get started on everything but the otter as soon as the furbearer season opens up next month."

"But how 'bout quail or trout; have you ever tried trappin' any of them?" Nate asked.

"No. But I'd be willin' to try. What'd ya have in mind?"

"Oh, nothin.' I ran across what I thought might be a fish trap in this stream a few days ago. I thought maybe the state had you doin' some tests with 'em or something. I found some quail in a box trap that same day. It just had me curious. You see anything strange like 'at?"

"No, but this is my first time here this fall. But speakin' of being curious, I gotta admit, you got me a bit puzzled," the trapper said. "I don't think I ever run across anyone out here, except durin' deer season, besides ranch hands, that is. What're you huntin'?"

"Well, I was quail and grouse huntin' when I came upon the traps I was talkin' about. Now, to be truthful, I was kinda hopin' to find the folks that set those traps. They were really crude and primitive. I reported 'em to the state police, but I guess they've got more pressin' matters to attend to than a little small-game poachin.'"

"What'd the fish trap you're talkin' about look like?" the trapper wanted to know.

"It was shaped like a giant letter 'M' in the stream bed. I'm not sure it was a trap, but I saw that crazy *Survivor Man* on the TV make something similar on his show, so I think that's what it was."

"I didn't see anything like that. But I did see somethin' I found a bit peculiar. I think I spotted a puff of smoke comin' from the bluffs upstream of here. Ya know where the cliffs are on the west side of the river about five miles upstream?"

"Yeah, I know where you're talkin' about. I've never spent much time up there though. The river is fallin' too fast for good fishin,'" Nate answered.

"The water is fallin' too fast for trappin' too. And it's tough movin' through that narrow ravine. But I had just finished makin' a set in the last big hole at the base of that fast stretch, and was just lookin' up and enjoyin' the scenery when I noticed smoke. It seemed weird that someone had a fire up there. Might have been my imagination too, I dunno.

"But right now, I gotta get that otter back to my rig. They won't pay for 'em if they've croaked, and it hasn't been cold enough yet for the pelt to be worth anything."

"Well, good talkin' to ya. And thanks for the information. Good luck with your trapping. I'm Nate, by the way," Nate said, extending his hand.

"My name's Clint. We'll likely run into each other again. Take care," said the trapper as he shook Nate's hand and then moved toward his pack.

The man slung his otter-filled pack onto his back like it contained nothing heavier than a pair of wool socks and headed downstream. There goes a strong guy, a strong guy in very good physical condition, Nate thought as he watched him hike off.

36

Eliab and Yanoa were summoned by the King. Though it had happened many times, the wonder of receiving instruction directly from the Almighty was always fresh and exciting. This assignment was clear: Go and engage the enemy in the northern portion of a quadrant of the area the mortals called "Chiloquin County." The lives of men were in the balance.

This battle fascinated the angels. The King was certainly able to speak all the troops of the enemy out of existence with a single word, yet He chose to use them and other angels to wage war. Their effectiveness was determined by the quantity of faith-filled prayer that the mortals sent up to the King. Eliab and Yanoa knew they had great assignments. Their mortals were people who prayed! Other angels, they knew, were assigned to mortals that prayed hardly at all. Those unfortunate angels rarely got in on the battle.

Nate would probably never know it, but his parents were on their knees in his behalf for the better part of an hour, requesting God's protection and wisdom for their son.

The story about the smoke fascinated Nate. Two months, or even a month ago, the sight of smoke in this country would have sent everybody scrambling. Forest fires caused major damage every year, so they were taken very seriously. But it was cool enough, and there had been enough rain lately, that fires wouldn't be a threat again until late May. Still, that smoke was very interesting. Especially in the area that Clint had described. No one went in there. It was too steep and too rough—and there just wasn't any reason to go.

Nate had been forced into that country a few years ago when he had shot a buck with his bow west of there. He'd gotten a bad hit on the animal and it had traveled farther than normal before piling up. He had found the buck in the area where Clint had seen the smoke. Getting the venison out had been a major undertaking. The terrain was so rough that he had spent two days doing what should have been a two-hour job. He was not particularly excited about climbing around in that brush-covered rock pile, but he was very interested in finding the source of that smoke.

Instead of following the stream up to the entrance of the canyon and then climbing up the rocks, Nate decided to skirt to the west. That way the climb would be more gradual, and he could have a look around from the top. The roundabout way up was mostly over shale rock, which made for noisy, difficult walking. The vegetation in this area was primarily badly stunted rabbit brush and bunch grass. It was a desolate stretch of country even by Central Oregon standards. He was glad that the sun's heat was leached out by its fall angle, since there wasn't a bit of shade to be found. Warm enough as it was, the climb would have been unbearable in the heat of summer. The only wildlife to be seen was an occasional songbird and a red-tailed hawk slipping the thermals in search of an early lunch.

Even though this route was less steep than coming straight up from the river, it was still steep enough and made for rough going. Nate was winded within an hour of leaving the river, and he was only about half of the way to the top of the cliff where Clint had thought he saw the smoke. He decided to sit down on a large rock and take a water break. As he sat, drinking from his bottle of water, he thought about the events of the past few months. Starting with Gail's horseback riding accident, life had certainly been interesting. Somehow, in Nate's mind at least, all those strange events were not as much about the pain or injuries, or even the killings for that matter, as they were about the circumstances leading up to Mike's decision to become a follower of Christ.

He couldn't help but consider that he might be out of touch with reality, maybe even crazy. Do sane people get so caught up in taking advantage of opportunities to talk about Jesus Christ that everything else is secondary? As a Christian, shouldn't he feel terrible about shooting that man? And how about that guy Gail killed; wouldn't a true follower of Christ be knee-deep in guilt and remorse for being involved in that? Instead, no matter what should be, in Nate's mind Mike's experience eclipsed everything else. He was even worse at the Christian thing than he was with a shotgun; and he'd been doing it almost as long as he'd been shooting. One of these days he was going to find something that he was good at.

But that day wasn't likely to be today, Nate thought, as he stood up to continue his trek up the steep incline. As he gained elevation, he was able to see more and more of the countryside. On other days, the view of the stream running through the meadow, fringed by pines and then giving way to the thousands of acres of sagebrush and junipers, had inspired awe. Today, in the frame of mind that he was in, the panorama merely reminded him of his insignificance in the overall scope of things. The perspective of viewing "the big picture" could sometimes be depressing.

In another hour of steady walking Nate had reached the plateau. It was an enormous flat plane that stretched south for several miles and a couple of miles to the west. It appeared to be as flat as a tabletop where nothing larger than a jackrabbit would be able to hide, but Nate knew from experience that this was one of those things where appearance was different from the reality. There was a break running through the plateau that, unless you viewed it from the air, you couldn't see until you walked right up to it; from a distance you looked right over the top of it, never realizing it was there. A good-sized fresh water spring formed the break as its water had run to the river for the past seven thousand years. During spring runoff it was a sizeable stream of water. By fall it was nothing more than a small seep. But it provided a valuable animal sanctuary. The water from the spring produced a small area of lush vegetation that attracted a variety of wildlife. It was a haven for mountain bluebirds, chickadees, flickers, and meadowlarks and a host of other songbirds. Rabbits, chipmunks, and golden mantels also took up residence in the hidden island of green. Deer and antelope frequented the area, too, especially in dry weather. The succulent vegetation attracted them like the dessert bar at a buffet-style restaurant attracted Nate.

It was in this oasis, an area of ten to fifteen acres, where Nate had shot the deer that led him down into the steep ravine a few years earlier. He had walked approximately two miles from the nearest dirt road and set up a stand in an aspen tree that was perfectly situated above the spring. A buck had come in to get an evening drink and found an arrow instead. Since he knew from that experience that he could go from the plateau to the river through that break, he decided to use it now. He didn't know of any other way down the cliffs to the river, and he was determined to find the source of the smoke that Trapper Clint had told him about.

He approached the spring from the north and was surprised at how thick the current bushes were on this slope, with its southern exposure. He hadn't noticed that when he was here before. The currents had obviously been loaded with berries, which would have been ripe in the first part of September. A variety of birds were feeding on the fruit that had dried on the bushes. Robins, with their red-orange breasts, were the most abundant, and Nate was surprised to see a few cedar waxwings here as well. He couldn't remember seeing them in Central Oregon before. There was plenty of bear sign around too. Those big brutes were sure to cash in on a berry bonanza like this.

Nate was thinking that he had better keep an eye out for bruins; he knew he wouldn't want to accidentally startle one of those fellows, when the bushes exploded. Quail were suddenly in the air, flying every direction. The Browning was on Nate's shoulder and barking almost automatically. He emptied the gun and reloaded five times before the covey quit erupting from the brush. It would have been a lot easier with the dogs; he had to search through the current bushes for nearly thirty minutes to retrieve the eight quail he had managed to bring down.

All the shooting erased any thought of stealth in his approach to the cliffs. The barrage of shooting made everyone and everything in the area aware of his presence. "That was brilliant," he said out loud. "I might as well have hired a brass band to announce my arrival." Disgusted with himself, he debated whether or not he should just turn around and take the easy way back to his rig or continue into the rough terrain. After a few minutes of deliberation he decided he was here, he may as well keep going.

Using a game trail that paralleled the small, nearly dry streambed, Nate moved eastward toward the river at a fast pace. The walking was easy, and he was making good time, until after about a quarter mile, he realized that down in this draw, in the fairly thick undergrowth, he wasn't going to see much of anything. "Another bright move," he said to himself. I gotta get outta this hole so I can see something, or I'm just wasting my time." He started searching for a trail that would take him back up to the rim for a look around. Within minutes another game trail intersected the one he had been using. He turned up it, and though it was steep, he was back up on the plateau within a few minutes.

He was only a couple of hundred yards from where the plateau ended when he got out of the draw. Looking toward the east he could see across the river to the rolling sagebrush-covered hills. Out in the distance, Nate guessed it to be about a mile away, a small herd of antelope was running up one of the hills. He couldn't see anything chasing them; they apparently were just running because they liked to run. They ran single file over the crown of the hill, and their white rumps looked like popcorn just before each one went out of sight. The sight of them made Nate grin. They looked nothing but graceful from this distance, but up close they always made Nate think of a clown. Their nostrils looked too big for their heads, and their heads looked too large for their bodies, and their brown coats with the white stripes seemed like a fashion statement gone wrong.

The sun was directly overhead, and when Nate checked his watch, he was surprised to see that it was already 12:30. It had taken him half the day to get here, so it was going to take the better part of the rest of the day to get out. That didn't leave much time for investigation. Being out in this country after dark wasn't his idea of a good time. Especially since it was the dark of the moon, and it would be so dark tonight that he would hardly be able to see past the end of his large Irish nose once the sun went down. He made his way over to the lip of the ravine and sat down on a boulder.

Finding a spot that allowed him a view both to the north and south as well as east, he decided to watch for smoke while he plucked and drew the birds he had shot. He didn't want their flavor to be tainted by having their entrails in them all day. They were delicious birds if properly cleaned and cooked. Nate thought that most people who didn't like the taste of wild meat probably had never had any that had been taken care of correctly. Busy at the task, the sun warm on his shoulders, he wished he wasn't in a hurry. He could be easily enticed into curling up on a nest of ponderosa pine needles and taking a nice afternoon nap if there were time.

The task of cleaning the birds had just got under way when a flock of Clark's Nutcrackers arrived. These noisy gray and black birds had an uncanny ability to find a handout. While their diet consisted mainly of pine seeds, they were more than happy to share whatever food was available. They apparently didn't have any qualms about cannibalism, since they eagerly jumped on the offal from the quail. Nate had often wondered how the birds located a food source. You might go all day without seeing one of them, but all you had to do was open a sandwich bag, and you'd have a flock of this small member of the crow family hopping around, filling the air with their trademark "*kraak*." The racket they made was annoying, but you couldn't help but find their bravery endearing. Normally, given a few minutes, these audacious twelve-inch birds would be eating out of your hand. But this flock, though obviously hungry, was not going to get too close.

By the time that Nate had cleaned his hands with a little water from the bottle in his pack the nutcrackers had finished cleaning up the quail parts. Now the birds were jumping around in a nearby juniper, "*kraaking*" in insistence for more. Breaking out his lunch, Nate shared some of the bread crust from his sandwich and a handful of his tortilla chips. As glad as the birds appeared to be at getting the quail, if their hollering was any indication, they were even more excited about the chips and bread, but they still kept their distance.

The racket the birds were making almost drowned out the noise that came from the direction of the river. From somewhere below, Nate thought he heard something. And then the sound came again. It was a noise that he knew he should recognize. It sounded like something halfway between a growl and a cough. The sound came twice, then a third time. Between Nate's hearing being well below average and the commotion that the birds were causing, he couldn't distinguish what the sound was, or precisely where it was coming from, but he knew it wasn't a normal sound from the forest. He scrambled to get the Browning, and his quick movement sent the nutcrackers flapping away.

Stuffing the remnants of lunch into the pocket of the hunting vest and tossing the field-dressed quail into the game pouch, he started trying to find a way down the cliff toward the noise. A straight approach was obviously impossible. Directly below him was a shear drop for around a hundred feet. The drop ended in a boulder patch, surrounded by currant bushes. Nate couldn't see what was on the downhill side of the boulders. To the left there was a steep shale slide that appeared to be far too steep to negotiate. It looked like the only option was to go back the way he came, get into the draw again, follow it to somewhere beneath the boulders, and hope there was a way to cut over to the source of the strange noise without going all the way to the bottom. Before taking off, Nate tried to orientate his position, and the approximate position of the noise, with some identifiable landmarks. Just to the north of the lunch spot was a ponderosa that had been struck by lightning. The tree was dead, the top gone, and a crooked break in its orange bark went half the way down the snag. Down the cliff, one of the largest boulders in the group had a small jack pine tree growing out of a crack on top of it. Nate tried to imprint these images in his mind so that he would have some points of reference when he crawled out of the draw down below.

Back in the draw, Nate tried to calculate how far he needed to go before he tried to side hill out and end up in the general area of where the noise came from. He counted out two hundred paces on the path that paralleled the little spring fed stream, thinking that it might be about the right distance. The sides of the draw were much steeper here, and Nate wasn't sure that he would be able to make his way out. While he was looking around for a trail out, his eyes caught on something unusual downstream. In a spot where the creek bed formed a small natural bowl, it looked like someone had made an attempt to put a small dam in the creek. Moving closer, he could clearly see that rocks, sticks, and mud had been used to block the stream's meager flow. The result was a pool about two feet long, a foot and a half wide, and eight inches deep.

Nate could feel the hairs on the back of his neck stand up when he noticed some crude steps cut into the ground on the steep slope of the draw to his left. Someone had gone to a lot of effort to make a passable trail down to this stream; someone who apparently was using the crude pool as a source of water. The question was, who?

Visions of pot growers and fugitive murderers were running through Nate's mind while he contemplated what his next move should be. He was inclined to make tracks out of here as fast as he could, report what he had found to the police, and let them worry about it. But what was he going to tell the police? That he had found a small primitive dam in a creek in the middle of nowhere? I'm sure that'll get 'em right out here, he thought. Really, what did he have? A lame story of what he thought were poacher's traps, a little dam in a trickle of a stream, and some earthen steps. It wasn't exactly earth-shattering evidence of crime. No, he needed to get his imagination under control, follow these steps, and try to figure out what was going on.

37

Even with the steps that were carved into the hard soil, it was a hard climb. In fact, after climbing just the first dozen steps, Nate had to stop for breath. It would be a lot easier going if he had both hands free, so he took off his belt and fashioned a makeshift gun strap out of it so he could use both hands for climbing. That made a big difference, and he made it twenty steps before he had to rest again. As he stood resting, he glanced at his watch—1:45. He had to get moving, or he was going to get caught out here after dark, and that would probably mean he'd be out here all night. He was too old for sleeping on the ground! Besides, if he didn't make it home, Amy would be calling out the National Guard—and she was persuasive enough to get them to come.

Another twenty steps and Nate stopped again. When he could breathe normally again, he caught the scent of a foul odor. There was a dead critter around here; no, that wasn't quite right. It was something rotten. No, it was sewage. He smelled sewage.

Not eager to continue into the scene that his mind was conjuring up, he rested longer than was really necessary. During the extended rest he noticed a pile of feathers that looked to have come from nutcrackers. No wonder they were more wary than usual. Then, while he was trying to convince himself to start moving again, he heard the sound. What was that growling, coughing noise? He'd heard it before today, but where? Then it came again, three times in quick succession and Nate realized where he had heard this particular sound before. On board a charter boat, on a bottom fishing trip. This was the sound of someone violently heaving. Someone was extremely sick.

Moving again, Nate took only a couple of more steps, and the ground began to level out enough so that the steps weren't necessary, and he hesitated long enough to un-sling the shotgun and put his belt back around his waist. Somehow he felt instantly better with the Browning in his hands. He moved cautiously forward, straining to see until his eyes burned, he realized that he was starting to hyperventilate. It was then that he did what he should have been doing throughout the day; he called out to his Lord God for wisdom and protection. Even while he was silently beseeching God, he noticed the dark opening in the brush, up against the rocks. It appeared to be the mouth of a cave. Moving closer, still unable to see past the black opening, he heard moaning from inside. He moved right up to the cave and tried to see in. All that he could determine was that there had been a fire here recently; in fact, it was still smoldering. The stench of sewage mingled with the scent of the dying fire.

Fumbling through the pockets of his shell vest he searched for the mini Maglite flashlight he always carried, hoping that the batteries were still good. He found it and twisted the top, and to his great relief, it lit up. Stepping forward, he shined the little beam inside the cave. At first he couldn't see anything in the cave; then, as his eyes adjusted, he was appalled to see the figure of a man lying in a fetal position against the wall of the cave. The man was shivering uncontrollably, and a low moan escaped him when the beam of Nate's flashlight hit his eyes.

Nate quickly stooped and stepped across the remnants of the fire.

He knelt beside the man, who was cowering against the rock wall, shaking uncontrollably. Nate leaned the shotgun against the rock and reached down and placed his left hand on the man's forehead. He was burning up with fever. Not knowing what to say, Nate said, "Are you okay?" and instantly felt like an idiot for asking that when the man was so obviously anything but okay.

The suffering man tried to say something, but Nate did not understand what it was. He looked him over more closely now and was mortified to see that the poor guy was dressed in nothing but tattered filthy rags and was hardly more than a skeleton. Nate pulled his water bottle from his vest and held it to the man's lips, but he seemed too weak to drink. Struggling to decide on an appropriate and effective course of action, Nate shrugged out of his shell vest, removed his flannel shirt, and threw it over the shivering man. He put the vest back on and moved to the fire and blew on the embers to see if it could be coaxed back to life. A couple of ruby coals responded to his breath, so he hurried out of the cave to try to find some firewood.

The wood in the surrounding area had been picked clean. This poor guy must have been living here for a while. Finally, Nate found a big old dead ponderosa whose bark had begun to slip. He pulled off a large chunk of the bark and placed several smaller pieces on top of it and pulled the whole mess back to the cave. The man was still lying just as Nate had left him, still moaning and shaking. Nate went to work on getting the fire going. He crumbled some bark into powder between his hands and blew on the ashes until he saw the glow of a live coal, then he gently poured a measure of the crushed bark on that coal. After a minute or two a wisp of smoke rose, and with a little huffing, Nate coaxed a small flame out of it. Then he added larger flakes of bark until he had a good-sized flame licking at the wood.

With the fire going, Nate turned his attention back to the suffering man. His stomach knotted when he realized that the shotgun that he had left beside the man when he went out to gather wood was gone. He frantically looked around the cave, hoping he was mistaken about where he had left the weapon. In his panicked visual search, the beam of the flashlight revealed that the cave was a lot larger than he had originally thought. In fact, there was another room connected to this one by a small opening. As Nate's beam illuminated this second room, he located his Browning; it was in another man's hands, and it was pointed straight at his face.

"Whoa there, fella," Nate said. His hands were raised and his voice was shaking. "I'm here to help you. I don't want any trouble. Just tell me whatcha want, and I'll do my best to make it happen." His statements were met with silence. He was left with his mind racing and his heart rate matching that of a frightened rabbit. Seconds passed, and nothing happened. The shotgun was still pointed right at his face, and the expression on the man's face that was holding it hadn't changed. As the initial fright began to subside, Nate's thought process cleared a little, and he realized that there were four others in the back part of the cave with the one that held the gun, so there was a total of at least six. Four were men, and two were women. It also registered in his malfunctioning mind that they all were dark-skinned with black hair. So, there was a possibility that they didn't speak English.

He decided to try again. "Amigo," he said tapping his chest. Still no response, so Nate decided to see what would happen if he just left. Half a step backward brought the distinct click of the safety on the Browning clicking off. Okay, leaving was a bad idea; but what to do? He couldn't just stand here until the guy with the gun needed to tighten his finger. After standing in place, enveloped in fear and indecision for several seconds, the sound of the safety clicking back on was very pleasing. There was more waiting, more wondering, a whole lot more sweating, and a little more observation. All these people looked gaunt and sick. They were starving to death.

When he couldn't stand the silence any longer, Nate started

again, "Look, I don't know what's goin' on here. And I really don't care to know. But it looks like you all could use some food. How long has it been since you've et anythin'? I've got some quail here in my vest, I'm just gonna take the vest off and get them out. If you'd like, I can roast 'em over the fire for ya. Would that be okay?" He slowly started to shrug the vest off his shoulders and there was no movement and, better yet, no sound of the safety, which Nate interpreted as a good sign—or was he confused about what click was off and what one was on? Trembling, he kept moving, taking the eight birds out of the game pouch one at a time and placing them by the fire.

Emboldened by the fact that there was still no comment from the cave dwellers, he reached into the front pocket of his Levis and took out his folding Buck pocketknife. He used it to cut the heads, wingtips, and lower legs off the birds. When the quail were ready to cook, Nate slowly stood and said, "I'm gonna go out now and cut some willows to use for a spit for roastin' these birds. Iffen you want to shoot me, have at it, but I'm not gonna stand around in here playin' Texas Hold 'Em all afternoon whilest you folks starve ta death."

He slowly moved to the opening of the cave and stepped out into the sunlight. He thought that the fact that he hadn't been blasted to raven food was another good sign. It took several seconds for his eyes to adjust to the bright sunlight; while he waited to regain his sight he considered just taking off at a dead run. He was old and slow, but none of the people inside the cave looked like they were in good enough physical condition to catch him. He could be out of shotgun range before the eyes of the guy with the gun adjusted to the light. Instead, he went to a nearby clump of willows and cut the components he thought he would need to construct a spit for roasting the quail.

When he got back inside the cave, he saw that one of his new friends had put some more bark on the fire, and the first man that

Nate had found had been moved to a spot closer to the heat. Despite the man being right in the warmth of the fire, he continued to shiver and shake, obviously seriously feverish. The shotgun was nowhere in sight. Before beginning to construct the spit, Nate again tried to get the sick man to take some water, sure that the man must be seriously dehydrated. This time the sick man managed to swallow a couple of sips of the liquid. When he was satisfied that the man would not drink any more, Nate turned to the task of putting a makeshift rotisserie spit together. It was a simple structure. He made a pile of rocks, gathered from those that littered the floor of the cave, on either side of the fire. These pyramids each held a forked willow stick in an upright position. Another willow, about an inch in diameter, skewering the birds, would lie across the forked sticks. This would hold the quail about four to six inches above the fire, close enough for them to cook but hopefully far enough away to not burn to a crisp.

Nate rubbed the small game birds with crumbs from the tortilla chips left over from lunch. It was the only way he knew of getting some seasoning on the birds. He preferred to fry quail when he was going to eat them, but he didn't notice a frying pan lying around anywhere. Busy at the task, he was shocked by the sound of a feminine voice asking, "Why you here?"

Not knowing how much English the woman might understand, Nate wasn't sure how to answer. The ensuing silence became uncomfortable. Nate supposed his silence looked like it was being used to construct a lie. In fact he was trying to compose a statement that would convey the truth. Finally he simply said, "Lookin' for you, I guess."

More silence, then, "Why?"

"Look, I wasn't lookin' for you, exactly. I heard about some rustling this summer, then I found a couple of traps. I'm just out here tryin' to figure out what's goin' on. What I wanna know now is, what are you doin' out here, and what's wrong with your friend?" Nate pointed at the man shivering by the fire.

Now it was the lady cave dweller's turn to hesitate as she tried to find a way to formulate a meaningful answer. Nate pushed the birds onto the willow skewer as he waited for her response. He glanced at the other four refugees who had come out into the front part of the cave to witness the exchange. Close up they looked even more gaunt and tired. Their clothes were tattered and dirty. It was apparent that they had been holed up for more than a few days. Nate was studying the group's spokeswoman as she struggled for the right words. Her age was hard to estimate. With her drawn look and unwashed hair, she could have been anywhere from twenty-five to forty. It was the same with the others; their haggard looks made guessing their ages impossible. Their clothes were nothing but rags, and the men all had scraggly beards. It was a rough-looking bunch, but somehow Nate no longer felt frightened. As a group, especially since they had his gun, they could certainly overpower him. But for some reason, he was quite sure they were not going to try to hurt him.

Finally, after the birds were in place over the fire, the woman spoke, and her answer was simple. "We is lost. Miguel," she pointed to the man by the fire, "he mucho sick. Throwing away, and other end, too. We all little sick, but he is bad sick."

"What's your name?" Nate asked.

"I Agripina. I called Aggie."

"Aggie, how did you get here?"

"We walk."

"No, I don't mean here to this cave, I mean here in Oregon, in the United States."

"We come from Mexico in the back of a truck. It was mucho long and mucho hot and mucho bumping."

"Did you all come here together?" Nate asked, waving his hand at the group that was now gathered around the fire over which the quail roasted.

"Sí. Together. We pay all our monies to get here. To get work. We has no good jobs in Mexico. We was gonna get work on ranch. Rosa," Aggie pointed to the other woman, "and me, we gonna cook. The mens, they gonna be vaqueros."

"So what happened? How'd you end up out here in this cave?"

"The man who bring us, he put us in barn. He say he gonna take us to ranch later. But then another man come, they argue, say no work on ranch, we gotta go back to Mexico. He say we hafta pay for truck…but we got no monies. So we wait till man leaves, then we go. Miguel," she pointed to the sick man. "He makes a hole in wall, and we go to the woods."

Throughout the conversation, Nate was slowly spinning the stick that held the quail. The eyes of everyone but the unconscious man were glued to the browning birds. These people didn't need to be able to speak English to tell him that they were hungry.

"And you ended up here? Why didn't you head south? There should be work in California."

"When we leave the barn, woman sees. She says she make to man take us back. She says we wait. But the man who says us to pay for goin' back comes out the woods and they fight. He puts rope on her neck. They is a big crack, and she dead. Then we run. Mans with guns chase, but we hide. Woman on horse looks. But we know to hide. We have hided at the border many times."

"Why didn't you go somewhere to get help?"

"We, how you say, illegals. No one helps. Man will say we kill woman. We must only hide."

"I'll help you. But you hafta trust me. Let me go get help. This man," Nate indicated the sick guy "has to see a doctor. And all of you, you can't survive in the winter. We get tons of snow here. There is gonna be nothin' to eat. And it will be very cold. You'll all freeze to death if you don't starve to death first. I'll go and bring people to help you."

For the first time since the conversation began, Aggie turned to her friends and began speaking to them in Spanish. Nate had no idea what she was saying, but as she gestured several times toward him, and then at the man on the ground, the tone of her voice belied the fact that she was pleading with the group. He hoped that she was pleading for them to let him go for help. Whatever she was saying was met with several verbal outbursts from the others. There was shouting and hand-waving and gesturing. Finally silence ensued.

After what must have been a full minute of silence, Aggie turned to Nate and looked him directly in the eyes for the first time and asked, "Why you wants to help us?"

Nate was struck more by the intensity of the woman's coal-black eyes than by her question. Her eyes were so dark in the fire-lit cave, he couldn't see her pupils. They were so piercing that he had trouble meeting their gaze. He felt that without really trying, she could incinerate him with those eyes. Like a third grader afraid of giving the wrong answer to the school's principal, he hesitated what he felt was too long before quietly replying, "You need help. Jesus said that when someone needs help, and you help 'em, it's just like you were helping him."

"You, how you say? You be Christian?"

"I sure hope so."

Aggie pointed to one of the men on the other side of the fire, "Pedro, he says he is Christian. Always saying Jesus take care of him. But Pedro, he is here just like us. Don't look like Jesus takes care of him!"

The tenseness of this conversation was broken by Miguel having a racking fit of coughing.

When the coughing subsided, Nate said, "Maybe that's why I'm here. Now, can I go and fetch you some help?"

Receiving no reply, Nate stood up and took the willow holding the skewered quail from above the fire. Five sets of eyes watched the now golden birds. Extending the stick toward Aggie, he said,

"Here, I know they're small and won't keep your stomach from thinkin' your throat's been cut for long, but it's all I got. I'm gonna take off now. You can jump me, or your buddy can grab my shotgun from wherever he hid it and shoot me, but unless somebody stops me, I'm goin' for help. I'd really appreciate y'all bein' here when I get back. And the sick fella there will appreciate it even more. 'Cause if he doesn't get to a hospital right quick, he's gonna die."

Aggie reached out and took the meat-bearing stick from Nate. Her large black eyes were filled with tears when she said, "Gracias. I don't know about them," gesturing toward the men with a sideways nod of her head, "But Rosa and I be's here. We is tired and scared. They send us back to Mexico is better than this."

Nate didn't know what he expected when he stepped out the entrance to the cave and straightened up, but what did happen he certainly didn't expect. A voice behind him said, "Here is gun." Nate turned around to find one of the men extending the butt of the Browning toward him. "I come wid you," the man said.

"Naw," Nate responded, "you keep the gun and stay here to help the others. And, oh—" Digging into the vest's pockets, he dug out about a dozen shotgun shells and handed them to the man. "Here's some ammo in case somethin' happens before I get back. Will ya be here when I get back?"

"*Sí,*" the man answered, "we is done. We starve. And Miguel, he need help!"

"What's your name?" Nate asked.

"Paulos."

"Paulos, I'm gonna get a crew of search and rescue folks back here for you just as fast as I can. But you need to stay here and take care of the rest of this crew till I get back. I'm leavin' the scattergun with you. You know how to use it?"

"*Sí.* I think."

Nate took a few minutes and demonstrated how to load, unload, and fire the gun, and then handed it back to the young Mexican.

38

Looking at his watch while he climbed down the crude steps that had been cut into the ground, Nate saw that it was after four in the afternoon. He was going to have to really beat feet to get back to his rig before dark! As he got to the small stream that he had followed down here, he decided that the best course of action would probably be to head due west toward the highway. He was acquainted with that route from packing that deer out of here. Once he got to the highway, maybe he could flag down a ride. He hadn't put his thumb out to hitch a ride in going on forty years, but he thought it still might work.

Climbing out of the draw was a lot harder than going down had been. Trying to move fast, he was huffing for wind within half a mile. He knew he was going to have to pace himself a little, or he was not going to be bringing help to anyone but the buzzards when they came to pick his bones. That'd be quite a meal, he thought, patting his ample gut. Traveling cross-country was a little different than jogging on the treadmill at the gym.

The rough, rocky ground out on the open area on the plateau slowed him down even more, but he couldn't afford to turn an ankle or fall out here in the middle of nowhere. It took the better part of an hour for him to cross the plateau and reach the old logging road that he had used on the deer hunt. The smooth surface of the old dirt road felt like heaven on his feet. From there, his memory told him, it was about three or four miles to the highway. He hoped his faulty old memory was right this time. He wanted to be on the highway before dark, and dark was less than two hours away.

Normally when Nate went for a walk in the woods, he had some type of prey in mind. Hunting and fishing, he moved slowly, observing the wildlife and their habitat. This hike had none of the components of one of those leisurely strolls. He was on a mission and not paying much attention to anything but the road. He was hoping with every step that he would hear the rumble of an eighteen-wheeler out on the highway, or catch a glimpse of a flash of chrome from a car headed to or from California. As usual when he was in a hurry, the road just seemed to be way longer than he remembered. Rounding each corner, he expected to see some evidence that he was almost to the highway, but around each corner was nothing but another corner.

A young Rough-legged hawk took off from its perch at the top of a forty-foot jack pine beside the road, and the sound of its wings beating to gain elevation startled Nate into noticing. It was a magnificent bird, with a wingspan of over four feet. The white and black mottled head and breast of the bird made him especially beautiful. In what seemed an effortless move, the raptor caught an air current that lifted him high, and pulled him to the west. Man, Nate thought, if I could move like that I'd be back to my rig in nothin' flat. The bird disappeared from sight, and Nate continued his hike feeling rested, somehow.

It was dusk when Nate finally heard the hiss of tires on pavement. He had begun to think that he was on the wrong road or had taken the wrong fork of one the spur roads back there somewhere. He had almost turned around and gone back a couple of times; but now that he could hear the highway traffic, he was glad that he'd been stubborn. "No surprise there," Amy would say.

Out on the pavement, Nate headed north. He'd walked about a hundred yards before he heard a rig coming from behind him. Making sure that he was well outside the fog line, he turned to face the vehicle and stuck out his thumb. It was an SUV, plenty of room for a passenger, Nate thought, but the light-colored Honda didn't even pretend to slow down. He knew it was a cliché, but he had a really lonely feeling as he watched the red glow of the taillights speed north.

He continued walking up the shoulder of the road as dusk turned to dark. Stars were fighting through the black curtain of the night sky. The distinct "pinging" of a hunting nighthawk surprised Nate. Normally the bullbats, as the bird was locally known, left Central Oregon sometime in mid-September. This late-leaving bird better get the trip south started pretty soon. The flying insects that provided the bird's diet were getting scarce as the high desert's nights began to get cold. Nate wondered what had kept this bird, with its white-barred wings, in the area so long.

What he wondered even more was why there wasn't any traffic on this normally busy highway. He'd been walking for half an hour, and the Honda SUV was the only northbound vehicle that he had seen. And there had been only half a dozen rigs moving south. It was kind of spooky, Nate thought. Had there been a catastrophe while he was cooking supper for the illegal aliens? Continuing to walk, he noticed a mile post sign that read 177. He knew that his rig was on a road that left the highway just this side of milepost 174. Three more miles of walking, and his calves were already on fire.

He heard the rattling before he glimpsed the headlights coming up behind him. Finally, he thought, now if he could only get this guy to stop and pick him up. As the rig got closer, the rattling got louder. This outfit was pulling a horse trailer, which made it highly likely that this was a local and more apt to stop and give him a lift.

The fact that it wasn't moving very fast was another plus. Nate held his hand up at chest level and extended his thumb high.

"All right," Nate said out loud as the truck and trailer slowed and pulled to the shoulder of the road ahead of him. He limped to the rig as fast as his tired feet would take him. Looking at the trailer as he went past he saw that it was a four-horse Featherlite that had seen a better day. There were more scratches than paint on the outside and a single horse inside. The old Ford truck made the setup a matched set. It looked like it may have been blue when it first rolled off the lot two and a half decades ago, but now the pickup was more dings and scratches than paint. In other words, Nate suspected that this outfit wasn't packing a gentleman rancher, but a workingman, a true buckaroo.

Nate wasn't surprised when he wrestled the passenger door of the truck open and started to crawl inside. The driver looked like one of the bad guys from an old Clint Eastwood movie. He was sporting a mustache that would have made a walrus proud, thick and hanging well below his chin on either side of his mouth. Long scraggly grey hair fell out from beneath a flat-brimmed Stetson. His pearl snap wrangler shirt was so faded Nate couldn't tell what color it had been when it was new. His Wrangler jeans couldn't have been any whiter if they'd been washed in battery acid. This guy was all cowboy, right down to his down-in-the-heel pair of roper boots. The only item of clothing the crusty old guy had on that looked like it may have been originally purchased in this century was the wild rag he was wearing around his neck; it was a deep royal blue and was tied in a perfect square knot.

"Howdy. You lost or sumpen? Ain't no houses fer miles," the crusty old man grunted.

"Nope. Ain't lost, but I sure do need a short hop ride. My rig is only a couple miles up the road. I'm sorry I stopped you for such a short lift, but I've got a kind of emergency goin' on. I didn't think anyone was ever gonna come by."

"That so? They's a big tangle of a accident down the road 'bout ten miles. Ain't no traffic bein' let through from either direction. I was sittin' in the string of parked cars tryin' to go south but finally decided to turn around and sit it out in Cindy's Kitchen up in Rosland. Might just as well nurse a cup of Joe and jack my jaws whilest I's waitin.' 'Specially since both the heater and the radio in this old pile are busted."

Well, I am glad you came along and picked me up. My dogs are sure enough barkin' at me. I've been walking 'most all day."

The cowboy groomed his mustache with his thumb and index finger before saying, "Ya said you are mixed up in some kinda emergency. What's goin' on?"

After debating how much information to dispense, Nate chose to play it safe and simply said, "Oh, not that big a deal. A friend is sick out in the woods. I'm tryin' to figure a way to get 'im out before he gets any worse."

"Where's he at?"

"Oh, back by the river on Forest Service Land. Ya know those cliffs just behind the Z?"

"Shore do. I've rode for the Z every fall roundup since I was a pup. 'At's some rough country, there now. Shot a big ole cat back in 'ere a few years back. T'was a two-hundred-pound male. Took to killin' calves one summer, 'bout '65 or '66 I think. Them cats'll take a calf a week once they get started. Easier than catchin' deer or elk I guess. Won't stop till their hide is dryin' on the side of the barn. Got a friend a mine to bring his pack of hounds out, and they run 'im fer miles till he went up a young ponderosa about halfway betwixt the river and the rim. 'At's where I finally punched that old painter's ticket. Rancher give me forty bucks for 'im. And that was a pretty good paycheck back in the day. All I had to pay for the use of the hounds was a fifth of Jack Daniels. What was you fellas doin' in that country?"

"Oh, we were just fooling around, trying to find some quail or grouse."

"'At's a fer walk for a few birds, ain't it?"

"We didn't really expect to walk so far, we just got carried away with the beauty of the day, I guess. Then he took sick. That kind of ruined everything."

"Where's your scatter gun?"

This old geezer is asking too many questions, thought Nathan. He's either suspicious or fishin' for something. "The loggin' road that my rig is parked on is just around the corner. Ya can drop me off anywhere. I 'preciate the ride."

"Not a problem. I'd take you on down to your rig but with this trailer hooked on the back, I'd never get turned around to get outta there."

"Hey, that's okay. I'm just glad ya saved my old feet with the ride ya gave."

Nate didn't even turn around as the truck and trailer rumbled off; he just waved over his shoulder and he walked in the direction of his pickup as fast as his sore and tired legs would carry him. "Man," he said out loud to himself, "I'm gettin' too old for this stuff."

It was totally dark by the time Nate got to his Dodge. He had to use his little mini Maglite flashlight a couple of times to keep on the trail. Even in his struggle to move quickly, the miracle of the enormous myriad of stars in the black velvet sky caught his attention. They sparkled like diamonds poured out on a jeweler's cloth. The diesel engine started without so much as a hiccup, and within minutes Nate was out on Highway 197 headed north. "Let's see," he mumbled, "first I need to get home and get a call in to the county. Try to get the search and rescue crew to go out and pick that ragtag bunch up and get them some medical attention. Amy's probably wonderin' what happened to me. She might already have 'em lookin' for me."

There was still no traffic on the highway. As he rolled through

Rosland he noticed that the Oregon Department of Transportation had barricades up detouring traffic around the accident by way of the High Lakes Highway. They must plan to have the road blocked awhile, he thought. That detour would take ya two hours out of the way.

Driving by Cindy's Kitchen, he observed that the old cowboy's truck and trailer were not in the parking lot. What he couldn't see was that the outfit was parked behind Vic's Tavern, and the old buckaroo was in the phone booth that hung on the side of the building, saying, "You still willin' to pay for information about the location of them Mexes that bolted on ya a couple of months ago? I think I might have somethin' for ya iffen ya are. I picked up an owl hoot on the highway this evenin,' and he's found somethin' tha' has 'im all fired up, and I got a sneaky 'spicion that it has somethin' to do with your runaways."

39

Amy was standing at the door when Nate climbed out of his pickup and started into the house. "Where've you been? I was startin' to think some old bear with poor taste finally swallowed ya."

"You know that ain't no bear in the woods big 'nough to swaller me. Four or five of 'em could eat for a week on my old carcass. They'd all likely die from high cholesterol, though."

"I wish you'd get in the habit of takin' your cell phone with you so you could call and tell me where you're at when you're gonna be late like this. I get worried."

"There wouldn't be reception if I did have that stupid phone with me. T'wouldn't do me any good. Ya had reason to be concerned this time, though. I'll tell ya 'bout it soon's I make a couple of calls."

"Ya want I should fix you somethin' to eat?"

"That'd be great, but it needs to be something quick. I'll probably be leavin' again shortly."

Amy's eyes got big, and her eyebrows went up. Nate rarely went anywhere in the evening, except to meet with their Bible study group. "Leavin' to go where? What's goin' on?"

Nate rubbed his forehead with both hands. "I'm sorry. I really don't have time to talk right now. Listen in on the phone calls that

I'm gonna make in the next couple of minutes, and you'll get the picture. Then I'll fill you in on the rest." He was rooting through the cabinet beneath the phone table as he talked.

"What're you lookin' for?" Amy asked.

"I thought we had a Chiloquin County phonebook in here," Nate replied with frustration in his voice.

"We do. Here, let me get it," Amy said. She pulled out the small book almost instantly and handed it to Nate.

"Thanks," he said and started thumbing for the Chiloquin County Sheriff's Department non-emergency number. Finding the number, he quickly dialed. "Ah, come on," he said, clicking the phone off. "They've got it on a recording!"

"Well, Nate, why don't you calm down and tell me what's going on, and maybe we can come up with a solution."

It only took Nate about ten minutes to summarize his day. He turned to Amy, nodded, and said, "So, I gotta get back down there and get that guy to the hospital. I'm tellin' ya, he's in bad shape. I don't know if he'll make it till morning without he gets some IV fluids."

"Well, before ya go runnin' back down there in the dark, why not give Gail a call and see if she has any ideas?" Amy was making a sandwich as she talked. Handing it to Nate, she said, "Here, work on this while I call Gail."

Nate hadn't realized how hungry he was until he started on the sandwich. He enjoyed the first one so much, by the time Amy came back into the kitchen he had made a second and was halfway through it. "What'd she say?" he asked around a full mouth of roast beef on sourdough bread.

"She said that she was gonna give Mike a call and see if there's any chance that he might be able to help out. But she said it's a little touchy since the group you found is outside Mike's county. He was on the 7 a.m. to 7 p.m. shift today, so she thinks she should be able to get a hold of him and call us right back."

"Okay, but I hope she hurries. I really don't want to go down there alone, but I will if that's what it takes to get those people some help."

Amy moved close to Nate and brushed some stray breadcrumbs from his beard. "Ya know, Nate, you can't save the world all by yourself. You're not eighteen anymore, and I hate to be the one to remind you, but you weren't ten feet tall or bulletproof when you were eighteen. You need to get some rest. How much help you gonna be to those folks if you pass out or have a heart attack or somethin'? You've been up since 5 a.m., and you walked all day. You gotta get some sleep."

"I got the rest of forever to sleep, but those folks aren't gonna even have a tomorrow if they don't get some medical attention."

The phone rang, and Nate involuntarily jumped. Amy answered, "Hello. Hey, Gail. Okay, here he is."

Amy handed the phone to Nate, "This is Gail."

"Hi, Gail. Were you able to talk to Mike?"

"Yeah. I got him on his cell while he was driving home from work. He said that you aren't gonna get any help from the Chiloquin County Sheriff's Department tonight, though. They have some big mess goin' on down on Highway 197 at the Highway 58 junction. A truck loaded with some kinda HAZMAT stuff overturned when the driver swerved to miss an elk. They've got every available officer on the scene tryin' to keep people away until a cleanup crew can get there and get the poison cleaned up. It looks like both the highways are gonna be closed most of the night, at least."

"Oh, that's great! I knew there'd been an accident and the road had been closed for a while, but I didn't know there was a spill. But I gotta get back down there and get at least the one guy out and to the hospital. He's in really bad shape, Gail."

The phone went quiet for a moment, then Gail said, "Tell you what, let me call Mike back and see if he's willing to round up some ATVs and go down there with us tonight. But he is just comin' off a twelve-hour shift, same as me. So I'm not too sure that he's gonna think that traipsin' around through the pucker brush in the dark sounds like a good plan. I'll call ya right back."

Nate paced from the dining room to the kitchen and back, then back into the kitchen, opened the refrigerator door, and then closed it without taking anything out. He was headed back to the dining room again when Amy grabbed his arm and whispered, "Nate, slow down. You're workin' yourself into a froth here. Come here," she took his hand and led him into the family room and pushed him into his recliner. "You think you're gonna solve this problem? You ever consider prayin' about this? Don't cha think that God might know about those people out there? Why don't cha spend some time askin' him what you should do?"

Nate's first response was irritation; but, after thinking about what she had said, he had to agree that she was right. He hadn't asked God about what he should do. He was relying on his own ideas and strength, and that usually didn't turn out so well. "Okay, you're right," he said. "Don't expect me to admit it tomorrow, though. I need to calm down and do some prayin.'"

It took him a quarter of an hour to slow his overactive mind and settle into a discussion with his God, then for the next hour he was washed over by the sense of peace that comes only from communing with your maker. If someone had asked what he had said to God, or what God had said to him, Nate wouldn't have been able to answer. But he came away with a renewed knowledge that God had everything under control.

"Feel better?" Amy asked when he came back into the kitchen.

"Yeah, a ton better. God just needed me to slow down long enough for him to remind me that he is still God, and I'm not. I'm sure glad I thought of givin' that a try," he said with his tongue stuck in his cheek.

"And, wow, the rest of us are all thankful for that!" Amy replied with a smile.

The phone rang and Nate picked it up. "Hello."

"Hey Dad, this is Gail. I talked to Mike again. He wants to wait until morning before doing anything. He said he'd take tomorrow night off if I would. That way we can head out at first light without having to worry about whether or not we'll be able to stay awake during tomorrow night's shift. Right now we're both exhausted. We wouldn't be able to do much in the dark anyway. We'll meet you at the Newberry Park and Ride lot in the morning. Right now I'm gonna get some sleep."

"Okay. Does Mike think that someone from Chiloquin might be able to help us out tomorrow?"

"No, I guess the spill is a real mess. It doesn't look like they'll get it cleaned up before noon tomorrow. The HAZMAT team isn't even on the scene yet."

"So what we gonna do for quads?"

Gail went silent, and for a moment Nate thought she'd hung up; then she said, "Well, here's the deal. We're not gonna have quads."

"Oh, boy," Nate muttered. "I'm gonna be so sore tomorrow from walkin' all day today. I'm not sure that I can walk all the way in there and back tomorrow. And how we gonna get the sick guy out of there without some wheels?"

"Well, that's the good news. Mike's bringing his horses. We're gonna go in by horseback. We'll take a fourth animal to carry the sick guy out. The others will have to walk."

"Gail, I haven't been atop a horse for over thirty years. And I can't say I ever enjoyed it. I'm not sure I remember how to get in a saddle."

"Well, I guess you can jog along beside us. But I'm ridin,' and you know how much I like horses these days."

"Yeah, yeah. I guess ridin' would get us there faster, but man, I was hopin' for some ATVs. No chance of borrowin' some from East Lake County?"

"No, I already checked on that. Mike says that the search and rescue squad has some type of training for their reserves tomorrow, so all their machines are tied up."

"All right, then. It sounds like there's no way around it. We'll ride those glue-factory rejects. But I don't gotta pretend I like it, now, do I?"

40

Jake and Jan lay silently in their beds next door. Neither one knew the other was awake. Both were locked in earnest prayer. Jake had had one of his "knowings," but he wasn't going to tell anyone the details. His chest was tight with knowing, and his pillow was wet from the tears.

Far away in a little town on the west coast of Mexico, a ten-year-old boy, Hector, and his twelve-year-old sister, Felice, were crying out to the same God as Jake and Jan. They had been introduced to their Lord Jesus Christ by a group of short-term missionaries that had conducted some daily vacation Bible classes at a local orphanage. Ironically, the missionaries had been from a small church in Central Oregon. They were praying for the safety of their father, an uncle, and an aunt that had gone north to find work. They had left over two months ago, and no one had heard from them since. The simple prayers of these children filled the throne room of the Almighty God with a sweet fragrance.

Two armies, invisible to the human eye but more real than any earthly army, were preparing for battle in a remote canyon in

Central Oregon. These warriors had faced each other countless times over the past millennium. The outcome of each of the battles was never in question, as long as people prayed and freed the angels of light to fight. When men and women of God failed to pray, the angels of darkness were able to wreak havoc at will. But people were praying this dark night. Eliab and Yanoa knew that the victory was theirs to present to the King.

Nate rolled over in bed and glanced at the red digital readout on his alarm clock. It was 12:45. Four hours before he was planning to get up. He'd been trying not to toss and turn and wake Amy up for the past half-hour. The mental image of the dehydrated man refused to be evicted from his mind. Was this God telling him that he was supposed to get moving? Maybe he needed to get up and get started, take some water to the camp in the cave. He could leave a message on Gail's cell phone telling her that he had left early and give her directions to the cave. He tried praying, but his thoughts were spinning too fast for him to reach that place of communication with God. Frustrated, he swung his legs over the side of the bed and got up.

Before going to bed the night before, he had laid out his clothes for the day so that he wouldn't bother Amy while he was dressing. He had practiced this technique for thirty-five years when he was going to work at 4 a.m. Within minutes, he was out of the bedroom, pouring himself a cold granola breakfast. He read a couple of chapters from the Book of Psalms as he ate, then knelt in front of a kitchen chair for a few minutes, beseeching God for his protection and guidance, and was out the door.

In the garage, he opened the gun safe and pulled out his Remington Model 700 .223 varmint rifle, a purchase made just this fall, and two boxes of shells. He loaded the shells, a carton of energy bars, a half-dozen bottles of Gatorade, and a hatchet into a backpack. A couple of flashlights, including one that could be worn as a headlamp, and their replacement batteries rounded out the load.

He had left a voice message on Gail's cell phone giving her detailed directions to the cave. And he told her to watch for smoke on the eastern horizon. He'd start a smudge with some green pine boughs.

The reader board sign, advising motorists that the road was closed, was superfluous; the absence of any traffic made the closure obvious. The truck's headlights picked up the reflective eyes of a doe and her two fawns that were standing on the shoulder of the road. Nate slowed almost to a full stop as he watched them cross. They were blinded by his lights, and the roadway was slick under their hard hooves, so they crossed slowly, awkwardly, nothing like the sleek athletic creatures that they were when you came upon them in the woods. No wonder so many of them were slaughtered by traffic on this highway at night.

By the time he parked at the end of the logging road that he had walked out on just a few hours earlier, the adrenaline in his system was surging at full strength. He had spent quite a bit of time in the woods in the dark, but if he was to be honest, he'd admit that he found it a bit frightening. You could never quite tell what was out there in the dark, just beyond the limits of your vision, or outside the beam of your flashlight. It was eerie. Pushing those thoughts to the back of his mind, Nate climbed out of his truck, pulled on the pack and slung the .223 over his shoulder. He fitted the headlamp over his Ducks Unlimited baseball cap but didn't turn on the beam. His illuminated dial on his watch said that it was a nearly 2:30 a.m. when he set out walking toward the cave. Slowed by the dark and his sore feet, he should still arrive there by 5:30.

A great horned owl let out a soulful series of calls to the south, and somewhere to the east another answered. A pack of coyotes added a chorus of ethereal howls to the night's background music. Since it was a new moon, the only light was from the stars, and the sky was full of them. Under different conditions, Nate would have been awed by this setting and its sounds, but tonight he was on a mission.

Nate chose a particularly bright star on the eastern horizon and set his course for it to keep from wandering in circles. He stumbled and tripped across the rocky landscape for about forty-five minutes without making any real progress. The headlamp flashlight proved to be of little help in trying to walk through this rock-strewn terrain. Frustrated, he sat down on a large rock and considered his options. He could stay where he was until daylight. Or, he could keep floundering around in the dark and maybe break some bones. Or he could…he decided there wasn't another choice. Sitting in the dark, the breeze that was blowing across the high desert felt a lot colder than it had while he was walking. In fact, he'd worked up a pretty good sweat while he was moving. As his sweat cooled it added to his discomfort. Moving to the lee side of the rock, he sat on the ground so he was sheltered from the wind. The ground was hard, but getting out of the wind made it a little more comfortable.

Guys over fifty are not meant to sit on the ground out in the wilds in the middle of the night, Nate thought. "I shoulda left this to the boy scouts," he said to himself. With more than two hours to wait for daylight, he decided to try to get some sleep, but he couldn't find a comfortable position. With no other options available, he decided to spend some time in prayer. He started out with the obvious requests for safety and success in this adventure. He followed with some intercession for the sick people that were waiting in the cave. The myriads of stars in the heavens incited some praise. But before he knew what was happening, he was pouring out his heart to his Lord in a way that he hadn't done for quite awhile. Tears poured down his face as he confessed some things in his life that he'd been trying to rationalize to God, or hide from him altogether. "Man," Nate said out loud. "How stupid am I to try to hide things or debate issues with the sovereign God?" Odd as it seemed, God was shining light on Nate's heart in the midst of the night's physical darkness.

Switching on the headlamp to look at his watch, Nate was surprised to see that he'd been sitting for over an hour. He was also surprised to notice that he could see his surroundings a lot better. In fact, he thought, he should be able to get moving again and be able to see the rocks and brush that had been tripping him earlier. So he set off toward the east again. The motion felt good, but what felt infinitely better was that he was at complete peace with God. "Why don't I take time to communicate with you more often, Lord?" he wondered in a quiet voice. "The world never seems more 'right' than after I have spent some real serious time in communion with you."

He made good progress for the next hour, and the first rays of the sun were reaching their long shiny fingers over the eastern horizon when Nate reached the brim of the canyon. He'd erred slightly in his navigation in the dark and had hit the cliff about a half-mile south of the draw that would take him to the cave. As he stood calculating how to correct his error, the few clouds that were scattered across the morning sky were lit brilliant orange, and silver highlights marked their edges. The magnificence of the view was well worth the extra walking that resulted from his mistake. Nate wished that he had a camera to capture the sight. He headed north and was delighted to feel the caress of the sun on his right check as he walked. The wonder of the morning almost made him forget the purpose of this hike.

Morning light hadn't reached to the creek bank, though. The trees that were supported by the water from the small stream blocked the sun quite effectively. In the semi-dark, Nate would have missed the crude steps up to the cave had it not been for the makeshift reservoir. As it was, he stepped in the small pond before he saw it; then it still took some searching to locate the steps that led up to the cave.

He'd been in such a hurry to get back to the people that were using the cave for shelter that he'd got out of a warm bed after only a couple of hours of sleep and stumbled around in the dark most of the night. Now that he was within yards of the cave, he found himself stalling, mainly because he didn't know what to expect. Both his calves were rippling with cramps as he stood contemplating what would come next. Would the refugees still be here? Would the severely sick man be alive? Would they use the gun that he'd left with them on him? Nate knew that the only way to get answers to the questions that were swirling around in his head was to climb the fifty or so steps out of this draw and look in the cave. Instead he found himself pausing to pray. After five minutes spent pleading for divine intervention and guidance, he climbed those hand-hewn steps and crawled out of the draw.

The stench of sewage still permeated the air, but it was mixed with the scent of wood smoke. A tendril of smoke hung in the mouth of the cave. The scent of the smoke relieved Nate. It meant at least some of the people he'd found were still here. As he moved closer to the dark entrance he could hear moaning. Nate switched on his flashlight and stepped past the fire. Even with the light, it took a minute for his eyes to adjust to the dark interior of the cave. When he was able to focus, the first thing that he noticed, to his relief, was that he wasn't looking down the barrel of his own Browning. He intentionally left his rifle slung on his shoulder. The next thing that came to his attention was that Miguel was in exactly the same place as when he had left. He quickly knelt beside the man and was encouraged to find a pulse. It was weak, but it was there.

Nate pulled a bottle of Gatorade from his pack. As he was wrestling with the comatose man, attempting to get him into a position that would allow some of the liquid to be poured into his mouth, Aggie knelt beside him and began to assist. "Hi, Aggie. Glad to see you're still here," Nate said.

"Is good to see you. We didn't know if you was come back."

Nate glanced around the cave while he worked on Miguel. "Where're the others?"

Aggie indicated the back part of the cave with a jerk of her head and replied, "Rosa and Paulos is there. They is very sick. Other two mens, they did left. They thought you bringing sheriffs to arrest them. They takes your gun."

"How bad are Rosa and Paulo? They aren't as bad as Miguel, are they?"

"No. Miguel is the mos' bad, but they is mucho sick. Why you no bring others to help?"

"Oh, that reminds me, I've gotta get a good smoky fire goin' outside so those others can find us," Nate said as he gently lay the sick man back down; they'd managed to get a only a few swallows of the Gatorade down him. "I've got a couple a friends comin' on horseback to help get you guys outta here." He took the rest of the Gatorade and the energy bars out of his backpack and set them on the ground. He handed a couple of drink containers to Aggie and said, "Here, I'm going to go out and try to start a signal fire. While I'm doin' that, why don't you see if you can get some liquid, and if possible something solid, into your friends?"

Outside, Nate scraped a big pile of pine needles together and lit them with his disposable lighter. Then he took his hatchet and cut a couple of armloads of pine boughs and threw them on the burning needles. It only took a few minutes to get a good-sized smoke plume rising into the air. Gail and Mike shouldn't have any trouble seeing that, he thought.

41

It had been light about an hour by the time that Gail and Mike pulled off the highway onto the sorry excuse for a road that was just south of milepost 171. "Man, I hope this is the right road," Gail muttered. "I don't know why that crazy old coot couldn't have waited a couple of more hours for us to come down here with him, instead of chasin' out here by himself and leavin' us hangin.'"

Mike laughed as he wrestled the steering wheel of his pickup truck and looked in his side-view mirror to make sure that his horse trailer was going to miss a tree beside the road. "Do you ever understand anything your dad does? You know he always does what he thinks is best. It just isn't always what anyone else thinks is best, that's all."

"Yeah, I know. But what'd he think he was gonna accomplish out here in the dark all by himself? We'll be lucky if we don't find 'im out here with a broken leg or somethin.' And the most he could gain was a couple of hours. What difference would that make to a bunch of people who've been livin' out here for a couple or three months?"

"I dunno, he's your dad! But I do know that his instincts were pretty good a couple of months ago when he saved our sorry butts."

"Well, I hope you don't ever tell him that! He's bad enough without any encouragement. Oh, there's his rig. But who do ya suppose belongs to that other outfit?" Gail said, pointing to pickup and flatbed trailer that was parked next to her dad's Dodge.

Mike pulled his rig behind the one Gail had indicated. "I dunno for sure, but I've seen the pickup around Rosland. I think it might belong to a buckaroo who works on the Z. But I wonder what it's doin' out here. The Z took their stock off this range a month ago."

While Mike was unloading the four horses from his trailer, Gail took a look at the outfit that was parked next to her dad's. She could see where at least two ATVs had off-loaded. The tracks looked really fresh. They cut across the tracks of the Dodge, so her dad had been parked here before this outfit arrived. Whoever was on the off-road machines had left just minutes earlier. She was turning to go help Mike with their mounts when something on the ground beside the flatbed trailer caught her eye. Her heart rate doubled when she realized that it was a cigarette butt, half buried in the soft soil.

"Mike, come here a second," she called. "Look at this."

Mike looked annoyed at being interrupted while unloading the horses, but then his eyes went big and round when he saw what she was pointing at. He didn't say anything; he just went to his pickup and pulled a Ziploc bag and a pair of needle nose pliers from his jockey box and bagged the butt. After tossing the improvised evidence bag onto the seat of his truck, he told Gail, "Mount up. Let's go."

Gail didn't feel very confident about getting aboard a horse since she'd been pitched off, and especially not at the pace that Mike was setting on his Morgan gelding, Clem. The chestnut-colored horse stood fifteen hands—on the tall side for a Morgan—and had both the strength and intelligence that had made the breed so popular in America when horses were bred more for working than for pets. Gail was on Lucy, one of Clem's half-sisters. The other two horses were mares that Mike had gotten through the program set up for adoption of wild mustangs. They were on long leads that were snubbed to Mike's saddle horn. They trailed behind Mike's mount like a couple of obedient dogs out for a walk. It had taken a lot of Mike's time to get the once-wild horses to this point, but, in his mind at least, it had been worth every minute.

Lucy obviously was not impressed or intimated by her larger brother. Though she was a full hand shorter than he, the mare matched his gait stride for stride. After the initial bit of panic that she felt because of the pace, Gail realized that this little mare was the smoothest-riding horse that she'd ever been on and actually began to enjoy the ride.

Off to the east, the smoke that Nate had promised to provide for navigational purposes was obvious against the brilliant blue of the October sky. The pair on horseback set as straight a course for the smoke as the rock-strewn landscape allowed. Their sense of urgency was only intensified by the fact that the tracks left by the quartet of ATVs was unerringly on the same course.

The sound of the first shot was the somewhat hollow boom of a shotgun. It came from what Gail and Mike judged to be about a half-mile south of the smoke plume. Mike had stopped when the sound reached them, and Gail rode up beside him and said, "What'da ya think, a hunter?"

Before Mike could respond to Gail's query, the sharp crack of a rifle, quickly followed by two more booms from the shotgun, and another crack from the rifle, provided fuel for more questions. "That don't sound like hunters," Mike said. "But it ain't comin' from the spot your dad marked with the smoke, either. What'da ya think?"

"I dunno what to think. Other than that, we better get over there and see what's goin' on, and quick."

Clem didn't need much encouragement to increase the pace to

a trot. Gail was convinced that they would have been galloping had the terrain allowed it. A variety of thoughts were running through her mind as she adjusted her rhythm in the saddle with her horse's gait. Her concern wasn't alleviated any when she watched Mike pull his rifle from the scabbard on his saddle and rack a round into the chamber. She felt more than a little frustrated by the fact that she wasn't on something with wheels or at least carrying a long gun. But there was some measure of comfort from the weight of her Sig Sauer in the holster on her hip and she let go of the saddle horn just long enough to reach up and pat the grip of the SP2022 nine-millimeter. It obviously wasn't a weapon to be carrying into a shootout with people toting rifles, but at least she was comfortable with it, and it was what she had. She just hoped she wouldn't have to use it.

Mike had been all business once they'd found the cigarette butt. But since the shots, his intensity had multiplied five-fold. She'd heard a lot of stories about his prowess in crisis situations from people who had served with him on the Central Oregon S.W.A.T. team. She couldn't help but wonder how much he was being affected by having been shot only a few months earlier. She knew she didn't feel anywhere near as invincible as she had before, and she'd just taken a round through the shoulder; he'd taken one to the head. Hopefully it wouldn't cause either of them to freeze up at a crucial moment, she thought. Nothing was ever quite the way that it looked on TV or in the movies.

42

Satisfied that the smoke would be visible for several miles and for a couple of hours, Nate went back to the cave.

Aggie was in the back. She was holding a bottle of the Gatorade as Rosa tried to drink. After a several small gulps, Rosa slumped back to the floor, apparently exhausted by the simple effort. Paulos was shivering uncontrollably on the floor of the cave just a few feet away, but a half-empty Gatorade sat beside him. Nate stooped, slid his hands and arms under the man, helped him stand; and then helped him shuffle out to sit by the fire near Miguel. He was shocked at how light the man was and doubted that he weighed more than a hundred pounds. Then Nate went out to look for more wood for the fire. Finding another downed ponderosa with loose bark only about a hundred and fifty yards from the cave, he cut two poles and pulled them through the sleeves of his coat, making a crude little travois to use to transport the bark back to the fire. Once the fire was burning well, Nate turned back to Aggie. "Do you know what's making your friends sick?"

"We is having nothing to eat. I thinks they is starving, maybe."

"I found fish and quail traps. Did they ever get anything in them?"

"Sí. Miguel, he did catch much food. Even cows sometimes. But since he is sick, we not haves so much. The others no good at catching."

Nate threw another couple of pieces of bark on the fire and asked, "How 'bout water? You been gettin' it outta the stream down there, haven't ya? Have you been boiling it?"

"No," Aggie answered. "We got only a few cans we find to carry water. We has no way to boil the water."

"I bet your friends have giardia. I just don't know why you aren't sick, but I'm glad you're not. We gotta figure out how we're gonna get the others out to where we can get 'em on horseback. Can you ride?"

"No," Aggie said, looking down. "I walk. Others ride."

"There'll be four horses, so all four of you can ride, if you want."

"No, I walk. I no like horses."

"Well, I'm not gonna argue with you about it now. We'll see how ya do once we get started. Got any ideas of how to get these three down to the creek?"

"Is very steep. I don't know if they can make it."

"We'll carry 'em if we have to. Mike's a big strong guy. Him and me should be able to do it. Right now, though, I better go out and see if I can meet them and show 'em how to get here. The smoke 'ill get 'em to the edge of the canyon, but gettin' down the draw and then back out of it is a little bit tricky."

Aggie put her hand on Nate's arm, looked him in the eye, and asked, "Tell me, Mr. Nate, why you doing this for us? We is just a bunch of poor Mexicans. We can't do nothing for you, maybe get you in big trouble."

"I dunno, really," Nate replied. "I've haven't been able to ignore anybody in trouble since I first understood that Jesus gave everything for me. And I don't know when I've ever had an opportunity to help someone who needed help more. I'm just thankful for the chance to give you a hand."

"You think Jesus is real?"

"I know he is. You better believe I do. More real than anything that you know," Nate said as he stood up. "Try to get some more liquid, and maybe even some food down your friends. They're gonna need all the strength they can get."

He stepped past Rosa, Paulos, and Miguel and into the morning's sunshine and turned to assure Aggie that he'd be back as soon as possible when the boom of a shotgun broke the stillness of the morning and froze him in his tracks. The shot was followed by a report that sounded like it was from a rifle, then two more blasts from the shotgun and one final crack from the rifle. As the echoes of the shots reverberated across the canyon, Nate un-slung his rifle. He quickly checked to make sure it was loaded and instructed Aggie, "You guys stay put. I'm gonna go and see what's goin' on, and then try to bring back some help."

He hit the steep trail that led down to the stream a little too fast and slipped, sliding to the bottom on his backside. Landing in an awkward tangle at the bottom of the hill, Nate quickly assessed all his limbs and concluded that aside from some serious scrapes and contusions, he wasn't really hurt. He wasn't sure about his rifle, but it didn't appear to be any worse for wear. "Wow. All I need right now is to break an arm or leg. That'd add some excitement to my otherwise dull day," he said to himself. He started up the trail that led out of the draw at a fast walk, fighting Charlie horses in both legs and debating with himself about what to do. The shots had sounded like they were somewhere to the south of where the trail exited the draw. He hoped that the shooting didn't mean that Gail and Mike had stumbled onto the two refugees that had "borrowed" his shotgun.

Nate stayed inside the tree line when he reached the spot where the trail angled out of the wooded draw and started across the rocky flat. From the last of the cover, he scanned the area to the south for movement. The only area that was visible was the rock-strewn open area, and there wasn't anything moving there, but he knew that the breaks and canyon walls could hide an army. Not wanting to leave Mike and Gail stranded if they were involved in the shooting, Nate moved in the direction that he thought that the shots had come from. He hugged the rim of the canyon and kept in the shadows as much as possible, alert for any movement that might provide a clue to what the shooting had been about.

Nate moved south with stealth as, a half-mile north, hidden from Nate's view by the giant boulders, Gail and Mike were trying to figure out how to get down the sheer face of the cliff to the source of the smoke that they had been using for a guide. When they had first arrived at the top of the cliff they thought there must be a direct way down, but once they had eliminated all the possibilities they went north in search of a trail. After an unsuccessful mile, they turned around and headed back, searching for some route that they had previously missed and getting more and more frustrated by the minute. When they finally found the trail that Nate had been using to go down the draw, it was too steep and the brush too thick to take on horseback. They dismounted and began leading the horses down the trail.

While Gail and Mike were dismounting and starting their hike down the draw that led to the cave, Nate was out of sight to the south hunting the source of the shots. He was moving slowly, straining for anything that might provide a hint as to what the shooting had been about. First he heard voices, too far away to be distinct, but near enough to tell him that he needed to be careful. Then he saw two men standing armed guard over a third man, who was digging.

Before he tried to get closer, he decided he'd check around and see if he could find the ATVs or horses these guys came in on. Disabling their transportation might prove to be a big help later.

Circling around, he located two quads that were parked on the brink of the hill about a hundred yards from where the digging was being done. Fortunately for Nate, they were far enough above the crown of the hill that they were out of sight of their owners. Nate intended to cut gas lines or perform some other sabotage, but when he got to the machines he grinned. The keys were in them! So he removed them from the ignitions and put them in his pocket. Those machines just might come in handy, he thought.

Now that he was confident that he had blocked their escape route, with painstaking deliberateness he began edging closer to the three men. He was convinced that the slightest miscue would invite disaster. After taking ten minutes to move less than thirty yards, Nate was in position to see that the man with the shovel was the guy from the cave that had taken his shotgun and pointed it at him. He was apparently engaged in the gruesome task of digging a grave for the blood-covered body lying face up off to the side of the nearly completed grave. The corpse was the second man missing from the cave, Pedro. The other two men, each armed with a rifle, were arguing the merits of killing the gravedigger and adding his corpse to the grave or keeping him alive long enough to lead them to the others.

Nate wasn't interested in seeing which side of the argument came out on top. Nestled among several large boulders, he took a good rest for his rifle and brought the scope to bear on the man on the right, knowing it was easier for him to obtain a new target to the left than to the right if needed. With the rifle's safety off and the scope's crosshairs centered on his target's back, Nate hollered, "Hey, don't either of ya do anything stupid! Just turn around real slow and put your weapons down!"

Both men flinched at the shout. At first it looked like they were going to comply, but then, as if on cue, they bolted for the cover of the nearby trees. Nate pulled the trigger on his rifle and was both horrified and relieved to see dirt fly up a yard and a half to the right of where the weapon was aimed; horrified because he realized that the scope on his rifle had been jarred out of alignment in his fall, relieved because he hadn't shot the man.

43

Mike called Gail over to look at the steps he had found in the steep bank of the draw. "Someone has been using the steps recently," he observed when Gail came over to inspect them. "My guess is that they lead to the cave your dad was talkin' about. I'm gonna tether the horses here. They'd go up the bank all right, but I don't want one of 'em gettin' hurt comin' back down."

They scrambled up the steep bank and both stood trying to catch their breath when a rifle shot rang out in the distance to the south. As they were looking at each other, trying to decide what the shot meant, and what their next move should be, Aggie stuck her head out of the cave, and the three caught sight of each other simultaneously. "Nate sends you?" Aggie asked.

"Sorta," Gail answered, "where is he?"

"He is gone to find you, I think. He heard shots and leave, maybe one hour ago."

Gail grabbed Mike's elbow and said in too loud a whisper, "Could you see what you can do about gettin' these folks to the horses and outta here? I'm gonna try to find Dad."

"Do ya think it's a good idea to split up?" Mike asked. "Wouldn't it be better if we both went huntin' for your pop, then we can come back here and figure out how to get these people outta here?"

Gail locked her eyes on the eastern horizon for fifteen seconds or more before being interrupted by Aggie, who said, "Please, señorita, Miguel is very sick. Nate say we must get him to hospital quick. I help get the others to the horses while you look for Señor Nate. But please, we must hurry, he is not breath so good."

Her mind made up, Gail swung into action. "I'm goin' after Dad, Mike. Please do your best to get these folks outta here and to the hospital. I'll catch up with ya as soon as I can."

"Okay," Mike conceded. "I've got some rope and other tack on Clem. I'll get it up here and work up some kinda rig to get the sick folks to the horses. I don't really like it, though. I think we should stick together."

Gail didn't bother to answer; she just started down the steep embankment. Mostly because she was afraid that Mike might be right. Maybe they should stay together. But there was too much to do in too short a time. She had to find her father, and these people, especially Miguel, had to get medical attention. When she reached the horses she muttered, "Pray that I find the old geezer fast!" But she was surprised when he answered. He had come down right behind her without her knowing it.

He nodded and said, "That I can do, and gladly," as he went to work gathering the equipment his horse was carrying.

44

Nate scanned the vegetation until his eyes were burning and watering, but he couldn't see either of the men that had been supervising the grave digging. The man doing the digging had disappeared too. Nate realized now that it was too late, that the position he had chosen offered good cover, but did not offer much of a view of the area. The two men could be flanking him on either side, and he would not be able to see them. Frustrated, and kicking himself for not planning better, he held his position and continued to scan the area into which the men had vanished.

Rocks clattered to his right, and Nate adjusted his position to get a view in that direction. Peeking out from behind one of the boulders, he spotted one of his adversaries. The man had his rifle in ready position and was moving toward him, obviously hunting him. Nate took aim at the man, and then adjusted that aim, hoping to compensate for the scope's alignment problem. He started to squeeze the trigger, but found he couldn't shoot from this ambush. Trying to rationalize shooting the man, Nate told himself that, were the positions reversed, the man would gladly shoot him. But still, he couldn't bring himself to pull the trigger. Only about thirty yards separated them, and Nate could clearly see the man's features through the lens of his scope.

Nate was looking right into the man's eyes and knew instantly when those eyes focused on him. The man deftly swung the rifle to his shoulder and fired. Nate had rolled to his right, and the shot missed. Four more shots immediately followed the first and the roar of the rounds and flying rock fragments forced Nate to keep his head down. A lull followed the fifth shot, and it convinced Nate that the shooter was reloading, and that gave him the confidence to change his position enough to try to get off a shot. When he looked out, he saw his guess was correct. The man was slamming a new clip into the rifle. Nate took quick aim and squeezed off a shot. In his panic he forgot to adjust for the scope being out of line and the shot went wide, but at least the blast sent the man diving for cover. Nate sent another round into the brush at a glimpse of the man, but he had little hope that it had connected.

Nate was searching for some sign of his target when his left leg was knocked out from under him, and there was a loud blast from behind him. He didn't feel any pain and wasn't sure why he was suddenly lying on the ground looking up at the sky. He looked down at his leg and saw that his right pant leg was already soaked blood red. Crimson spatter was all over the dirt and rocks. Nate had tracked enough wounded game animals to recognize that a major artery in his leg had been severed. He struggled to get the belt out of the belt loops of his jeans and around his thigh, but before he could tighten the makeshift tourniquet, his ears were buzzing, his vision was going black at the edges, and his hands wouldn't perform the tasks that his brain was requesting of them. Then he was spinning down a black tunnel toward an intense light.

As he began to regain consciousness, Nate thought, I gotta shovel snow. But he couldn't get his eyes to open. The sunlight that was apparently reflecting off the snow was blinding, even through his closed eyelids. He had to get it off the sidewalks before someone slipped. He couldn't get his arms or legs to work. What was wrong with him, and what was the source of the beautiful music that was filling his ears and washing over his senses?

45

Gail couldn't find any tracks to help her determine where her father had gone, so she just moved south toward the sound of the last shot, keeping to the cover along the lip of the canyon. All of her senses were at full alert, and her nerves were strung tight. When she caught a glimpse of sunlight reflecting off of chrome, her heart started beating faster. She moved closer and realized that the chrome was on the handlebars of a quad; her pulse began to race. She was trying to see the person who had rode in on the machine when the sound of a nearby shot nearly sent her into orbit.

The silence that followed the shot was almost as frightening as the sound of the shot had been. Gail had her Sig Sauer in her hands, locked and loaded, as she cautiously made her way in the direction from which the shot had come. She had the advantage, since she held the high ground and her quarry wasn't aware of her position, while she knew theirs. Moving laterally on the hillside to maintain the advantage of elevation she caught sight of a man with a rifle who appeared to be stalking someone or something that had taken refuge in a patch of boulders. As she watched the near man move, she saw movement on the other side of the rock pile as well. It was another man with a rifle, apparently also concentrating on something hiding among the rocks. At first she thought they might be stalking each other, but as they moved it became obvious that they were working in conjunction with each other against whoever had taken refuge among the rocks.

Suddenly the man nearest her threw his rifle to his shoulder and fired a shot. The echoes of that shot were still reverberating across the canyon when he fired four more rounds as quickly as they could be chambered. Gail was watching the man get a new clip into the rifle, trying to come up with a plan of action, when a shot came out of the rock pile. The guy she had been watching dove into some nearby cover, and a second shot came out of the rocks. Gail was trying to digest all this information when a blast came from a third position. She figured that it had come from the man on the opposite side of the rock pile.

She was trying to decide what to do when the far man hollered, "Hey, he's down. Have ya seen the Mex?"

"Nah, haven't seen 'im since this jerk took the potshot at us. He obviously went rabbit on us. Let's get back to the machines and get outta here quick. I'm hit," the near gunman yelled back.

"What'da ya mean you're hit? You're shot?"

"Yeah, I'm shot, you idiot. What'd ya think I meant? I gotta get some help."

"Where did he get you?"

"It's a through an' through in my side. I don't think it hit anything vital, but I'm losin' blood, and it hurts like crazy. I gotta get outta here while I can. But what about the turkey in the rocks, ya think he's out for good?"

"Yeah. He went down hard and hasn't moved. You know these Nosler ballistic tips don't mess around. They make a hole ya can put your fist in."

Gail was having difficulty breathing. She knew she had just been witness to her father's murder, and she didn't intend to let these guys get away with it. Every instinct in her wanted to go in with her Sig blazing, but she knew that it would only get her killed. So instead she tightened her resolve, headed back to where the quads were parked, and began to plan how to trap her father's killers. She assumed an ambush position behind a huge old growth ponderosa pine and waited for the men to arrive.

It seemed to Gail like an eternity, but in reality she didn't wait long. They came up fast, confident that they could do whatever they wanted with impunity, not paying much attention to anything but getting to their machines. One of them was walking hunched over, clutching his side but still moving fast, and Gail figured him for the one that had been hit. The other man was giving his injured comrade a wide berth. It was obvious that he didn't want to rile the wounded man any more that he already was.

Gail intended to wait until the men put their weapons in the scabbards that were mounted on the ATVs to make her move, but before the weapons were stowed the men realized that the keys were missing from the ignitions of the machines. "Hey," the wounded man yelled at his partner. "What'd ya do with my keys?"

"I didn't do anything with 'em. I left 'em in the ignition of your machine just like I did with mine. That jerk that tried to ambush us must've swiped 'em before he jumped us. The question is, what'd he do with 'em?"

"Hustle back down there and see if they're on 'im, will ya? I'm gonna stay here and see if I can slow the bleeding." He put his rifle in the scabbard, got astraddle of the machine, and pulled his shirttail out of his jeans while the other man jogged back to the site of the shooting.

Gail stepped out from behind the ponderosa when she figured that the man who went to fetch the keys was out of earshot. She had her Sig Sauer in both hands, and the sight was centered on the wounded man's chest. He didn't appear to know she was there until she said, "Keep quiet and ya just might live another thirty or forty seconds. Get your hands in the air and crawl off the machine." He calmly looked up and then complied. She continued in a tone of voice that carried a volume of authority, "Now, get on your face and get your hands out to your sides." She was moving closer to him while she talked, and as soon as he was on the ground with his arms spread wide, she got a zip-tie out of her pocket and holstered her Sig so she could get the makeshift handcuffs around her prisoner's wrists.

It was while Gail was preparing to cuff him that he made his move. He rolled over and kicked her legs out from under her and then reached for the .38 that was in his coat pocket. He had it half out when Gail slammed into him with her shoulder, knocking him down. She tried to kick the wrist of his gun hand when he scrambled up, still trying to get his pistol into action. Fortunately for Gail, the front sight of the pistol hung up on the fabric of her opponent's coat. It gave her time to get her Sig out of its holster. Three shots from the nine-millimeter decided the contest. The man went down and stayed down. Strange, Gail thought. It didn't make her feel any better.

There wasn't time for Gail to react to what she had done. The other shooter would be on the move to take her out. And she wouldn't have the advantage of surprise with him. To make the odds against her even worse, he had a rifle and she had a handgun, unless she could grab the long gun out of the scabbard on the ATV. She scrambled to the machine and grabbed the weapon. She could almost feel the crosshairs of the man's scope burning a tattoo on her back as she pulled the rifle free and headed back to her hiding spot behind the ponderosa.

She spent a minute getting familiar with the weapon. It was a semi-automatic Browning, a pretty straightforward weapon. She located the safety on the forward part of the trigger guard. A lever on the left side of the breech released the clip, which she confirmed was fully loaded. While the clip was out, she pulled the bolt back and found that there was a round in the chamber. She let the bolt slam back into place and reinserted the clip. Satisfied that the rifle was set to go, she sighted through the scope and found it a fair fit. So, she was set; now, if she could only see the guy before he saw her.

Birds chirped and flitted about in the bushes, the tails of squirrels twitched as they scolded from their front row seats in the trees, and insects buzzed around her ears, but aside from those and the scurrying of a couple of golden mantels that were busy gathering seeds, Gail didn't see any movement. Minutes passed, and her anxiety began to grow, but there was still no sign of the other man. Convinced that he was counting on her to get antsy and move first, she was determined to use the lessons her father had taught her through countless hours in a duck blind. She was completely confident that she would win the waiting game. The tough part was keeping her mind from drifting to her dad's body lying in the rocks less than a quarter mile away. The corpse of the man she had just shot was a bit of a distraction too. Her subconscious kept expecting it to rise up off the ground like some ghoul in a horror flick. She just had to concentrate and focus on seeing the man before he saw her.

A flock of juncos erupted from a patch of bitterbrush that was growing about halfway to where her father had been ambushed. Gail suspected that they had been spooked by her adversary. She swung the confiscated rifle to her shoulder and viewed the spot through the scope. The variable powers of the optics were set on nine, which brought everything right up close, but gave a view of a very narrow area. She cranked the scope's magnification down to three and felt much more comfortable.

She was slowly sweeping the scope across the landscape when something caught her eye. She stopped the movement of the rifle and concentrated on a spot where she thought she saw movement. After a moment of searching, a man's hand came in to view as it reached around a tree trunk and gripped the rough bark. Gail snapped the rifle's safety off and put her index finger through the trigger guard. As the man's shoulder became visible from behind the tree, she placed the crosshairs on it and began to take up the slack in the trigger. As soon as the man's torso came into view she intended to take the shot. She was tired of playing fair and taking chances.

The man was moving incredibly slowly and cautiously. When his face finally came into view from behind the tree trunk, Gail's finger was about four ounces from dropping the hammer on the round in the rifle's chamber. It was her training as a police officer and the experience of nearly shooting her father two months earlier that saved the man's life. She had made sure of her target before applying that last bit of pressure to the trigger. The face that peeked out from behind the tree was not that of the man she expected, but instead it was the face of the guy who had been doing the digging. Gail relaxed her trigger finger and watched as the man crept out into the open.

The newcomer was rail-thin and dressed in tattered clothing. He was carrying a shovel and wielding it like a weapon and not at all like a garden tool. He kept coming with remarkable stealth, moving slowly and silently toward her. Gail suspected that this was one of the men that her father had found and that they had come out here to rescue. The question was, what was he doing sneaking around and carrying a shovel like it was a broadsword?

He kept coming, and she remained silent, studying the man to see what he was up to. He crept up on the ATVs, flinched, and raised the shovel for a strike when he saw the body of the man Gail had shot. Realizing that the man no longer posed a threat, he nudged the body with the shovel blade, much like you might treat the body of a road kill varmint. He then stopped and slowly pivoted his head, cautiously studying everything in view. Finally his eyes focused on the rifle that Gail was holding, and he froze, obviously realizing his vulnerable position. They were less than twenty yards apart. That's when Gail said, "Let's just keep this real quiet. I'm not anxious to let that guy's partner know where I'm at."

"*Sí, señorita*. But you no have to worry about him. I take him with the shovel."

"What?"

"He comes down to the other man, the one they shoots, I hide there. When he puts his gun down, I hit him with the shovel. He dies, I think."

"The other man," Gail shouted as she started running. "Is he dead?"

"*Sí*, they shoot him. He bleeds much. This is sad, he was very good man. He tries to help us, I think," her new ally grunted as he ran beside her. "He is your friend?"

Gail hesitated to make sure her voice didn't fail, and said, "He's my father."

"I am sorry, señorita."

Even though she had been hoping against all hope, it was obvious to Gail that there was nothing that could be done for her father as soon as his body was within sight. She had taken enough "dead body" calls in her years with the Bend P.D. to recognize the signs from a distance. That didn't stop her from rushing to his side or repeatedly checking for a pulse. Five long minutes later, her heart had to finally give in to what her head already knew.

It wasn't the same with the guy that Ramon had used the shovel on. In fact, when Gail felt for a pulse she found a very faint one beating in the man's carotid artery. She was disappointed. As much out of revenge as to be safe, she zip-tied his wrists behind his back and then fastened one of his ankles to a three-inch juniper tree. Once he was secure, she checked his pockets. She found a .38 revolver in his coat and a wallet in his jeans. The name on the driver's license that was in the wallet was Ron Shear.

"You know this man?" she asked Ramon.

"Sí. He is the man who brings us here. He is bad man. He keep us in a barn with no food and little water. He takes all our monies and is supposed to get us work, but we never get no work."

Satisfied that the man posed no danger, Gail turned back to her dad. She rolled him onto his back, straightened out his legs, folded his arms over his chest and picked up his Ducks Unlimited cap from where it lay in the dust and covered his face with it. There was a huge lump in her throat and she had to keep running her tongue between her upper teeth and lip to keep from crying. This seemed so impossible! This man who had always seemed bigger than life was nothing but a cold empty shell.

Ramon stood off to the side, looking out across the canyon, giving Gail her moment alone. He jumped, startled, when Gail came up beside him, held out her hand, and said, "I'm Gail."

He took her hand and answered, "I is Ramon. I is very sorry for your father."

Gail dragged her sleeve across her eyes and said, "Thanks. We need to get back to the cave. A friend of mine is trying to get your friends out to safety. I think he'll be needin' our help."

"Okay, *señorita*. We should take the…" He gestured with his hands, searching for the word. "The motor carts."

"Oh, the ATVs. Good idea. But the keys aren't in 'em. And these guys were tryin' to find the keys when I ambushed 'em. So I think we're walkin.' Hey, wait a minute, the guy you whacked with the shovel was comin' down here to see if my dad had the keys on him."

Turning back to her dad, she gently checked his pockets and found the keys.

"Will ya look at that?" she said as much to herself as to Ramon. "The old codger grabbed the keys to keep these guys from gettin' away. Looks like we'll be ridin' after all. Let's go." Gail set a fast pace back up the hill. Minutes later, they had the ATVs fired up and were headed back to the north. Gail had an impulse to go make sure that Shear was no longer wounded, then she felt a twinge of guilt about thinking that way, and for leaving the wounded man laying out in the elements, but she controlled the impulse, and the was guilt was fleeting.

Her thoughts became fixated on the desire to finish the job of getting the refugees to safety, the job that had cost her father his life. If they didn't get these people out it would be a failure that would haunt the rest of her life.

46

Mike was gnashing his teeth. Getting these people out of the cave and down to his horses had been a major undertaking. Even though Aggie had managed to get some Gatorade and granola bars into each of them except Miguel, they were still too weak to be much of any help. And poor Miguel hadn't even gained consciousness despite all the bumping and jostling that had taken place.

Once he had the four down to the creek bottom, the challenge was figuring out how to use the horses to move them. He'd seen enough old westerns on the TV to know that a travois would be the answer, but he wasn't too sure how to make one with the tools and materials that he had on hand. Besides, considering the rocky ground between here and the road, it would make for a very rough ride. Finally, he decided to simply sling Miguel over the saddle. He knew it couldn't be good for the poor guy, but he couldn't think of any alternatives. Everyone else would have to hike out, but at least they'd have a stirrup to hang on to while they walked. The good news was it wasn't that far until everyone could mount up.

This ragtag crew was almost out into the open, and though Mike had known these people for less than two hours, he was as proud of them as he could be. There hadn't been any whining or complaining at all. Each of them had done exactly what he asked of them, once the language barrier was broken, and they understood what that was, at least.

The big cop was thinking he might just pull off the impossible and actually get these people out to the rigs when he heard the sound of ATVs somewhere close. He couldn't think of any way that having visitors could be a good thing, so he motioned for everyone to stay put and be quiet and he sprinted up the trail, hoping to get into a position to see who was coming. He was still in the draw, and unable to see out, when the machines shut down at what sounded like the approximate location of where the trail started down into the ravine.

His rifle was locked and loaded, and Mike was hidden in an ambush position beside the trail, ready for the worst, when he caught a glimpse of a pair of people coming down the trail doing double time. They were even with him and less than twenty-five yards away before he realized that one of the two was Gail. The other was obviously another member of the group that he was working on getting out of the woods. He was surprised by how glad he was to see Gail, alive and in one piece. "Hey," he called out from his hiding spot. "Slow down before you break your necks."

Gail spun around, and from the look on her face she wasn't quite as glad to see him as he was to see her. In fact, her face was a mask of torment. In spite of how she looked, she said, "Oh, Mike. Man, I am glad to see you! Where are the others?"

"They're down the trail a hundred yards or so. Where'd you pick your partner up?"

"That's kind of a long story. I'll fill you in as we go. For now, let's concentrate on gettin' this crew out of here."

Mike took the lead, heading back to his horses and the rest of the crew. Gail quickly told him about her dad and saw the big man wince, but they just kept moving. Somehow the movement made the terrible news easier to handle. "And, oh, you might be interested to hear this," Gail added. "The guy Ramon took out with the shovel was carrying ID that says he is Ron Shear."

That bit of news stopped Mike for a second. "Are you kidding me? So this whole mess is tied together with our other adventures? I knew it!"

"Yeah, according to Ramon, Shear brought them up from Mexico and then didn't come through with the work he had promised them."

When they got to the others, Aggie had Miguel off the horse and was cradling his head in her arms; tears were running down her face. "He is died," she said, sobbing. "He was choke, and Paulos help me get him down from the horse, and he is gone." The woman's obvious grief and despair set Gail off on a crying jag of her own.

47

When Nate finally got his eyes to open, it wasn't snow that he saw. The radiant light that was blasting his senses was coming off the man standing before him. When his eyes recovered enough from the light to focus, they focused on the brownest, most compassionate and powerful eyes that could ever be seen. Wave after wave of sweet emotion washed over Nate, and he was simultaneously filled with awe and worship and praise and thanksgiving like nothing he had ever before felt. This was his Savior, his Counselor, The Almighty God! The King. When Nate thought that his emotions could experience nothing higher, this most awesome man reached out a calloused and pierced hand and lifted him to his feet without effort. The touch of the Master surpassed the experience of sight of him, and Nate thought sure that he would explode with pleasure and peace when he was embraced and heard a voice like the sound of many waters say, "Well done, Nate, well done. Come with me. I want you to witness a celebration, for you were the instrument that I used to bring my message to the one that I greet next."

Nate stood, listening to the unimaginable beauty of the voices of a myriad of the hosts of heaven singing praises to this King of his, and theirs. His shock and awe only intensified as he watched the

King reach out and welcome another man into the Kingdom, and he recognized the man: a healthy and whole Miguel!

This was confusing. (And that compounded the confusion. You weren't supposed to be confused in heaven, were you?) He had never even spoken to Miguel, so how could he have been an instrument of the King in this man's salvation? The King recognized Nate's feeling of bewilderment and said, "Miguel was listening while you spoke of me to Aggie. Miguel, please explain to Nathan how his words influenced you."

Miguel walked over to Nate and began to tell of how he had heard the good news of the King from a missionary in Mexico but had never responded until he lay dying on the floor of the cave. When the man was through with his short and remarkable story, Nate realized that he had understood perfectly but he also knew that the man had not been speaking English. This was indeed going to be an adventure.

Eliab and Yanoa sang with the rest of the hosts of heaven as they witnessed the homecomings. The King had brought them in so they could take part in the celebration. Then it was back to the battle. And they went back with eagerness and vigor, refreshed by seeing the results of the work in which they played some small part. Theirs was the Powerful King of Creation!

48

Gail and Ramon were on the quads, and Aggie was behind Gail, and Paulos was behind Ramon. Mike and the other two migrants were on horseback. Miguel's body was draped across the fourth horse. Crossing the rock patch was a rough ride any way you went about it. Mike hoped they were strong enough to hang on.

He had checked his cell phone to see if service was available so many times during this mess that pulling the little unit out of his pocket had come to be a ritual. He did it again as the pathetic band headed toward the highway. He glanced at the screen and was so sure that it would say "no service" that he had the phone back in his pocket before he realized that the message hadn't been there. He reined Clem to a stop and hit the speed dial button to his captain.

"Cap, it's Mike. I don't know how long this phone's gonna work so I'm gonna talk really fast, and I'd appreciate it if you'd just listen and not interrupt. We need you to arrange for a couple or three ambulances, plus transport for a couple other semi healthy vics. And we'll need a recovery team big enough to handle four DBs and one critically injured man. We need all this to meet us at the end of the old logging road that heads west off Highway 197 just south of milepost 171. Having a good team of homicide investigators on hand wouldn't be a bad idea either. Gail and I, plus the four needing medical attention, will be there in about an hour. It'd be real nice to have at least one of the buses waiting for us when we get there. One of the guys with us is in bad shape."

The captain was shouting when he replied, "Four dead bodies! What'da ya been doin,' having a private war?"

Mike didn't feel up to explaining, so he just closed his phone and clucked Clem back into a walk. The others hadn't stopped when he had, so it took a few minutes to catch back up to them. When he did, Gail made eye contact with swollen, bloodshot eyes. He swallowed the lump in his throat and nodded a silent response.

The sick, tired, and bruised little band was a quarter-mile away from where the rigs were parked when they first noticed the rotating lights of the ambulance parked with the other rigs. Red and blue lights never looked so good. Within minutes, the EMTs had assessed the condition of the migrants and had the sickest of them loaded up and on their way to the hospital in Bend. A rig from East Lake County Sheriff's Department set out for the same destination with Aggie and Ramon. The sound of the vehicles' motors retreated, and Gail and Mike were left alone, waiting for the recovery crews to arrive.

"Ya know, Mike," Gail said. "People are gonna start talkin' if we keep meetin' like this."

"If we keep meetin' like this, ain't gonna be anybody left to talk," Mike replied.

The tears that had been building in Gail for half a day burst to the surface, and before Mike knew what he was doing, he had her in his arms, mumbling words of comfort into her ear. Gail felt safe for the first time this day when the big bear of a man was holding her. While she was still in shock over the loss of her father, she couldn't help but think that God was using the arms of this mammoth cop to comfort her. They broke their embrace when they heard the vehicles that were carrying Mike's captain and a sergeant from Chiloquin County Sheriff's Department growling up the dirt road. Right behind the brass was the first of the recovery teams and an Oregon State Police Homicide team.

"Okay, Mike," the captain said, walking over to the pair but staring directly at Mike. "You've put me off long enough. I wanna know what's goin' on here."

Before responding, Mike looked Gail right in the eye asked, "You all right?"

"Yeah, go ahead and brief your boss," Gail answered.

Mike spent the next fifteen minutes bringing his captain up to date. Gail used the time to get acquainted with the recovery team members, putting on the dog in a barely veiled bid to make sure she was invited to accompany them when they went in to pick up her father's body. She really needn't have bothered. Since she knew exactly where the bodies were, they were more than happy to have her accompany them. It made their job a lot easier. The homicide detectives held a different opinion, but they finally relented in face of the recovery team's argument since time was of the essence, considering there was still a wounded man out there.

Ron Shear, the man that Ramon had cracked with the shovel, was still breathing when they arrived, and a paramedic went right to work on him and said that there was no reason he shouldn't recover. The trip in and out was a simple, uneventful mission. The only casualty was her emotions when they picked up her dad. Watching them zip him into a body bag made his death all the more real, and she found herself wishing that she hadn't come along. But her presence did allow her the opportunity to witness the detectives discover a half-buried cigarette butt near where the ATVs had been parked. She advised them to be careful with that bit of evidence, but they didn't as much as acknowledge her comments with a nod.

49

It was dark by the time Gail drove up the driveway of her parents' home. Since she had ridden with Mike that morning, she had talked the state police incident commander, who was on the scene when she got back with the recovery team, into letting her take her dad's pickup home. She was certainly not looking forward to facing her mom. It was tough enough dealing with her grief; she didn't feel capable of dealing with her mother's also.

Gail didn't know who the car parked in the driveway belonged to, and she didn't know what to expect when she walked into the house. Whatever she expected, it wasn't what she found. Amy was seated in the family room with a cup of coffee. Across the room from her sat her best friend, and pastor's wife, nursing a cup of java of her own.

"Hi," Gail said simply as she walked into the room. Amy rose and crossed the room, and mother and daughter embraced. They held each other and wept silently for a long time. Finally Amy stepped back and said, "Your sisters are both supposed to fly in tomorrow. Do you think you could pick them up at the airport? I'm gonna be tied up making arrangements."

This was typical Mom, Gail thought, always organizing, and

always thinking of everyone else, even when she had every reason to be focusing on herself. "Sure, Mom, I'll be glad to. Do you know what time they'll be at the airport?"

"Not yet. They're both supposed to call back later and give us the details."

"How are Gramma and Grampa doin'?" Gail asked.

"They're okay, I think. Your grandfather somehow knew this was coming, so he wasn't surprised. But still, it's just not natural—or easy—for parents to outlive any of their kids."

"I'm sorry," Gail said, sitting down and addressing the woman who had been sitting silently through Gail and Amy's interchange. "How've you been, Carol?"

"I'm fine, Gail. The question real has to be: how are you?"

"Confused. Stunned. Exhausted. Take your pick. This has been a very long and crazy day."

"I'm sorry. I'll get outta here and let you get some rest." Carol turned to Amy. "Call me if you need anything."

Amy walked Carol out to her car. As Carol opened her door, Amy said, "Thanks for comin' by and sitting with me. I'll give you a call in the morning."

"Amy, it'd be all right if you grieved. Jesus cried over Lazareth's death, ya know."

"Oh, I'm grievin',' all right. Don't you worry about that."

"I'm not gonna worry. But I will be praying for you. Goodnight, Amy." Carol hugged Amy quickly and climbed into her car and drove away.

Amy went inside and found Gail still sitting where she'd left her, head back, staring at the ceiling. "Gail, why don't ya go on to bed? You look exhausted. We'll talk in the morning."

Gail didn't say anything for several minutes. She just sat there, head back, staring at the ceiling. Finally, she softly said, "It's just so frustrating. It shouldn't have happened! All he had to do was wait a couple of stinking hours, and Mike and I would've been with 'im. Why'd he have to go out there all by himself?"

"There are a hundred whys in this deal, Gail. I dunno why any of it had to happen the way it did, but we just have to believe that God is in control. I'm gonna have ta tell myself that a thousand times a day to get through this."

"In control?" Gail asked, her voice rising with emotion. "How can you say God is in control of this mess when everything looks like it is completely out of control?"

"I'm sure that I'll be asking those same questions at times in the weeks and months ahead, and I don't think God minds us asking. But right now God is giving me the ability to believe that He knows what He is doing. I'm not saying I understand, I'm just saying that I can accept it, right now, tonight, anyway."

"I think you're in shock or something. You should be a basket case."

"I was earlier, and I'm sure I will be again. But right now I have a real sense of peace. And I'm thankful for that."

"Whatever. I'm glad for you. But I sure don't understand. Right now I think I'll try to get some sleep. Maybe things will make more sense to me in the morning."

Gail was headed to her room when the phone rang. Amy answered, and from listening to one end of the conversation, Gail knew that it was one of her sisters. She waited for her mom to hang up so she would know the plan for the next day.

"That was Erin. Her plane is due into Redmond at ten in the morning. She talked to Beth, and she's due to arrive at eleven fifteen. If you could pick 'em up, it'd sure be a big help."

"No problem. Are they both coming alone?"

"Yeah. They wanted to get here as quick as they could. Both their families are comin' in by car later. Do you think that havin' the memorial service next Saturday would be okay? That should give everyone time to get here."

"I guess. Dad always said he didn't want a big funeral or anything, though."

"I'm not plannin' a funeral at all. Just a service to give everyone a chance to get together and remember your father's life and celebrate his going home."

"Is Pastor Bob going to officiate?"

"I haven't had a chance to ask yet, but I'm sure he will."

"Okay," Gail said through a yawn. "I'm gonna go to bed and try to get some rest. Don't you think you should do the same?"

"A little later," Amy answered. "I have some prayin' to do first. Thanks for all your help, Gail. I hope you can rest."

Gail's mind raced through the events of the day at three hundred miles per hour as soon as her head hit the pillow, and she was sure that she'd never get to sleep. Exhaustion, however, took over, and before she knew it, the chirping of her cell phone was dragging her out of a deep sleep.

The screen on the phone told her that it was seven in the morning, and the caller was Mike. She answered gruffly, "This had better be good."

"I'm sorry I woke you, but I think you'll be interested in this. The state police investigators went to Ron Shear's place last night. What they discovered verifies what Ramon had already told you. They found records that indicate that he'd been smuggling Mexicans into Central Oregon for the past couple of years. He charged the immigrants to bring them up here, and then he charged ranchers a fee for providing them with cheap labor. It looks like he was also running drugs in from Mexico. He's a real sweetheart. And he has regained consciousness, so the boys from the state will be giving him a chance to tell his side of the story real soon."

"Did they find any clues about the horse woman?" Gail asked. "She has got to be involved up to her eyebrows!"

"I don't think so, but I will fill the interrogators in on that part of the story so they can ask Shear about her when they chat with him. How are you holdin' up, by the way?

"Okay, I guess. The whole thing is just so surreal."

"Is your mom all right?"

"So good it's scary. Reality is bound to set in any second, and then we'll see how she is."

"She may be stronger than you think. Anyway, I'm gonna go. Let me know if there is anything I can do."

50

The King had summoned Eliab and Yanoa and instructed them to take the battle to the south part of East Lake County again. They were far from alone in the battle this time. The air was filled with a host of their peers as the saints of the little town of Rosland were unified in prayer in preparation for the celebration of the life of one of their own.

For Amy and her daughters, the week went by in a whirlwind of activity connected with planning and organizing the memorial service. There really hadn't been time for grieving or reflecting. Now, somehow, it was time for that service to begin, and they were seated in the Rosland High School auditorium, listening to the people from the community file in and find seats.

The big surprise was the attendance of the four surviving migrant workers who Nate had been trying to rescue when he died. They had pleaded with the officials of the immigration department to allow them to attend, and miracle of miracles, permission was granted.

When Pastor Bob took his place at the podium and greeted

those in attendance, the auditorium was filled to capacity. At the end of celebration of Nate's life, Bob followed the instructions that he had received from Nate several years earlier and presented the simple gospel message of the love of Jesus Christ. When he opened his eyes after giving the benediction, Bob—and nearly everyone present—was shocked to see that the aisles were filled with people, including two of the Latinos who had come to the front in response to that simple message.

In the Throne Room of the King, myriads of heavenly beings were celebrating the new birth of one hundred and three saints in the little town of Rosland, Oregon. Nate was filled with awe as he not only observed, but also participated in the amazing celebration.

e|LIVE

listen|imagine|view|experience

AUDIO BOOK DOWNLOAD INCLUDED WITH THIS BOOK!

In your hands you hold a complete digital entertainment package. Besides purchasing the paper version of this book, this book includes a free download of the audio version of this book. Simply use the code listed below when visiting our website. Once downloaded to your computer, you can listen to the book through your computer's speakers, burn it to an audio CD or save the file to your portable music device (such as Apple's popular iPod) and listen on the go!

How to get your free audio book digital download:

1. Visit www.tatepublishing.com and click on the e|LIVE logo on the home page.
2. Enter the following coupon code:
   342e-db7a-bc71-d8b6-e094-0ade-7661-4320
3. Download the audio book from your e|LIVE digital locker and begin enjoying your new digital entertainment package today!